Cursed Mates

By

Cara Marsi

Nick Radford is a reluctant werewolf who's been fighting the Beast within for nearly 500 years. He's never killed a human, but the Beast is gaining strength and Nick may not be able to ward off his inner demon much longer.

Kyla Yaeger is an elite were-hunter with a scarred past. Her life's mission is to slay the werewolves that slaughtered her parents. Her quest has brought her to Maine, where she's been summoned to destroy the werewolf terrorizing the quaint little village of Heavensent. The last thing she needs is to get distracted by her mysterious—not to mention hunky—new neighbor, Nick Radford.

By the time Kyla learns Nick is her target, she's already fallen for him, making her task of killing him that much harder. She is torn between her love for him and her duty to kill her sworn enemy. Nick fights his forbidden love for Kyla, knowing she is duty-bound to kill him. Kyla and Nick must join forces to fight an even bigger threat—one that will destroy all humanity. Only by their combined powers, can they destroy the evil and bring an end to a centuries old curse.

This book is dedicated to real wolves, those much-maligned, magnificent creatures who have been hunted almost to extinction through the centuries.

CHAPTER ONE

There was nothing angelic about Heavensent, Maine. Kyla Yaeger felt evil all around her, watching, waiting. A hell of a lot more was going on here than one werewolf. Her stiletto heels clicked on the sidewalk as she hurried up the street, but she couldn't outpace the feeling of malice. She had to block it out. Nothing could distract her from her mission. As an elite were-hunter, she had a contract to fulfill—slaughter the werewolf haunting this strange little town.

Anticipation of the next hunt pulsed through her. She hungered for it as an addict craved the next hit. Maybe someday she'd find the peace she longed for, but that couldn't happen until she avenged her parents' murders.

The fresh smell of pine from the surrounding woods wafted by on the slight breeze. The aroma brought the memory of that hunt in the Adirondacks. Determination flowed over her like ice through her veins. If she met the black wolf again, this time she wouldn't miss.

Quickening her steps, Kyla reached the homey-looking restaurant, a welcome touch of normalcy in this place tainted by wickedness. She hoped she could get a table for her and Todd while he parked the car. As she grabbed for the door handle, someone on the other side pulled the door open. Losing her balance, she wobbled in the entrance as a hand cupped her elbow, steadying her. An electric charge shot up her arm.

"Sorry." The deep voice was definitely male, with a trace of a British accent, and so close to her ear she could feel his warm breath. She inhaled his scent of spice, familiar yet exotic.

The timbre of his tone ignited a spark of recognition in her. She was eye level with a very masculine chest covered by a black T-shirt that stretched over hard muscles and defined biceps. Slowly raising her gaze she met deep topaz eyes—eyes shadowed with sadness that spoke of pain and unbearable loss. Thick black hair framed the rugged beauty of his face. The large jagged scar on his neck saved him from being too perfect. She didn't know him, yet she felt as if she did.

How odd.

He stood holding the door, not moving. The awareness in his eyes gradually changed to shock, then fear. Rooted to the spot, Kyla couldn't look away.

A roaring noise filled her head and pain stabbed her temples, signaling a vision. The man, the restaurant, the street wavered. Disjointed scenes flickered before her.

A tall man, his face hidden in shadows, his long black hair blowing in a rush of wind, stood before an empty grave. She felt his crushing grief as if it were her own.

She blinked and the vision left her. And so had the mysterious stranger. The restaurant door closed slowly, leaving her alone on the sidewalk. She looked both ways down the street, but the man seemed to have disappeared.

"Hey, I thought you were going to get us a table. I found a parking spot a few blocks away." Todd, her best friend and business partner, sauntered toward her. He frowned. "What's wrong? You look like you've seen a ghost, or maybe a werewolf."

"I don't know what I saw." A shiver ran through her.

* * * * *

As if he could outrun the image of the intriguing woman from the restaurant, Nick Radford drove his Jag fast, too fast, along the winding road that led from the village up to his cliff-top mansion. He rounded a sharp curve and glimpsed the churning sea below. One tire hit gravel and spun. Fighting for control, he propelled the car back onto the road. Too bad he couldn't control his thoughts as easily.

The woman's face flashed into his mind again. Long black hair and pale, fine-boned features. When he'd looked into those clear green eyes, recognition, longing, and lust had shaken him until fear overrode all other feelings. But fear of what?

Home in record time, he jerked the car to a stop on the circular drive, cut the engine, pulled the keys from the ignition, and jumped out. Fighting to banish the picture of the black-haired beauty, he ran up the stone steps leading to the old manse. The fast drive and the physical activity couldn't dislodge the mysterious woman from his thoughts.

He entered the cavernous living room, threw his keys on the nearest table, strode to the sideboard and poured a tumbler of whiskey. He drank it in one gulp, then poured another.

Pacing, he stalked to the window and stared at the darkening sky streaked with deep gold and purple. Too agitated to stand still, he paced again. Soon the moon would be full and the Beast inside would struggle for freedom; freedom to roam the deep woods, to run along the wild, winding path that led to the seething ocean below. Bloodlust stirred. The Beast craved the hunt. And Nick hungered for revenge.

The Beast sensed the demon Montague was near. Nick had always been able to control The Beast, but it grew stronger with every full moon and he feared he couldn't control it much longer. Soon he'd leave the mortal world. But first he'd destroy the demon who'd cursed him.

Montague's stench had begun to creep over the wilderness below Nick's window. He would annihilate his enemy and send the shapeshifter back to Hell where he belonged.

Regret for all he'd lost at the demon's evil hands cried out deep in Nick's soul, but he dared hold one last flicker of hope. Hope that Antica's prayers would be answered and his soul would find rest.

"Stop it," he ground out. He pounded the stone wall until pain shot up his arm. "There is no hope."

A scuffling noise caught his attention and he turned. Antica. The ancient witch had saved his life and been like a mother to him all these centuries.

"What has disturbed you, my son?" She gripped the black crystal hanging from a gold chain around her neck. "My crystal speaks to me."

Nick tossed back the last of his whiskey and set the empty glass on a small table. "I saw a woman in the village. I've never seen her before, yet I felt as if I knew her. I sensed danger from her as well." He couldn't tell Antica about the lust that had also stirred when he'd looked into the woman's eyes. She was danger and desire in one package.

Fear crossed Antica's weathered face. "Is she a hunter?"

"I don't know. The most powerful can disguise their true nature." He turned away and leaned his forehead against the cold windowpane, fighting his despair. Immortality hadn't been all bad. He'd amassed a great fortune, and through the Radford Foundation he'd contributed to life-saving causes all over the world. He could leave this earth knowing he'd left a worthy mark.

But he had to die. And soon. It was the only way to kill the Beast.

Exhaling a resigned breath, Nick walked to the fireplace and grabbed the poker, stoking new life into the flames. The fire sputtered and popped in the huge stone fireplace. He inhaled the calming scents of pine and rosemary wafting from the hearth. His gaze skimmed the walls adorned with ancient tapestries, their colors now muted. Nick had moved Radford Manor from England to this safe corner of Maine. His lips tilted in a wry smile. Heavensent, Maine. Not so safe anymore. And far from heavenly.

"My crystal is telling me something," Antica said. "But it is not yet clear." She moved closer and pressed her fingers into his arm. "Rest. Your trips to Switzerland tire you overmuch."

He barked a harsh laugh. "I'll have eternity to rest."

"No, Nicholas. It is not time. Wait. You will know when the time is right."

"It is time when I say it is time." He reached out to stroke her parchment-like cheek. "My powers are strong enough now to destroy Montague. And if God is merciful, He'll take my soul."

Her face tightened. "It will not end that way. The prophecy will prevail." She gave him a sad smile and rubbed the large black crystal. "Another force is here, one that could destroy you. Perhaps it is the woman you saw today. Mayhap she is one of Montague's."

Nick shook his head. "She is not with Montague. But she

may be more dangerous."

* * * * *

Todd stopped the SUV in front of the small two-story seaside cottage he and Kyla had rented. "A blue cottage with white picket fence. Quaint. What is it with werewolves? Why do they pick the most God-forsaken places to hang out? Would it kill them to haunt Milan for a change? Or Paris. Think of the shopping."

Kyla laughed and unbuckled her seat belt. Todd, the brother of her heart, always knew how to lighten her mood as she battled the inner demons that bedeviled her even more than were-creatures. She opened the car door and jumped out. Standing on the walkway, she scanned the small house, a true fairy tale cottage nestled in thick woods and perched about thirty feet above the ocean. It would be their home while she searched for the werewolf terrorizing the area. Since Todd wasn't a hunter, he'd work on the new video game their software company had already contracted.

The SUV door slammed as Todd got out and came to stand next to her. She raised her arms in a stretch. "It was a long drive from Manhattan. I'm glad we stopped to eat before settling in." Thinking of the restaurant brought to mind the hot guy she'd nearly bumped into. Through dinner she hadn't been able to shake his image or the vision he seemed to have triggered.

Rolling her shoulders to relax her tense muscles, she turned to Todd. She had more immediate worries. "There's something weird about this village. You must feel it too."

He shook his head. "I don't feel anything. But don't worry. You can handle whatever's here." He yawned. "It's late. Let's get our stuff into this gingerbread house."

As he turned toward the car, his gaze swept upward.

"Holy shit. A wolf's lair if I ever saw one."

"Wolf's lair?"

"Radford Manor," he whispered in reverent tones. "Eerily authentic." He pointed to the gothic mansion clinging to the cliff above them. "That's the setting for our next game."

"Radford Manor." She followed his gaze and froze. "You know that place?"

"I'm a computer geek. I do my research. Why do you think our games are so kick-ass popular?"

Kyla strained her eyes to take in the grandeur of the dark stone monstrosity high above them. Turrets speared into the blue-black sky. Rugged and ominous, a menacing sentinel, the house seemed to command everything around it. Her whole being trembled as cloudy memories surrounded her.

The hairs on her neck bristled against her sweater. She had seen this mansion before. Those turrets were familiar. She knew gruesome gargoyles, hidden by the darkness, stared from the rooftop. Thirty-four cracked, uneven steps led up to the parapets of the cliff house. The only thing she didn't know was how she knew all those details. She stiffened against the knot of panic that formed in her chest.

"They brought that stone by stone from England," Todd said. "It's positively ancient."

Pain, sudden and intense, pounded in her temples. For the second time that day she saw the empty grave. Instead of the shadowed man in her first vision, the face of the handsome stranger from the restaurant flashed before her. The vision disappeared.

Struggling for air, she lifted her eyes to the stone building. One small light flickered in a high window. Wind gusted around her, a forewarning of unknown forces gathering, waiting, in the dense woods?

"What is it?" Todd asked. He grabbed her arm. "Did you have one of your visions? Your face is white as that picket fence."

"Forget it. Just my imagination doing crazy things." She yanked free and pulled open the car door to haul out her suitcases.

"You've been jumpy as all hell the last six weeks." He dragged out his own suitcases and followed her up the brick walk to the door.

Kyla put the key in the lock and turned it. The door unlocked with a loud click. "Six weeks ago was the Adirondacks," she said, twisting to look at him. "You know what happened there."

"Damn it, woman, quit beating yourself up over that."

"My hand trembled." She looked down at her hands, searching for renewed strength. "My hands don't tremble." The memory of that hunt in the Adirondacks haunted her like a horror movie with no end. She'd missed.

She never missed.

Heaving a shaky breath, she pushed open the door and strode into the small living room. After placing her luggage on the rag rug, she faced Todd. "Something's wrong. I've felt it since the Adirondacks. The feeling got stronger in Geneva. Something's out there, Todd. And I don't know if I can conquer it." She tugged at the suddenly tight neckline of her sweater.

Todd pulled his suitcases into the living room, then straightened and met her gaze. "You're the group's best were-hunter. You always get your beast."

"Not always."

"You bagged the alpha in the Adirondacks. That's what Hunter-Wolf sent you to do." Todd shrugged. "So you faced another werewolf and he got away. So what? Don't sweat it."

"But there was something different about that werewolf. I felt more danger and darkness from him. What if he wasn't a werewolf at all, but something much worse?"

CHAPTER TWO

Kyla jerked awake, heart thumping. She sat up and pulled the bed covers to her chin as if she could protect herself against the nightmares. They were back. She'd finally stopped dreaming about that hunt in the Adirondacks. Why had the nightmares started again? The answer she feared pushed through her sleep-addled brain. The black wolf was here, in this weird little town. Waiting for her.

Confusion and dread formed a knot in her chest, stifling her breath. She licked her dry lips. Her gaze scanned the small room, its coziness at odds with the remnants of her dream. Pearl fingers of dawn poked through the slit in the drapes and crept into the shadowed corners, a mocking reminder that she'd lost the fight for sleep. Pushing hair back from her face, she slid out of bed.

Fifteen minutes later, Kyla sat at the small dining room table and nursed her mug of strong coffee. She'd been on numerous were-hunts for Hunter-Wolf, but never had she felt this pervasive sense of doom, this feeling that something big was about to happen.

Sipping her coffee, she gathered her doubts close. She'd never failed Hunter-Wolf, except that once. Member of an ancient and revered sect of were- hunters, she was ever mindful of the family legacy weighing her down, as it had for the ten years she'd worked for Hunter-Wolf, Ltd. An ordinary looking law firm much like hundreds of others in New York City, Hunter-Wolf hid a dark secret. Deep in the bowels of its high-rise headquarters, hunters and warriors lived and trained for battle against the demons, vampires, were-creatures and other supernatural beasts threatening the world order.

"What are you doing up so early?"

Startled at the voice behind her, Kyla jerked her hand holding the mug. Coffee spilled over the lip of the mug and splashed onto the table. She turned in her chair to face a yawning Todd. "My God, don't sneak up on me like that."

He frowned. "Little jumpy, aren't you? Who else would be in this house?" He shot her a sly grin. "Unless you've got a guy in your bed, which wouldn't be a bad idea. You need something to take the edge off."

She rolled her eyes. "There's coffee in the kitchen."

"I'll get the paper first." Todd headed to the front door to retrieve the local daily paper they'd ordered before they left New York.

He came in minutes later, a look of annoyance on his face, and slapped the paper on the table in front of her. "Would you look at that headline?"

"What?" Kyla grabbed the paper from the table, quickly scanning it.

Girl Disappears. Wolves suspected.

With a snort of disgust, she threw the paper back onto the table. "What the hell is wrong with these people?"

Todd shrugged. "It sells papers."

She stood. "Damn it. Real wolves don't carry people off. There aren't any friggin' wolves left in Maine. And werewolves sure as hell don't attack weeks before the full moon. Something else is going on here. I'm going to find out what it is."

"Where are you going?" Todd asked.

"Into town."

"And do what? Slow down. What do you expect to find? Do you know what you're looking for? You just going to go up to people and say, 'there's something evil here and it ain't wolves'?"

"I'll know what I need when I find it." She strode out of the dining room, heading to the stairs. "I'm leaving as soon as I change," she called over her shoulder.

"Then I'm going with you." Todd ran after her.

* * * * *

"What can I do for you, beautiful?" The butcher tore off his blood-stained apron and threw it into the straw basket behind the counter. Smiling at Kyla, he grabbed a clean apron and tied it around him.

"Just a little information, Neil," she said, reading the man's nametag.

In a blur of movement, he hauled a slab of beef onto the wood block table and cleaved it in half with a huge knife. Wiping his hands on his apron, he leaned over the large wooden table and stared at her chest. "I'll be glad to give you whatever you need."

Ignoring his leer, she gave him a faint smile. She needed information. No butcher, baker, candlestick maker, or whatever, would stop her. "You're a butcher and a baker?" With a quick glance around the shop, she suppressed a shiver of distaste as the gamy smell of fresh meat mingling with the cloying scent of sugar tripped her gag reflex. "I've never seen a shop like this before."

"I make the best Bismarks in these parts." Neil nodded across the room to where Todd stood munching on a cruller.

"I'm a man of many talents," the butcher added, then plunged a knife into the meat in front of him. "So, what do you want to know?"

"Is it true you have wolves here and they carried off a teenage girl?" she asked.

He tensed. An unearthly coldness descended over the small room, its frosty grip tinged with the faint odor of sulfur. Todd had moved closer, chomping on his pastry, oblivious.

"Where did you hear that?" Neil's eyes darkened.

"It was in the paper this morning."

He snorted. "Stupid editor is always stirring up trouble. Can't believe everything she prints. Wolves don't carry girls off here. This is a peaceful town." He leaned toward her. "Stay out of what don't concern you." Venom colored his voice.

"What do you mean?" She stepped back and bumped into Todd. He grabbed her arm, steadying her.

Neil's thin lips curled into a snarling grin, exposing jagged yellow teeth she'd not noticed earlier.

"I mean our lives here ain't none of your business." His eyes glinted with a malevolent light.

Kyla leveled her gaze at him, refusing to look away. Her instincts had been correct. Something much worse than werewolves had infected this place. If Neil thought to frighten her away, he was sorely mistaken.

Neil blinked.

She smiled.

The door opened. An elderly couple walked in and helped themselves to the free coffee on a table near the large picture window. The air lightened and the scent of sulfur dissipated, as if swept out the door.

Neil looked over at the elderly couple. "Be with you

folks in a minute." When he turned back to Kyla, his teeth were white again. "Anything else I can do for you today?"

She shook her head, recognizing a dismissal. She was glad to oblige. "No, we're good."

"Weird," she said when she and Todd were outside.

"What?"

"Neil isn't what he seems. His teeth went from white to yellow and back to white. Odd."

"Downright creepy." Todd's brow furrowed. "I didn't feel anything other than a guy being smarmy. But you're the one with the second sight."

She looked toward the newspaper office across the street. "I'm going over to talk to the editor."

The acrid smell of ink and paper hit Kyla's nostrils when she and Todd walked into the cramped office. The odors made Kyla cough. An older woman, her silver hair in a bun, looked up from a desk in the back of the room.

Adjusting her half-glasses, the woman rose from her chair and approached them. "What can I do for you folks?"

"Your paper's headline this morning. The missing girl." Kyla glanced around the small room. A decrepit computer rested on a desk from another era, and yellowed newspapers were piled in every corner. On the front page of the nearest one she saw the turrets of Radford Manor. She reached for the paper, but the older woman grabbed her hand.

"Name's Sally Weston," she said. "Who might you be?"

Kyla looked into Sally's inquisitive brown eyes. "Kyla Yaeger and this is my business partner, Todd Bailey." She shook Sally's proffered hand.

Sally gave each of them a quick once over. "What kind of business?"

"We own a software company," Todd said. "We're

researching a new video game."

"What kind of video game?" Sally asked.

Todd opened his mouth to speak.

"A game about wolves," Kyla answered, anxious to allay the other woman's suspicions. "That's why I asked about the missing girl."

Sally relaxed her stance and pushed aside papers on a heavy worktable, perching on the edge. "Now let's have the truth. What paper do you write for?"

"We're not reporters," Kyla said.

Sally sniffed. "But you want to know about the wolf attacks."

"There's been more than one?" Kyla shuddered.

"Been a few," Sally said.

Kyla feigned surprise. Hunter-Wolf knew of the attacks and suspected werewolves. If she did her job well, the townspeople would never know the true monsters in their midst.

"We only heard about the poor girl who's gone missing," Kyla said. "Thought we might work it into a game. We asked the butcher across the street, but he didn't want to talk about it."

"Neil's an ass," Sally said. "He's probably scared like the rest of 'em."

"Scared of what?" Todd asked.

"Hell if I know," Sally said. "Doesn't take much to scare folks around here."

Kyla frowned. "You wrote the story about wolves carrying the girl off."

Sally shrugged. "The public has a right to know. People have been mauled and killed. Some swear they've seen wolves in the woods. Wolves are as good an explanation as anything."

"But there are no wolves in Maine," Kyla said. *At least not natural ones*.

Sally shrugged again.

Kyla walked around the crowded room, touching ancient inkpots and scanning years-old headlines. The paper with the photo of Radford Manor rested on the top of a pile. She reached for it, then turned to Sally. "What do you think is going on?"

Sally pushed her glasses farther up the bridge of her nose. "People say it's druggies who went too far into the woods and disturbed wolves or some other animals. I report what I hear. We even have some New York detective sniffing around."

The hairs on Kyla's nape prickled in warning. She dropped the newspaper she held. "New York detective?"

Sally's lips tilted in a wry grin. "I guess they don't have much crime down in New York."

"I guess not." A New York cop checking out wolves in Maine. Very odd.

The door opened, ushering in a gust of wind that made papers fly off a small desk. A middle-aged woman, large and rawboned, entered the room and studied Kyla and Todd before turning to Sally. Faint sunlight slanted off the golden badge pinned to the woman's khaki jacket.

"Sheriff," Sally said with a slight nod. "Have you found the girl?"

The sheriff let out a derisive laugh and waved her hand. "She's probably some runaway, off to the big city. Happens all the time."

Sally's features tightened. She opened her mouth to speak, but the sheriff ignored her and turned to Kyla and

Todd.

"You must be the new tenants at Raven Cottage. We heard you were here." Holding out a hand, she walked toward them. "Maxine Sanders, town sheriff. Everyone calls me Max."

"Kyla Yaeger, and this is my partner, Todd Bailey." Nodding, the sheriff shook Todd's hand, then turned to Kyla, hand outstretched. The woman's crushing grip made Kyla's hand tingle in pain. Warnings fluttered in her stomach.

"Raven Cottage?" Kyla freed her hand and rubbed it down the side of her jeans. "What an intriguing name. The real estate agent who rented it didn't tell us the house had a name."

"Agent probably didn't think it was important," Max said. "Glad to have you both here." Despite her welcoming words, her glacial eyes, sharp as blue icicles, bore into Kyla.

Kyla had met her share of self-important officials before and wondered if Max was filled with her own importance, or just cautious with strangers. Kyla resolved to keep a low profile around the sheriff until she knew more about her.

"Got those flyers for me, Sally?" Max asked.

"Right here, Sheriff." Sally twisted around to the desk behind her, pulled out a sheaf of papers and handed them to the sheriff.

Without a backward glance, Max hurried from the shop.

"I've got news to put out," Sally said.

"Thanks for your help." Kyla headed for the door, Todd close behind.

Her gaze swung toward paper with the picture of Radford Manor. She stopped and turned to Sally. "We noticed the huge house on the cliff. Who lives there?"

"Can't help but notice that old monster." Sally rolled up

the sleeves of her flannel shirt and picked up a pen from the desk. "Radford family. Newcomers. Only been in these parts about one hundred years. Keep to themselves. Old man died last year. Son lives there now. Nick. He comes into town now and then." She grinned. "A real looker, like his father."

"Thanks, Sally. We'll leave you to your work." Kyla hooked her arm through Todd's and steered him outside.

Nick Radford. Could he be the good-looking stranger outside the restaurant yesterday?

"I'd sure like to meet this Nick Radford," Todd said. "Maybe he'd give us a tour of the house. It'll help my game."

"I think I may have seen him at the restaurant the other day. The guy was hot." *And he might have caused me to have a vision.* She couldn't tell Todd that, not yet.

Todd grinned. "Hot, you say? Maybe you ought to get to know him. You need to loosen up a bit and have some fun."

"I'll have fun after I've bagged my alpha." She scanned the sidewalk lined with small shops. A clock tower dominated the town square across the street. A little past noon, people hurried about their business and cars rolled by on the narrow road. Banners announcing the town's upcoming tri-centennial celebration fluttered in the breeze. Real life in a normal town, no more, no less.

Taking Todd's arm, she led him away from the flow of pedestrian traffic to stand near a small gift shop. "This is a strange town. Or maybe it's me. My instincts have been skewed since the Adirondacks. I'm imagining depravity lurking in the heart of a butcher and suspect the sheriff is hiding something. What the hell is going on?"

"I think you're reading too much into things. Heavensent is like any other small New England town. Except for Radford Manor."

The mention of Radford Manor drew her attention toward the distant hill where the turrets of the old mansion bit into the sky.

"There's something about that place." Her gaze locked with Todd's. "I feel dizzy when I look at it, as if the old pile of stones is trying to tell me something, something important."

"Hell, woman, it's saying you need a vacation. And a good lay."

She scrunched up her nose and gave him a gentle punch on the arm. "Stop it. We've wasted too much time already today."

Kyla and Todd spent the rest of the morning wandering the town, pretending to be curious tourists. When they asked about the missing girl, they met resistance and frightened looks. No one spoke her name or seemed to care what had happened to her. An ache formed in Kyla's chest. She knew how it felt to be a misfit.

The townspeople proved eager to talk about Nicholas Radford though. Village royalty. Lord of the manor. The name and the title suited him. Nicholas.

* * * * *

Afternoon shadows were deepening when Kyla left Todd working on the video game and got into her SUV. She needed to get out, to do something. Answers waited among the dark trees. She had the strange feeling she held some of the answers deep inside, unfocused and just out of reach. Uneasy at the thought, she quickly backed the car out of the driveway.

It was the time of the waxing moon. The monsters would be stirring in anticipation of the full moon. If werewolves were here, the evidence would be in the thick woods. She needed to find it.

She parked the SUV at the end of an abandoned logging road, settled her pistol in the shoulder holster under her denim jacket, stuffed her car keys into her pocket, then tramped along the rutted trail. Sunlight couldn't penetrate the dense foliage. The early April air held a chill and she shivered with cold.

Nerves on high alert, she picked her way carefully over the narrow path. A slash of waning sunlight, bright fingers pointing the way, broke through the trees and illuminated a small clearing. Anticipation made her pulse jump and she hurried toward the clearing, stopping at the edge.

A large circle had been traced in the soil. Moving to the middle of the circle, she sniffed the air. Excitement coiled like a snake in her stomach. She recognized the faint scents of nightshade, belladonna, and alcohol mingled with charred wood from an old fire. Werewolves had been here not more than a night ago, preparing for the transformation. She glanced around, as if expecting them to burst from the bushes. Who were they? Townspeople? The butcher? She touched her gun.

The stillness surrounded her, kicking her apprehension up a notch. No twittering of birds or rustling of small creatures disturbed the silence. A whisper sighed through the trees, but the leaves high in the sky were unmoving. The fine hairs on her arms rose up. She pulled her gun from its holster. Holding the gun in readiness to shoot, she turned slowly, covering every direction.

"Planning to use that thing?" The mystery man from the restaurant, his topaz eyes dark and intense, stepped out of the shadows.

"Should I?"

Surprise softened his features and he threw back his head

and laughed. The sound rang through the trees, waking the forest from its unnatural slumber. Branches swayed in the breeze and birds flapped toward the sky.

His laugh unleashed a mixture of anxiety, longing, and recognition in her. She knew that laugh. But she couldn't. It wasn't possible.

Dressed all in black—black leather jacket, black sweater, black jeans, and black boots—he looked dangerous. And exotic. He didn't belong in this time.

Arms folded across his chest, he moved into the clearing with the lithe grace of a powerful cat. Or a wolf.

"I don't often get beautiful gun-toting women on my property," he drawled. "I like it, though."

Awareness shimmered in his golden eyes, and something else, something dark and forbidding that woke an answering darkness in her.

She studied the sharp planes of his face framed by wavy black hair worn a trifle too long. Should she fear this man? Relaxing her stance, she holstered her gun. "Your property? I should have known."

"Why is that?"

"I suspected I was on Radford property. You're Nicholas Radford of Radford Manor, I presume."

"I've not been called Nicholas in many years. Nick Radford at your service, ma'am." He gave a slight bow, then offered his hand.

She held out her own and his hand closed over it. A scene flashed into Kyla's mind. *Swirling cape, muscular calves covered in thick stockings, long black hair tied in a queue.* Her legs wobbled as if she stood in a fast-moving stream. The firm grip of Nick's hand and his steady gaze finally tore her from the surreal sight.

He released her hand and stepped closer until they were only a breath apart. He stood a foot taller than she, but she had bested larger men. She wasn't afraid.

She inhaled his woodsy scent. Memories, soft and shaded, filled her with an overwhelming need to touch him again.

"I saw you at the restaurant yesterday." She looked into his fathomless golden eyes and felt herself falling into a well of longing and mystery.

"Why are you here?" His friendly expression had become wary and cautious.

A frisson of trepidation slid over her. The thought that he knew about the wolf circle and had a part in it leapt into her mind. Her instincts urged caution. "I felt like a walk, and your property is so beautiful. I'm sorry to trespass."

He leaned toward her. "Be careful. The woods can be a dangerous place."

"I'm not afraid." They stood close, neither moving. Heat throbbed between them.

He took a step back. "You know my name. But you haven't told me yours."

"Kyla Yaeger."

He stilled. "Yaeger? German for hunter."

She nodded. "The spelling is slightly different, but yes. You speak German?"

"I speak many languages." The tightness around his mouth eased. He touched her hair where it fell over her shoulder and let the strands slip through his fingers.

A fleeting picture floated in her mind. Another time, another forest. A man's soft lips. A tender kiss. She swayed toward him.

The loud cry of a crow broke the spell. She met Nicholas'

gaze. An image appeared in the golden depths of his eyes. Snarling snout with fangs bared. Yellow eyes. Wolf eyes.

She backed away.

"What is it?" he asked.

"I-it's nothing. I have to go." Head high, she turned and followed the trail back to her car. She knew he watched and forced herself to walk slowly. When she felt free of his gaze, she collapsed against the trunk of a towering tree.

What had just happened? She hardly knew Nick Radford, yet a part of her did. She'd nearly allowed herself to be seduced by a pair of topaz eyes, eyes that showed a wolf in their depths. Perhaps a warning. First Radford Manor, now Nick Radford himself, seemed to be playing with her mind.

Nothing or no one would keep her from her mission. Not even a wildly mysterious man who provoked her with unnamed yearnings.

CHAPTER THREE

Trying to keep warm in the chilly night air, Kyla rocked back and forth on the ancient rocker. The rickety chair squeaked its protest at her invasion. Her breath misted in the faint porch light. Shivering, she wrapped the thick wool blanket tighter around her as if she could gather her tangled thoughts close enough to make sense of them. Disturbed by her reaction to Nick Radford in the woods this afternoon, she'd been unable to sleep and sought refuge in the cold outdoors.

She looked up at Radford Manor, hanging on the edge of the cliff, dark and forbidding and dominating all around it. Like Nicholas Radford, compelling and mysterious, who dominated her waking thoughts and her dreams. Tucking her legs beneath the blanket, she stared at the rows of darkened windows.

Nicholas. The Old World name suited him. She would call him Nick.

Did he sleep or did he toss in his bed, replaying their encounter this afternoon, as she did? Did he waken with the same unfulfilled desire and longing that twisted through her? Her frustration had driven her to find her own release, alone in the down-covered bed as fantasies of Nick played in her head. It hadn't helped.

Somewhere deep in the woods, a creature cried. Another

death by nature's hand? Or perhaps by an unnatural force. She pulled the blanket tighter.

Nick once again filled her thoughts. From deep in his eyes the wolf with the glowing yellow eyes had watched her. White fur had covered its snout. An old legend came to mind. One her father told. Her heart beat a little faster and she pushed her legs from the confines of the blanket and sat straighter. Werewolves who had never killed a human had yellow eyes. A rare species. If Nick Radford were such a beast, she dreaded the idea that her mission might be to kill this rarest of werewolves.

The thought exploded through her, propelling her from her chair. No. It couldn't be. She would have some inkling, some feeling, if he were her prey. But she no longer knew if she could trust her instincts in this strange place. White werewolves were said to possess uncommon strength and mystical ability. Did they possess the ability to hide their true nature from an elite hunter?

As if in answer, a sudden gust of wind whipped the blanket away. She lunged to catch it and banged her knee against the railing.

"Damn it all to hell!" She grabbed the heavy post for support. The blanket dropped to the steps. Leaves skittered along the porch, brushing her bare feet like bristles. The wind chimes hanging from the beams rang a furious warning. Something cold blew against her neck, licking her with malignant power. A lot of power. Heart pounding, she snatched the blanket and hurried into the house, bolting the door behind her.

* * * * *

A hairy, muscled creature, red eyes shining, fangs dripping blood, flew at Nick, knocking him to the hard

29

ground. The fangs descended, ready to rip the flesh from Nick's neck.

"No!" Nick woke, trembling, to the darkness and despair he'd known for five centuries.

He sat up and drew a ragged breath. Bed sheets twisted around his waist. Wrapping a sheet over him and holding it close, he left the bed to pad barefoot to the large windows. The pre-dawn gloom beckoned to the darkness within him. The waxing moon hung from the sky, waiting. The Beast stirred, releasing a low rumble deep in his throat.

"Soon," he said, not knowing if he meant the inexorable curse of his existence or the benediction of its end.

"Catherine." The word, borne on a tortured whisper, hovered over him. He closed his eyes, seeing his dead wife in his dream, before the monster had sliced through his sleep.

Catherine, so alive, so beautiful, gazing at him with love in her clear blue eyes. He could almost believe she still lived. The hardened peaks of her nipples had thrust through her curling masses of red hair. He'd always loved her hair.

But Catherine was dead.

The ravages of his dreams flitted through his mind as he stared at the dark valley below. The valley seethed with mystery, like Kyla Yaeger. Kyla, alive and vibrant. He'd dreamt of her too. Green eyes, hair black as a moonless night. In his dream, Kyla had smiled at him and held out her arms in open invitation. He'd reached for her. Laughing, she'd disappeared.

He stared now at his reflection in the dark glass, familiar and unchanged. But things were not the same. He felt within him an odd coalescence of forces.

Catherine. Montague… And Kyla. Did Kyla play a role in this ancient, deadly game? She'd invaded his dreams and his thoughts since the first time he'd seen her.

He'd touched her yesterday, let her silky hair slip through his fingers. Out of curiosity or a need to know if she as was warm and pliant as his Catherine had been? Kyla was both, only hotter, pulsing with life. She had bewitched him.

She couldn't belong to Montague. He'd recognized the demon women his enemy had sent to taunt and tempt him over the centuries and Kyla was not one of them. But a small nugget of doubt settled in his heart.

A soft knock at the door made him turn from the window. "Come in."

Antica, her figure small and bent, slipped through the door and shuffled toward him. "The dreams are back. I heard your cries. The time is near." She touched his arm.

He shrugged free. He wanted no comforting. "Another invades my dreams. Kyla."

"Kyla?" Antica's voice trembled and she clutched the crystal around her neck. "Who is this one whose name makes my crystal burn?"

"She's a visitor to the village. Nothing more."

But some force deep inside him knew her.

Still gripping the crystal, Antica pulled her flannel robe closer. She stared into the distance, her eyes clouded, seeing something he couldn't. "This Kyla brings the dreams. I am sure of it. Will the hunts follow?"

Nick put a hand on one of Antica's thin shoulders and shook her until she glanced at him with clear eyes. "This isn't Salem. Or Barbados. No witches will hang or burn."

"No one can be sure. People destroy what they fear."

Antica's frail body quaked. She'd lost a daughter in Salem. And a son in Barbados. Antica and her clan had escaped Barbados with an angry mob in heavy pursuit. The ship Nick had purchased carried them to France and the safety of his mother's family chateau. The memory haunted them still.

He squeezed Antica's shoulder. "It will be all right. We're safe here."

"These people are afraid and they hunt more than witches. My crystal protects you, but you must be careful." Worry darkened her eyes and she rubbed the gem.

He kissed her forehead. "Back to bed with you." He caught a glimpse of himself in the dresser mirror. "At least I no longer need your witch charm. I can appear as myself." Through the centuries, Antica had cast spells to disguise his true features. Her spells had allowed him the freedom of seeming to age normally. In truth, he'd not aged at all since that night long ago.

"You will go out now," she said.

He nodded. "The house stifles me."

"I know. Have faith, my son. That which was prophesied will come to pass."

* * * * *

Nick inhaled the earthy dampness and pine scents saturating the awakening forest. The air around him stilled as if the very wind felt the evil in him. Sadness overcame him as he tramped along the narrow hiking path.

Not evil.

Cursed.

He'd fought the Beast inside him all these years since the terror-filled night Charles Ashbrook, the Earl of Montague, had cursed Nick to a living hell.

He stopped and lifted his head toward the crescent moon peeking between dark branches. The promise of its fullness made him recoil in disgust, but the Beast trembled with anticipation. Nick yearned for the freedom to run through the woods, to feel the wind in his fur and smell the blood of prey. It had been that way from the beginning. Like an addiction, he hated what he craved.

The horrific memory of that long-ago night plunged pain into his chest as surely as the monster's fangs had ripped into his throat. Antica's son had found him and carried his damaged body to her small hut at the edge of his estates. Better if they'd let him die.

Needing release from the memories and the pain shackling his heart, Nick sprinted through the thick woods. His eyes, tainted with the mark of the wolf, allowed him to see in the darkness. Running faster, he tripped on rutted vines but didn't stop. The moon watched and mocked him as he wove in and out between the trees. He ran as if he could outrun the Beast. Fool. Finally, gasping for air, he fell against a tree trunk.

When his breathing slowed, he looked around. He knew this place. In the nearby clearing, dimly illuminated by the slowly brightening sky, he saw the wolf circle. Too consumed with the bewitching Kyla, he'd not noticed the circle yesterday.

He moved closer. Chills that had nothing to do with the forest's dampness penetrated his skin. They'd been here. Was Montague with them? His old enemy had meant for him to find this. Nick let out a bitter laugh. Clever of Montague to use Radford property for his malicious purposes.

Nick walked around the circle. The familiar scents of nightshade and belladonna churned violent need deep in the recesses of his heart. Memories assaulted him. The centuries peeled away.

Germany's Black Forest. The full moon. They had

anointed their bodies with the sacred oils and drunk the vile alcohol. They'd feasted on small animals. Filled with bloodlust, they'd searched for bigger prey. The woman was young and blonde. Howling, the pack had surrounded their frightened, screaming victim. Nick had fought his own bloodlust. He wouldn't take human life. Sensing Nick's weakness, the pack had turned on him and left him for dead. The next morning, he woke and crawled away, barely alive. What was left of the woman lay close. The years had not diminished the vivid picture of her ravaged and bloody body.

Nick hurled away the remembered pain and released a low growl. Kyla had found the circle. Her beauty and vitality hid dark secrets that had drawn her here. He would discover them.

A soft cry, like the mewling of an injured kitten, reached his ears. He sniffed the air and smelled blood. Lust roared through him at the scent. Senses on alert, prepared to attack whatever hid, he approached the thick bushes next to the trail. The figure, dressed only in a bloody white shirt, lay sprawled just beyond the thicket.

The Beast reared up, demanding freedom. Nick stiffened and filled his lungs with the clean air. He closed his eyes and used all his powers to force the Beast back, deep inside him. Still shaking from the strength of his exertions, he brushed aside thick foliage to approach the still figure.

The young girl opened frightened eyes and screamed, but no sound came. She tried to slide away, but her broken body couldn't move. Purple bruises marred her smooth skin. One eye was blackened and blood caked her private parts. Whimpering nonsense, she put a hand up to ward off blows.

"I won't hurt you," Nick crooned. He slipped off his jacket and covered her, then knelt beside her on the soft leaves.

She whimpered again. "He hurt me. Monster. Red eyes."

Nick tried to brush her matted long blonde hair from her face. She cried out and pulled away.

"Stay quiet," he said. "I'm calling for help."

He slipped his cell phone from his pocket and punched in the emergency number. After giving the operator his location, he agreed to meet the ambulance at the entrance to the old logging road.

"What's your name, sweetheart?" he asked the girl, laying a gentle hand on her shoulder.

She sniffled. "Emily."

Emily. The missing girl.

"We've been looking for you." He couldn't save that woman so long ago, but he would save this one. "Emily, I have to leave you for just a little while to meet the ambulance."

Terror filled her eyes. "No." She grabbed his hand.

"I'll be back, with help," he said. "Understand?"

She nodded, closing her eyes.

Nick began to stand. Emily pulled him down. Surprised at her strength, he bent close.

"Devil raped me." Tears rolled down her cheeks.

His breath grew shallow with the anger that pummeled him. The Beast stirred. Nick willed calmness, for his sake and the girl's. "You imagined it, sweetheart. Don't think about it."

"I saw him. He had red eyes. They glowed. He did things to me. Horrible things. Please don't leave me. Please." Her slim body jerked and she screamed, a wailing cry filled with unspeakable horror and pain.

"I won't leave you, sweetheart," he soothed. "I'll wait until I hear the ambulance."

Nick held her and brushed hair from her face as she cried. His heart cried with her. Montague had done this. He would pay.

* * * * *

Todd entered the small cottage and set two brightly colored shopping bags on the living room floor. He smiled at Kyla, seated on the sofa cleaning her gun. "I just met the young couple who owns the antique shop. I bought some interesting things for our Manhattan place. Surprising to find such cool stuff, along with cool people like them, in this backwater town. Even more surprising, the shop owners recently moved here from Manhattan because they felt Heavensent is a better place to raise their kids." He lifted an eyebrow. "If they only knew. Let's hope we can make this a safe place for them."

"You got that right."

He picked up his bags and headed for the stairs. With a foot on the bottom step, he turned to her. "Did you hear the news?"

"What news?"

"They found the missing girl."

"Is she alive?" She held her breath for the answer.

He nodded. "Barely. But don't worry. Your secretive Mr. Radford isn't a suspect."

"What do you mean?"

"He found her."

Kyla carefully set down her gun and stood. "Found her where?"

Todd's features tightened. "In his woods. Early this morning. She was in a bad way. Bloodied, her face battered and broken. Beaten, raped. You name it. Rumor is she's spouting stuff about being raped by the devil. Townspeople think she overdosed on drugs. They say it's her own fault she's in this mess."

"Was she bitten?"

"I don't know."

Kyla shuddered. "Remember the girl in Pennsylvania last year?"

"Yup. Kept saying the devil raped her right up to the moment she died."

"No one believed her."

"And they'd had a problem with some particularly vicious werewolves down there."

She stared at him. "Could it be the same pack?"

His shoulders twitched. "I don't know. Let me think about it." He held up the shopping bags. "Want to see the great loot I got?"

"In a minute. I can't let this go. Packs are territorial. If they are the same as the Pennsylvania pack, they're on the move. We're dealing with something bigger than anything I've seen before."

"We'll worry about that tomorrow. I don't want to think about werewolves and monsters now."

* * * * *

Kyla eased her SUV around the circular drive of Radford Manor and cut the engine. She told herself she had come only to ask Nick about finding the girl in the woods, but she'd struggled against the need to see him since meeting him in the woods yesterday. He was an attractive distraction. Or perhaps something more deadly.

Gripping the steering wheel, she gaped at Radford Manor, bathed in the soft glow of dusk. The old house was even more impressive close up. Strategically placed lights shone on the weathered stones, once dark gray but buffed to pale silver by the years. Somehow she knew that. Chills, like gargoyle claws, slid up her spine.

Pain and piercing anguish, and great love too, throbbed from the thick walls of the house. Lights flashed before her eyes. The house knew her. The heavy beat of her heart pounded in her ears. This was a mere house, she told herself. A pile of well-placed stone and mortar, that was all. But she knew somehow that Radford Manor was much more than that.

The urge to flee overwhelmed her, but she reached for the keys still in the ignition and yanked them out. She would not run. She jumped from the car and strode to the stately mansion. The steep steps, the stone smoothed with age, led her to a heavy wooden door, dark, almost black. She touched the door, but she already knew the feel of its cool, rough wood. Shivers ran up her arm.

A brass knocker in the shape of a wolf's head confronted her. Perfect! A nervous laugh bubbled up. Wolf's head. Of course. Why would she imagine anything else? Next she expected the door to creak open and reveal Lon Chaney, in all his hairy werewolf glory, on the other side. Drawing a deep breath, she lifted the knocker and tapped lightly. No answer. She tried again, harder this time. Footsteps. The door opened a crack. Then wider.

No Lon Chaney glared from the doorway. A very real flesh and blood Nick Radford stood smiling down at her. The heat in his topaz eyes and the curve of his full lips sent her pulse into a tailspin.

"I've been expecting you," he said.

"What?"

Not answering, he stepped aside to allow her to enter.

"I need to ask you about the girl…" Kyla moved into the

cavernous room and gasped. She'd gone back in time.

Exquisite tapestries covered thick granite walls. Mesmerized, she studied a tapestry portraying the goddess Diana at the hunt. The colors were faded with age. But she knew at one time the heavy fabric had glowed with brilliant reds, blues, deep greens, and yellows. Diana's bow and arrows had been burnished gold. Kyla gazed at the other wall hangings and saw them new and bright. She shook her head against the strange double vision of new superimposed over old.

The hissing fire in the oversized fireplace drew her. An image, like an opening to another dimension, blazed in her mind. *A woman wearing a long cotton dress and a stained white apron stood next to the fireplace, stirring the contents of a black kettle hanging over the flames.*

Kyla could smell the beef, onions and potatoes bubbling in the kettle. Exhaling a breath, she blinked and looked again. The woman and kettle were gone. But they'd been so clear, the scents of cooking food so real.

She turned to find Nick quietly watching. Dressed in faded jeans and a gray T-shirt that strained against his hard-muscled chest, he looked like any normal hunky male. But he possessed a vitality and presence no mere mortal could capture.

"Who are you?" she whispered.

"A man admiring a beautiful woman." He moved closer and reached out to brush a strand of hair from her face. He touched her as if they were acquainted. Well-acquainted. She didn't back away. His finger skimmed her cheek, sparking a fiery need low in her belly.

Unsettled by her response to his touch, she swept a hand around the room. "Your house is amazing."

He laughed, a rich, full sound. She liked his laugh.

"The house is a bit much for Maine." He shrugged. "My grandfather brought the old place over from England. It's all we have left from the Radford estates."

"I would say it's quite a lot." She tipped her head and stared up at him. "You were born here?"

"I was born in York, England."

"You have only a trace of British accent. Have you been gone from England long?"

The sadness in his eyes arrowed straight to her heart. She put her hand out, ready to touch him, to offer comfort, then quickly withdrew it.

He lifted a shoulder. "I've been gone a very long time. But I've stopped my roving. I intend to stay in Maine until the end."

End of what she wanted to ask, but his features tightened and she suspected he'd said more than he'd intended.

She had come to ask about the girl, nothing else. "I heard about that poor girl."

He tensed. "Have a seat." Ignoring her reference to the girl, he indicated a very modern red leather couch set in a corner of the room. "Can I offer you some wine? Tea? Coffee?"

She shook her head. "No, thanks, I'm fine." But she knew she was not.

His eyes, brandy laced with honey, hypnotic and compelling, held hers. She couldn't look away.

He smiled, releasing her from his spell. "I have to share a glass of wine with my famous neighbor."

"You know who I am?"

He laughed. "I know exactly who you are."

The air around them thickened. He couldn't have guessed

40

her secret. Even the most powerful werewolves couldn't recognize her as a hunter. And Nick was no werewolf. Or perhaps she denied what she didn't want to believe. She would think on that later.

Giving him a glance through lowered lashes, she sank slowly onto the couch. She had to ask him about the girl, but so far, he'd done a clever job of changing the subject.

He walked to a side table, poured two glasses of ruby wine from a crystal decanter and handed her a glass. He sat next to her, so close she felt his heat and inhaled his outdoors scent of leaves and pine. Maybe she shouldn't have come after all.

"To my beautiful neighbor who designs the most incredible video games." He saluted her with his glass.

She let out a breath. "My video games. That's what you meant."

He studied her. "What did you think I meant?"

"I wasn't sure." She sipped the burgundy wine slowly. Its rich taste and warmth seeped through her, relaxing her, but not enough to control her body's heady response to his nearness.

"Then you're familiar with our games," she said.

He nodded. "They're the best on the market. You and Todd Bailey are legends in the gaming world."

Feeling in control again, she relaxed. "Todd is the real genius. He creates the games and designs most of the graphics. I just help with the concept. And we have a talented staff."

Nick smiled. "You don't give yourself enough credit. Concepts? How do you know so much about werewolves?"

She stiffened, wondering if he was toying with her, but his expression remained friendly.

41

"Designing video games isn't the same as your real-life heroics of saving that poor girl," she said, determined to get the information she needed.

Pain shadowed his eyes and he drew a ragged breath. "I wasn't a hero. Anyone would have done what I did."

She shook her head. "Not everyone. Where is the girl now?"

"Her family had her committed to a psychiatric facility."

"How terrible for all of them."

"It's worse than you can imagine."

"Oh." Did he suspect, as she did, that something unholy had possessed the girl? Her instincts told her if she peeled back layers she would find a very different Nick Radford from the one she saw.

"What do you think happened to the girl?" she asked.

He looked away from her, not answering.

A shuffling noise drew her attention to the doorway leading into an adjoining room. An ancient crone, gray-haired and bent, stood silently watching her. Confusion and shock creased the old woman's wrinkled face.

Their gazes locked. The woman's small, dark eyes widened and she gasped. Her hand went to the large crystal pendant hanging from her neck. A shimmering aura in shades of silver rose from the crystal and surrounded the old woman.

A witch? Hunter-Wolf knew of no witches here. A primitive instinct to protect herself flowed through Kyla. She put a hand to her chest, feeling the rapid tattoo of her heart against her hand.

"Antica," Nick said with a nod toward the old woman. "This is our neighbor, Kyla Yaeger."

Antica, the ancient one. Nick Radford lived with a witch?

It couldn't be. But the old woman had strong powers. They vibrated through the room. With a smoldering look, Antica rubbed the black crystal again.

The crystal held magic, but Kyla had no idea what kind.

Without a word, Antica turned and left the room as quietly as she'd entered.

Narrowing her eyes, Kyla glanced at Nick.

He shrugged. "Antica's been with the Radford family for a very long time. She gets a little protective."

Despite his dismissive words, he furrowed his brow and turned toward the now-empty doorway.

"That's understandable," Kyla said. The woman was more than protective, she thought. But she'd let it go for now. "Nick, about the poor girl you found. What do you think happened to her?"

He continued to watch the doorway. "No one knows yet. She was badly beaten and sexually assaulted. Maybe she was involved with a group of druggies as the townspeople seem to think. It's a tragedy any way you look at it."

His voice held suffering and a tone of finality and she knew he didn't want to discuss the girl further.

Sipping her wine, she studied Nick's strong, aristocratic profile. His straight slash of a nose and his firm jaw spoke of a man accustomed to getting whatever he wanted.

He turned to find her staring. Something deep and primal simmered in the depths of his eyes, spiking her lust.

Rather than the answers she'd sought, she'd found more questions. Draining the last of her wine, she stood. "I really shouldn't have barged in on you unannounced like this. I'm sorry to intrude. I was concerned about the poor girl. Thanks for the drink. I should go."

He stood and faced her. "No need to apologize." His

voice, rich and smoky as the finest wine, slid over her.

"All the same, I really shouldn't have bothered you." She started for the door.

He took her arm and pulled her gently back until they were a whisper apart. Heat arced between them like a powerful electrical storm. A small voice cautioned her to be careful.

Taking her chin between his fingers, he looked into her eyes. "Stay." He bent his head.

She lifted her face. Fear of losing herself intruded into her desire. But her body recognized him and responded, wanting the feel of his lips.

He mouth took hers in a slow and gentle kiss, giving her the choice.

Warmth flooded her traitorous body. On fire for him, wanting more, she wound her arms around his neck. He pulled her against his hard contours and deepened the kiss. She opened her mouth to him, unable to do anything else, welcoming his silky invasion.

Their bodies fit perfectly as if they were made for each other. As if they knew each other.

Fear of losing herself intruded into her sensual haze. But her body recognized him and responded, welcoming the feel of Nick's tongue expertly probing her mouth. His hands trailed a lazy path down her back, their touch silencing the ever-diminishing warnings in her brain.

Moaning softly, she skimmed her tongue along the silky smoothness of his mouth and raked her fingers through the crisp hair at his nape.

He left her lips to press searing kisses along her neck. Tremors shook her and she gripped his shoulders. His hands massaged her ribcage.

The exquisite torture of his lips and hands melted the last of her resistance. She'd waited a lifetime for this man. Waited a lifetime? The thought threw ice water on her passion.

She pushed away. Breathing hard, she gaped at him. She didn't understand why she should desire him with a longing that overwhelmed all her senses.

"Kyla," he said in the same thick voice that had weakened her defenses. He reached for her again.

"I shouldn't have come here." Head high, she retreated from the house.

* * * * *

Nick stood in the open doorway and watched her walk gracefully away from him. Without a backward glance, she got into her SUV and drove off. He closed the heavy door and leaned against it, trying to calm his breathing.

"You know who she is." Antica's voice, thin with age, crackled through the quiet room.

Nick raised his gaze slowly. Antica stood at the far end of the room. Lights sparked from the crystal at her throat. "I need time," he said.

She touched the crystal. "You are bewitched by her beauty. Your powers tell you, but you refuse to see."

He shook his head. "She isn't one of Montague's"

Antica's gaze caught his. "She is more dangerous."

CHAPTER FOUR

Something was wrong. Icy foreboding tingled up Kyla's arms and across her shoulders. Leaning closer, she peered at the computer screen again. The tight muscles of her lower back ached in protest, as if warning her away. A thought began to form.

The front door slammed and she jumped. She quickly closed her laptop. The thought was gone.

Todd ambled into the room and dropped his hooded sweatshirt onto the nearest chair. Wiping sweat off his brow with his arm, he plopped into another chair and swigged water from the bottle he held.

"Have a good run?" Kyla asked.

"Yeah, but I'm not sure I can handle all this clean air. Give me the exhaust fumes in Manhattan any time. What's up with you?"

"Not much." She couldn't tell him about her visit to Radford Manor. Her feelings about Nick were too confusing, too raw.

Frowning, Todd studied her. "What's wrong?" He glanced at the computer. "You closed it real quick."

With a frustrated sigh, she ran a hand over her hair. After a restless night, she hadn't the energy to do more than tie it into a hasty ponytail. Maybe Todd could help make sense of what she'd found. "I did some research on the Radford family. There's something strange about them." She opened the computer and motioned him over.

Grinning, he moved his chair closer. "You're doing research on Radford? Now, that's interesting."

"This is serious."

"Sorry. Hit me with it. I love good dish."

"You and your gossip," she said, rolling her eyes. "I don't know if you'd call this good dish." She turned back to the computer. "The Radford's have been major philanthropists for generations. Apparently they have billions of dollars at their disposal. But there are very few references to them in the financial papers." She tapped the screen. "This is the only photo I found."

He peered at the computer and let out a low whistle. "Looks like Radford in Fifties garb."

"I think it's his grandfather."

"Amazing resemblance." He shook his head. "I can't tell you what it means. What do you think?"

"I don't know, but there's something I'm not getting. I have the feeling the answer is here, just out of my grasp."

He grinned. "I get that you're hot for Radford. Don't worry about his family."

She stiffened. "I'm not hot for him." *Liar.* "I'm merely curious."

"Then why bother to check out Radford? Lighten up. Have a little fun while you're waiting for the smelly beast to show up." When she gave him a light punch on his arm, he flung up his hands. "Okay. You're not in a teasing mood. I'm sorry. What can I do to help?"

"I don't know if anyone can help. Damn it, I can't make sense of this. The men are always named Nicholas. I couldn't find anything on female relatives." The fine hairs on her arms stood in warning.

"Sounds downright repressive to me," he said.

"Sure does, but it's got to be something a lot more than plain old sexism. Why the hell can't I figure it out?" She grabbed a pencil off the table and chewed on the end. Giving herself a mental shake, she looked at Todd. "There's something else. The current Nicholas has personally funded several well-respected research projects to discover cures for some rare but deadly diseases. The Radford Foundation is based in Geneva, Switzerland."

Todd's mouth formed a circle. "Geneva."

She nodded. "Geneva. We had those reports of werewolf sightings, but nothing was there."

"This gets curiouser and curiouser," he said, waving a hand.

Kyla bit down on her lip. Nick and Geneva. White wolves with yellow eyes. And black wolves with glowing red eyes.

Her own eyes hurt from staring at the computer screen and her head ached from the unanswered questions rumbling around her mind. She threw the pencil across the room. It landed against the wall with a soft thud, then plopped onto the floor.

Todd laughed and leaned back. "I don't think that pencil is your prey. Settle down. I've never seen you this upset before a hunt."

"Damn it, damn it," she said, slamming a fist on the table. "I don't know what to believe. My instincts are off-kilter in this place." Narrowing her eyes, she turned to him, as if through sheer force of will and concentration she could figure out what was going on. "My visions have gotten stranger and stronger since I first looked at Radford Manor."

He touched her arm. "You're making too much of things.

You're tired. That's all. It's really a coincidence though, about Geneva."

"Huh! You know it too. There's a lot more here than what we can see." She pushed up from the table, scraping her chair on the wooden floor, and walked to the window. Early spring buds poked their delicate white heads through the branches of the Dogwood trees, signaling new life. But beyond their little house the blackness of the woods surrounded them, watching. She felt as if the very earth oozed malice.

"Odd things are brewing here," she said, her back to him.

Todd's chair creaked along the wood floor as he pushed back from the table and stood. "Stop imagining things. It's not doing you any good. There's nothing more here than your garden variety werewolf."

"I hope you're right," she whispered. She continued watching the garden, but instead of birds and trees, she saw red eyes. He was here, waiting. Was there a white wolf as well, she wondered, and considered what connection he could have with Nick. She heard Todd close behind her and turned to face him.

His brow furrowed. "You're a were-hunter. Trust your skills."

She exhaled a shaky breath. "You're right."

"I helped you after all." He released a loud yawn. "I have no ready answers for you, but I'll think about what you said. Right now, I'm going to take a shower, then work on that new video game."

"Ready to tell me about it?"

"Let me mull it over a little more. It needs a lot of polishing." He brightened. "I have an idea. How about we make the werewolf look like your Nick? I haven't met him, but you say he's hot. The townsfolk say he's hot. He lives in that creepy old mansion. Definitely the tortured hero type. With a hunky hero, we'll attract more females to our games."

He snapped his fingers. "And you can be his prey. We'll make it real sexy. Our male fans will suck it up."

She froze. "Leave Nick out of it. I don't want him in our game. And leave me out of it too."

"Little touchy, aren't you?"

"Drop the subject, Todd."

He saluted her. "Okay, but you protest too much about Radford. Take him to bed if that's what you want. That way you'll get him out of your system."

She raised her chin. "He is not in my system. And I don't need a man." She glanced away. "I gave up any dreams of happily ever after a long time ago. You and Hunter-Wolf are all I need, all I want."

"Kyla."

She turned to him.

He stood in the doorway, his eyes soft. "Deep down inside you're still the vulnerable little girl I met twenty years ago. You can't fool me. You want it all."

"Let it go. I have all I want." She inhaled a calming breath. "Men leave. You know that."

"Not all men are the kind to walk out on a woman. Stop running, Kyla."

"I don't want to talk about it."

His steady gaze, filled with love, held hers. "Your father didn't abandon you, dear. A werewolf killed him just as surely as if he'd died the night of the attack."

"He didn't have to die. He could have chosen to live."

Todd shook his head. "He had to finish what the werewolf started. Killing himself was the only way your father could protect you. It's time you accepted that."

"Right, my father protected me so much he left me to spend my childhood in foster care. That's some kind of love."

"If it weren't for foster care, we wouldn't have each other," he said softly.

"I know, and I don't know what I would have done without you."

"Me either." With a nod, he strode from the room. She turned to the window until she heard his footsteps on the stairs.

In her head, she knew Todd was right. But she grieved her father's desertion. She'd never love any man so much that his leaving could devastate her the way her father's had. And the day she took her vow to rid the world of all were-creatures, she'd abandoned her youthful dreams of family, marriage, and love.

She closed her eyes. She needed to relax and she needed advice. Black Fox. Her Spirit Guide would help.

* * * * *

Kyla lit the white candles ringing the tub and slipped into the warm sudsy water, inhaling the sweet scent of gardenias wafting from the candles. With an expectant sigh, she leaned her head against the rim of the tub and let the soothing water swathe her.

With another deep inhale, she tried to free her mind of all thought. But images of Nick intruded. His eyes, the color of rich honeyed brandy, invaded her consciousness. She recognized the pain in those eyes. It had been there a long time. Nick kept his secrets well.

She swished her hand through the water, imagining herself brushing a lock of his black hair from his forehead and soothing the tension from his chiseled features. Perhaps if she knew his secrets, she could make his pain disappear.

With an effort, she forced thoughts of Nick away. Obsessing over him took her from her mission. Clutching the edge of the tub, she sank lower into the warm water.

Closing her eyes, she concentrated harder on clearing her mind. And waited. A light breeze drifted through the open window. The fresh pine scent of desert mountains mingled with the gardenias and the loamy scent of the Maine woods. Languidness stole over her until her bones and muscles seemed to melt into the warm water.

A ball of light appeared in her mind's eye. The light grew closer. Vivid reds and blues sparked from it. A shadow appeared in the light. Her breathing slowed. The shadow grew stronger, gaining form.

She stood before Kyla, dressed in colorful Navajo garb. Turquoise and silver jewelry adorned her wrists and hung suspended from a heavy chain at her neck. Her long gray hair blew loose around her high-cheekboned face.

Welcome, Black Fox. The words formed in Kyla's mind.

Black Fox smiled. *You are troubled, little sister.*

The lilting voice of the elderly Navajo, her Spirit Guide since childhood, wrapped around Kyla, filling her with peace and warmth.

There is evil here, she said. *Unlike anything I've felt before. I don't know if I can fight it.*

The old Indian's dark brown eyes bore into hers, seeing into her soul, reading her deepest thoughts. *You will know what to do when the time comes. You are meant to be here in this time and place. That which was foretold will happen. All is as it should be. Do not be concerned.*

I don't understand.

You will, little one. Trust me, as always.

Black Fox's image wavered.

Kyla held out a hand. *Please stay.*

Black Fox gave her a tender smile and was gone. Only the sphere of light lingered. Then that too disappeared.

Kyla counted to ten and opened her eyes. The candles had burned low and the water had cooled. A chill invaded the room. She shivered. What had Black Fox meant? Could she fight whatever was out there waiting for her? Yes, she must and she would. She stood and reached for the towel. The full moon was in less than two weeks. She had work to do.

* * * * *

Kyla trudged slowly through the darkening woods, careful to keep the old logging trail in her sight. Small clouds scudded across the stars, blocking the half-moon and hiding her from those who might be lurking. Above her, the trees creaked in the wind. Perhaps it was an omen. She breathed the pungent scents of balsam and earth, and something else that hung heavy in the humid air. Fear or evil—she couldn't tell. She patted her gun in its holster beneath her leather jacket.

She would go to the wolf circle and wait. Werewolves in their human form were known to visit the circles in the weeks before the full moon. The monsters within them stirred, anxious for the hunt. The most evil of them welcomed the transformation and the killing.

Would the alpha visit the circle? If she knew his human form, she would follow him when the moon rode high and full. Bloodlust and hatred clogged her throat. She would hunt and kill until she found the beast who'd slaughtered her parents. Then she would finally have her revenge. And peace. Inside her, a small voice whispered that revenge would never bring solace, only more killing.

Needing to focus her concentration, she pushed all other

thoughts aside. When she reached the circle, she hid among the thick foliage. The realization dawned that no night creatures skittered through the underbrush. No night birds called to each other. Yet she knew she wasn't alone. Dread shot up her spine.

She slipped her gun from its holster and pivoted. Too late. A hand snaked around to cover her mouth and pull her back against a wall of powerful muscles. Her gun flew out of her hand. The stench of animal and fresh blood made her gag. She couldn't tell if man or beast held her. The pressure on her mouth threatened to cut off her air. Anger pumped adrenaline through her veins. With a loud grunt, she stepped hard on her assailant's instep with the sharp heel of her boot.

She took advantage of his loosened grip to jab an elbow into his ribs. Cursing, he released her. Fists at the ready, she swung around. His huge bulk, shrouded by the clouds, shook with fury. She delivered a swift kick to his balls, followed by a hard right to his jaw. He howled in pain, a sound not entirely human.

Ignoring the fear curdling her blood, she swung. The crack of cartilage greeted her whack to his nose. He howled again as his blood spurted over her jacket. Feinting on the balls of her feet, she kicked and hit ruthlessly, using all the skills her martial arts master had taught her.

Her assailant regained his strength and lunged. His ham-like fist made contact with her gut. She doubled over. He slapped her hard across the face. The metallic taste of blood filled her mouth. Fury, like a hissing snake, curled inside her, propelling her upright. She danced around him, avoiding his fists. When she got close, she gave the monster a sharp hand chop to the neck.

He shrieked and reached for her. She evaded his grasping

hands and faced him, crouched and ready to spring. The clouds freed the moon, allowing a shaft of light to touch her attacker's face. Recognition sliced through her. She gasped. Neil, the butcher-baker, his lips curled and blood dripping from his sharp yellow teeth, snarled at her. Neil? A werewolf? A demon? A growl rumbled from deep inside him.

"Come on," she said. "You want a fight, I'll give you a fight, you fucking bag of shit."

With a roar, he sprang. She ducked to avoid him, scooped up her gun and trained it on him.

"Still want to fight?" she asked.

"Leave her be, you fool." The harsh voice came from behind Kyla. She whirled toward the sound. Something hard hit her head. Her body folded. She saw thick black boots before she passed out.

* * * * *

Nick sipped the strong brandy. The liquid rolled down his throat and slid through his body. It should have warmed him, but nothing could warm the coldness in his soul this night. The flames in the fireplace danced and licked at the hearth, as if daring him to face the truth. A chilling truth.

He darted a glance at the blank computer screen across the room. Earlier, he'd spent hours playing Kyla's video games, not knowing what he'd expected to find.

Cradling his brandy snifter, he turned back to the fire. She knew so much about werewolves. Too much. If only the humans who played her games knew how accurate they were.

Perhaps Antica was right that Kyla's beauty had bewitched him. He laughed at his foolishness. He was allowing video games and Antica to fill him with doubts. Kyla was nothing more than an extremely sexy woman. Lust throbbed through him as it always did when he thought of her. He wanted her.

He tossed back the rest of the brandy, trying to wash away a reality he couldn't deny. Somehow his soul recognized Kyla. He refused to think beyond that, but one thing he knew for sure—possessing her body would never be enough.

He slammed the empty glass on the table and stood up. Enough thinking for one night. A sudden cold draft, bringing the stench of evil, blew over the room, scattering the papers on his desk. His glass fell to the floor and rolled along the Oriental rug. The fire abruptly died as if a huge hand had smothered it.

He froze. His head pounded and his heart pumped wildly. Kyla. The woods. Danger. The words reverberated through his mind. He ran from the room and out the front door.

CHAPTER FIVE

"Kyla, wake up." Nicholas' voice came from very far away. His strong arms were around her, carrying her. She inhaled his scent, fresh, like the outdoors, with no hint of horseflesh or wood smoke. She snuggled closer, letting warmth and contentment curl through her. She always loved it when Nicholas held her.

But who was this Kyla he called to? She tried to open her eyes, but they were so heavy. And Nicholas felt so good. She began to drift off to sleep again.

"I'm taking you home," he said.

Home. A blazing fire, a soft bed, and Nicholas. She hadn't been home in a very long time.

Branches slapped her cheeks, rousing her. Her dream faded into wakefulness, dissipating her contentment like smoke in the cool night air. Kyla opened her eyes and stared at Nick's strong face, shadowed by the half-moon. The beginning of a wicked headache throbbed. Flashes of memory shot through her. The raspy voice, the thick black boots in the soft dirt, then blackness. She moaned and struggled for release.

Nick stopped and looked down at her. "Thank God, you're awake." He kissed her gently on the forehead and pulled her closer.

She wanted to go to sleep again, away from the pain and

back to her wonderful, sensual dream. She closed her eyes. The dream she'd had while unconscious played in her mind. The man holding her in the dream had looked like the man of her visions, with his long black hair and black cape.

She was missing something. She'd called him Nicholas. The woman in the dream wasn't her, and yet she seemed familiar. Being knocked on the head must have caused these strange hallucinations.

But she'd needed no knock on her head to see her other visions. She'd always had visions before a hunt. But they were of werewolves, guns, and demons, not disjointed images of strangely familiar people. Her visions here were stronger than they'd ever been. There had to be a reason.

The hulking form of Neil surfaced in her memory. Safe in Nick's arms, she slowly opened her eyes and fought to remember. It had seemed to be Neil, but she had felt something very powerful back there, and it might have blocked the truth. She needed to go home to the cottage, to think, to figure out what the hell was happening. "Home," she rasped.

"Stay still," Nick said. "You need medical attention." He pressed her firmly against his chest. "My place is closer."

"No."

"Don't worry. I'll take care of you." He continued his long-legged trot through the woods, shielding her from the vines and foliage that dotted the trail.

The pounding in her head grew fiercer and she pressed a hand to her aching temples. Until she knew better, she would trust no one but Todd. "Todd," she whispered.

Never breaking his stride, Nick looked down at her. "I'll send someone to let Bailey know where you are when we get to my place. Once I know you're okay, you'll tell me who attacked you."

She tried to respond, but everything remained fuzzy. He'd think her insane if she told him Neil, the butcher-baker, attacked her. But the real questions were who sent Neil after her and how had Nick found her. Her jumbled thoughts made her head pound harder.

"Don't know who it was," she said.

They reached Radford Manor. Welcoming lights circled the driveway, as if the old manse waited for them. Nick looked down at her with anger blazing from his eyes. "I will deal with whoever attacked you."

His words provoked a shiver in Kyla.

* * * * *

Kyla had fought him when he'd tried to lay her on his bed, but her exhaustion had gotten the best of her, and she'd stopped fighting and fallen into a deep sleep. She hadn't even stirred while the doctor examined her. Now the doctor had gone, leaving Nick alone with the sleeping beauty.

She looked like a fairy tale princess, innocent and provocative, with long dusky lashes shadowed against porcelain skin. Her thick blue-black hair fanned over the pillow, inviting him to touch the silky strands.

She lay on her side, with one slim white hand resting on her smooth cheek. Her full lips were parted, as if she waited for his kiss. He bent over her, smoothing a hand through the softness of her hair and tracing the line of her lips with a finger, assuring himself she breathed.

When he'd seen her still form lying on a bed of leaves, he'd howled from fear and rage, rousing the Beast. The Beast would have its revenge.

Kyla needed rest now. She'd have a wicked bump on her head, but she was strong and would recover quickly. He smiled. One of the benefits of great wealth was convincing the best doctor from the local hospital to make a house call. A little extra money had assured the man's silence.

The urge to touch her again overcame Nick. He leaned closer, then quickly straightened and backed away. Kyla wasn't Sleeping Beauty and he lived in no fairy tale. The thoughts in his mind as he stared at her curvaceous body covered by the thin sheet proved him less than honorable. He was no prince.

The despair that was his constant companion rose up. The centuries had brought wealth and power and all that came with it, including wrenching loneliness. Immortality had its privileges; he'd helped a lot of people. But, he was so damn tired of it all.

He sank into his bedside chair and settled down, ready to keep watch over her. Leaving this world meant never seeing her again. He gulped deep breaths to dislodge the strong knot of regret that tightened his chest. He could change both their futures. Like a siren's song, her soft neck tempted him, pulling him into the darkness of his soul. The Beast cried out for something familiar it recognized in her, to make her his wolf-mate for eternity.

"No!" Nick hissed, propelled from his chair by self-loathing. He would not condemn her to his damned existence. But the Beast grew stronger. The Beast wanted Kyla.

Needing release, he strode across the room and pounded a fist into the thick stone wall. He welcomed the pain that shot through his hand, driving away the wickedness that had overtaken him.

Kyla groaned, the sound filling the quiet. On a ragged breath, he approached the bed. She stirred, but didn't waken. Golden fingers of dawn slid through the openings in the heavy curtains and reached into the room, caressing her face and gilding her satin skin to ivory.

Fighting to control his lust, Nick reached out and brushed a strand of soft hair from her face. Like Catherine before her, Kyla was a treasure he felt bound to protect. Anguish coiled around his heart, a reminder of his failings and his loss. He'd not protected Catherine. He would not fail another woman. No harm would come to Kyla while he still lived.

An uneasy chuckle escaped him. If she heard his thoughts, she would tell him in no uncertain terms that she had no need of his protection.

He knew she was very capable of taking care of herself—his people in Geneva had checked her out. Orphaned at a young age, her childhood had been spent in harsh foster care. He thought that vulnerable little girl still hid behind the sophisticated façade she showed the world. He'd like to find out if he was right, but his time here was short. Sadness lumped in his throat. He sank into the chair.

His people in Geneva also reported some disturbing rumors. Wolves were said to have killed her mother. Her father, injured in the same attack, had committed suicide soon after. The same wolves were rumored to have killed Bailey's parents. Not wolves, Nick suspected, but werewolves.

He knew what Antica feared, but he wouldn't believe it. Yet, Kyla and Bailey had spent their childhoods together in foster care. He wondered if that had been to protect them from demons who sought to harm them.

Kyla's soft and gentle sigh wrenched him from his thoughts. He leaned forward.

She opened sleep-clouded green eyes and smiled at him.

Her smile edged through his mind, letting light into the dark emptiness of his soul. Distant memories stirred in him, as if she'd smiled at him in the same way in another time and place. But it couldn't be.

She blinked in confusion and her smile faded. His world seemed to grow a little darker.

Putting a hand to her head, she tried to sit up. "Where am I?"

He gently pushed her back onto the bed. Wariness flashed over her features. "You're safe here. You're fine," he said in a soothing voice. "You have a nasty bump on the head, but the doctor says you'll be okay."

"Radford Manor," she whispered. "I should have known." She sank onto the pillow. "You carried me."

* * * * *

Kyla drew the soft bedcovers tighter and studied Nick. Funny how he'd known where to find her. She didn't want to believe he had conspired to hurt her. She barely knew him, yet something about him gained her trust.

He leaned closer and put a hand out, as if to touch her, then pulled back. "Do you remember anything of what happened last night?"

"I've been here all night?" She sat up quickly and grimaced as a wave of dizziness washed over her. She closed her eyes until it passed. "I need to get home. Todd will be worried."

Nick's jaw tightened. "You're not in any condition to leave yet. Bailey knows you're here." His intense gaze held her. "Who attacked you?"

She shook her head. She would keep quiet until she knew whom to trust. Anger, like a claw ripping her gut, stabbed her. Neil hadn't been quite human. He'd wanted to kill her. And she meant to find out whose harsh voice she heard before she blacked out.

Drawing a deep breath and trying for calmness, she sat straighter and clutched the sheet, then glanced around the large bedroom. The sun's early rays bounced off the burnished copper-colored walls. An ornate wooden armoire stood against the far wall. Her boots lay next to a claw-footed chair, and her clothes were carefully folded on the thick silk cushion.

Face burning, she looked at Nick. "You undressed me?"

He laughed. His teeth were white against the tan of his face. "Does that bother you?"

The thought of Nick slowly undressing her heated her down to her toes. She was no innocent where men were concerned, but Nick had a way of making her feel virginal. The knock on her head was definitely creating havoc with her thoughts.

His gaze darkened. "The doctor said you'll have some bruises, but you're lucky. It could have been worse. Who did this to you?"

"You got a doctor to make a house call?" she asked, ignoring his question.

"It doesn't take much to get a doctor here."

She looked around the room and back to him. "I guess not." Rubbing her aching temples, she said, "I appreciate all you've done, but I really need to go home."

He looked at her with narrowed eyes. She felt she'd somehow disappointed him.

"I can't force you now to tell me who attacked you, but you will tell me later." His firm voice brooked no further argument.

She bristled. Nick was used to getting his own way. He'd learn she wasn't a woman who took orders from any man.

With a sigh of resignation, he picked up a glass of water

on the bedside table, along with two white pills and handed them to her. "The doctor said you need plenty of liquids and aspirin for the headache."

Their fingers brushed as she took the glass and pills. His touch seared her and made her heart pound so loudly she was sure he must hear it in the quiet room. Clutching the sheet and pills in one hand, she scooted away from him. She popped the pills in her mouth and drank greedily. The liquid slid down her parched throat, cooling it, soothing her. Still holding onto the sheet, she handed the empty glass back to him. "Thanks. But I really need to go now."

He stood, his expression closed. "I'll send Antica to help you dress."

"No!" She shook her head, triggering a new round of pain. "I can dress myself."

"I'll be outside the door if you need me." His shoulders tight, he walked out of the room.

She watched his retreating back. Nick Radford was a proud man. He wouldn't rest until he had the truth from her. Not that she knew the truth herself.

* * * * *

Montague pressed against the shadows of the house and watched the couple descend the steps and get into the black Jag. Radford held onto the woman's elbow as if she would break.

Montague laughed, a low growl that sent small animals in the underbrush scurrying for cover. He'd seen the woman fight. She was far from delicate. Damn that idiot Neil. They hadn't expected the huntress to sneak up on them. They weren't ready to show their hands yet. He'd deal with the fool butcher later.

He shaded his eyes from the weak sunlight. The

sensitivity of his eyes told him they hadn't morphed yet into human form and still gleamed red.

He watched as the huntress folded her long slim legs into the car. Although he knew who she was, the stunning brunette incited an overwhelming lust in him. He wanted her. Death had freed Catherine from his possession, but the huntress would not escape.

Revenge and hatred slammed into him like a burst dam. It was Catherine's fault he'd made his pact with the devil. He would have given her the world if only she'd loved him and not Radford.

Radford would die.

Montague's ears pricked up the sound of a mouse rustling in the brush. He kicked the creature, then crushed it with one thick black boot until blood oozed from its lifeless body.

He edged closer to the house as the Jag sped away. The huntress stared straight ahead, her profile strong and her thick black hair brushing her shoulders. Her beauty stirred a hunger he meant to satisfy. The brilliant red of his eyes reflected off the stone walls of the old manor house, catching a spider in its light. The spider dropped from the wall, dead.

* * * * *

"You need to rest, Kyla. Stay home."

Kyla pulled on her boots and faced Todd. "I'm fine. My nap helped." She gave him a wry smile. "I was winning last night until I was hit from behind."

Skepticism worried his face. "You don't know who hit you. It could be anyone from the village."

"I aim to find out who was working with Neil."

"Neil," he said, shaking his head. "I thought he was your average leering butcher-baker. Who knew?"

"I'm ready to believe anything in this place." She

touched his arm, feeling the tenseness of his muscles under his knit shirt. "Hunter-Wolf is counting on me. I won't let them down."

"Be careful. You don't know who Neil's partner is."

"Until I know more, I'll be careful around everyone."

"Even Radford?" Todd grinned. "He can't be involved. He brought you home."

A strong dose of doubt clogged her throat, making her cough. "Things have gone to hell since the Adirondacks. And then in Geneva I felt a presence, but I was wrong. I don't know what to believe about Nick."

"Damn it, stop beating yourself up. If Nick were involved, he wouldn't have taken you back to his house and sent for the doctor."

"Maybe Nick is playing me."

"You don't believe that."

Kyla rolled her shoulders to loosen her tight muscles.

Todd grinned. "You should have seen the big lumbering dude Radford sent over with the message you were at his place. Looked a little like Frankenstein."

"And I think the old crone who lives with Nick is a witch."

"This gets more interesting all the time. A Salem, hanged-from-a-tree witch?"

She nodded.

"Why would Radford live with a witch?"

"It makes no sense. Nothing makes sense anymore."

"Witches, monsters, werewolves, and who knows what else," he said. "Lots of game material here."

"And you need to work on that game. If all goes well, I'll bag my werewolf at the next full moon and we can go back to New York."

New York. Far from Nick. She felt a hollowness in her heart. In such a short time, Nick had managed to intrigue her to the point of obsession. She sensed an innate goodness in him that spoke to a need deep inside her. The barely concealed pain in his eyes drew her in further. And he possessed a savagery that unleashed an answering wildness in her. She gave a short laugh and grabbed her car keys. Her imagination was out of whack. Todd was right. She needed a vacation.

* * * * *

"What can I do for you?" Sally Weston asked, coming around the desk to greet Kyla.

Kyla smiled and glanced around the cramped newspaper office. Same dusty furniture. Same smell of ink and musty papers. But none of the yellowing papers had the picture of Radford Manor she'd seen the other day.

She turned back to Sally. "I wanted to buy some pastries, but the Steak and Cake is closed. Do you know when Neil will be back?"

"Haven't seen that scoundrel for a few days now." Sally pushed papers aside and settled on a corner of the desk. "Man never was too dependable. Fish are probably biting. Neil can't pass up a chance to fish."

Kyla leaned against a case brimming with books and ancient newspapers. Trying to appear unconcerned, she folded her arms across her chest. She couldn't let Sally guess she had another interest in Neil.

"Has Neil lived here long?" she asked.

"Family's been in these parts about 300 years. Neil ran off to places unknown about twenty years ago. Came back last year when his old man died. Took over the family business. Whole clan's a little touched. Too much inbreeding."

Kyla laughed. "Does Neil usually take off like this to go fishing?"

Narrowing her eyes, Sally said, "Why do you want to know so much about that idiot?"

"Just curious," Kyla said with a shrug. "I'm not used to small town ways where proprietors take off whenever they want."

"Happens all the time around here."

"I guess I'll have to find another bakery to get Todd his Bismark's."

Kyla turned to leave and bumped into a hard bank of muscles masquerading as a man's chest. She hadn't heard the door open.

"Are you okay?" asked a deep, male voice. Large, strong hands gripped her upper arms.

"I don't break easily," she said, freeing herself and backing away. She raised her gaze to a pair of blue eyes that studied her with open admiration. The stranger's raw animal magnetism caused a shiver of warning to slide up her spine. Warning of what she couldn't guess. "I didn't hear you come in."

"Door's real quiet," Sally said, coming closer. She tilted her head toward the tall man. "Kyla Yaeger, Dan Taylor, NYPD."

Dan Taylor gave Kyla a friendly smile and scanned her face, lingering on her mouth. "I don't mind running into a beautiful woman." He brushed back a strand of thick, light brown hair that had fallen over his forehead, giving him a *little boy lost* look, yet there was nothing *lost-looking* about him. "What brings you to these parts?"

"Kyla and her business partner are renting Raven Cottage for a while," Sally quickly answered.

Dan grinned at Kyla. "Raven Cottage. Enticing place for an enticing woman. I look forward to seeing you around." Despite the boyish charm of his smoothly handsome face, she shifted uncomfortably under his intense scrutiny.

Deciding she was being paranoid, Kyla forced a smile. "What brings a New York detective to the wilds of Maine?"

He laughed. "That's what I keep asking myself."

"He's hunting for a wanted fugitive from Manhattan," Sally said.

Dan nodded. "We had a tip he's hiding out here."

Kyla frowned. "And Sheriff Sanders can't go after him?"

"A fair question," he said. "The fugitive is a serial killer I've been tracking for ten years. When we got the tip, Sheriff Sanders invited me to help."

Sally snorted. "Sanders invited you here because she's too damn lazy to do any actual police work. I've been hearing reports about young girls who have gone missing from some of the towns around here. Think Sanders followed up on that? Not on your life"

Dan stilled, his features tight. "I don't know anything about missing girls. I've got enough trouble tracking my killer."

Missing girls from nearby towns? A serial killer? This place gets weirder all the time. Kyla looked toward Dan again. "A serial killer in Heavensent?"

"Don't worry," he said softly. "I won't let anyone hurt you."

She flared her nostrils, ready to tell him she could take care of herself. Some instinct urged silence. With an effort, she relaxed her stance.

"Do you have any leads?" she asked.

He rubbed a hand over his face. "Not yet. Townspeople

aren't too cooperative. Don't like to talk about their neighbors. You know how these New Englanders are." He turned to Sally. "No offense."

"None taken," Sally said. "We're a closed-in bunch here."

Definitely a strange bunch in this town. She'd keep her thoughts to herself. Kyla needed to stay on Sally's good side. The newspaper woman seemed to know everything that went on there.

"Did you print up those posters?" Dan asked Sally.

"I've got a newspaper to get out. I'll have them for you tomorrow."

"I'll be back then." He turned to Kyla and smiled. "What business are you and your partner in?"

"We own a software company that specializes in computer games."

He let out a low whistle. "I'm impressed. Join me for a cup of coffee? I'd like to hear about your company."

She wanted to refuse. Her head hurt. And the awareness shining from Dan's eyes unnerved her. She had no interest in him or any man.

Except Nick.

The jarring thought came unbidden. She needed to get over her preoccupation with Nick Radford.

"Okay," she said.

* * * * *

Nick locked the Jag and hurried down the street. He'd had to get out of the house and be around people because the attack on Kyla had awakened the Beast. It wanted blood. He dragged air into his lungs. The Beast was gaining power. He had to control it until he confronted Montague. The demon's death would at last free Nick from the Beast.

As if he'd conjured her up, he saw Kyla sitting at a table near a window in the coffee shop. Smiling, he walked toward the shop. He stopped with his hand on the doorknob.

She sat with a light-haired man whose back was to Nick. She was laughing at something her companion said.

The sight of Kyla with another man roused the Beast. Nick tightened his grip on the doorknob. His muscles began to stretch. A low growl escaped him. His heart rate sped up and blood rushed through his veins, hot and thick. The Beast wanted freedom. He watched Kyla through the golden haze of his wolf eyes. She was his mate. No one else would have her.

Someone trying to enter the shop shoved against Nick, breaking the trance that had overcome him. He turned and ran down the street. Others stared at him, but he didn't care. The Beast had just demonstrated its burgeoning power.

* * * * *

Chills scurried up Kyla's spine and she jerked her attention to the window. Something or someone had been watching her. Her gaze searched the street through the window, but only the quiet tree-lined sidewalk greeted her. Pedestrians rushed by, oblivious to the unworldly forces surrounding them.

"Is everything okay?" Dan put his hand over hers where it rested on the table.

Her skin crawled at his touch. She gently extricated her hand. But when she looked into his eyes, she saw only curiosity and friendliness. Yet she had felt the sting of evil. Perhaps Dan's involvement with the serial killer had darkened his soul. Or perhaps he harbored his own darkness.

CHAPTER SIX

His transformation had begun. Through the darkened panes of the window, the low-hanging moon called to Nick. A sliver of moon remained in shadow, cursing him with the promise of its fullness. He balled hands already thickened and dug sharp claws into his palms. His face, still human, but shadowed with the Beast's features, reflected back at him. A mockery. White fur wove through the black strands of his hair and sprouted along his jaw like macabre snowflakes. The muscles of his face begin to pull and stretch in hellish alteration, forming the long snout of a wolf. He groaned with the sheer agony of contracting muscles whipping him like twenty lashes from a cat-o-nine.

Bones cracked and splintered as his arms and legs shifted into canine proportions. Pain-racked, he bit down on his tongue and drew blood. The taste stirred the ravenous Beast's lust. Tremors shook Nick as his body curved and twisted. His heart rate accelerated and his lungs expanded to the bursting point. The Beast wanted freedom. The Beast craved blood.

The dark woods beckoned. The sounds of small animals scavenging in the brush far below pricked his canine ears. A low growl of anticipation rumbled from his throat.

"It is time, Nicholas." Antica's voice came from very far away, as if through a tunnel. He stared into the glass, startled to see her bent body and anxious face reflected there. She stood close behind him.

"No." The word came out guttural, barely human. Soon he would not be able to speak at all. "I will hunt."

She touched his arm. Her fingers pressing into his burning flesh seared him with pain. He cried out.

"No," she croaked. "You must go to the cell. Mother Moon will not wait."

He snarled at her. "Destroy Montague tonight."

She pulled at him. Nick broke free of her grip. She ducked from his slashing claws.

Antica rubbed the crystal at her neck. "Wait. You must first see the scar and know the human form he has chosen. Thus your powers will increase."

Nick howled.

Her gaze—steady, sure— locked with his. "Have patience. Another month. You will find Montague. And the one prophesied will appear."

Her eyes darkened until no white showed. She looked at something beyond him. "A new danger lurks in the woods now. You are safe here."

"No." He forced the word out with his last bit of humanity.

Antica shook her head, releasing her trance. "You must go to the cell. When it is time for Montague, you will know."

His soul churned in agony. He wouldn't hurt Antica. He wouldn't hurt any innocent person. The Beast roared inside, tempting him with the desire to kill.

Fighting his malicious cravings, he bared fangs. His body ached with the power of his will, but he wouldn't bow to the Beast. He forced himself to follow Antica from the room. His claws clicked on the wooden floor, harbingers of the pending horrors.

* * * * *

Ancient timbers shivered at the onslaught of Nick's cries. Antica and her sons exchanged glances and went about the business of the house. His mournful wails as he completed the transformation filled her with sadness for him and his plight. She had heard these same cries for nearly five hundred years, but every sound wrenched her heart anew.

Had Nick's strength grown so powerful he would break free from his prison? At the last full moon, he'd wrecked his cell in Geneva and escaped into the woods. Her sons had found him and hid him from the hunters. Antica trembled and sent a silent prayer to Mother Moon that he would not escape this time.

* * * * *

Nick paced his dank cell and howled against the excruciating torture of muscle and bone expanding and contracting. With razor-sharp teeth and claws, he shredded the last of his garments from scorching flesh and fur.

The face of his enemy swam before the golden haze of his eyes. He would rip out Montague's heart and devour it. He threw himself against the steel doors of his prison. The impact hurled his wolf body to the floor. He picked himself up and stormed the door again. Unlike Geneva, it held fast.

The cursed moon, full now, watched him through the high window. Lifting his head, he bayed at his tormentor. He jumped, trying to gain the window and liberty. He fell back against the hard stone of the floor.

He lay there, bones and muscles aching, pulse racing. Lust rose in him, darkening his soul with unnatural urges. The need to kill consumed him, a living thing that wrapped around his heart, squeezing out the goodness. He craved the wind in his fur and the dirt beneath his paws. Craved the taste of blood and flesh.

A slice of humanity gleamed through the blackness of his spirit. Kyla's image appeared. Clear green eyes implored him through the veil of his torture. Loneliness and despair tightened a knot of desperation in his gut. Forewarning shivered through his body. Danger waited for her. He couldn't help her.

Tears slipped from his eyes. He stood on muscled wolf legs and howled angry curses at the moon. But peace wouldn't come to him this night or any other.

* * * * *

The light of the full moon danced on moss-covered rocks and lush foliage and shone a silvery path along the earthen floor. A lover's moon. But not tonight. Hidden among the bushes, darkness pressed against Kyla. The monsters would be prowling in full force this night.

Beyond her hiding place, the moon's brilliance illuminated the wolf circle, as if the heavens waited for the beasts. Someone had brushed the area clean and traced a second, smaller circle within the larger one. Bundles of larch and black poplar were stacked close, ready for the fire. Ceramic pots stood to the side. She knew they contained ingredients—opium, hemlock, aloe, henbane, poppy seeds—that would be thrown into the fire as the wolves danced to summon the powers of Hell.

Thoughts of Nick invaded her mind. Apprehension that he would appear in the wolf circle pierced her until it became a physical ache. She shook her head. He'd given her no reason to think that.

It had been almost two weeks since he'd found her unconscious. She'd been back to the wolf circle hunting for clues, something to identify the villain, but found nothing.

The pendant at her neck burned through her clothes, as if giving her courage. The ancient gold amulet, a cross suspended between two diamond circles, had been handed down through her family. It would protect her from wickedness, yet her mother had worn it the night she'd been attacked and killed. It hadn't saved her. Kyla had forgotten to wear it the day two weeks ago when she was attacked. Always so careful, since she'd come to this strange little town her senses were skewed. Rubbing the pendant, she sent a silent plea to the heavens for success and the end of her hunt.

Moving deeper into the brush, she waited. Dressed completely in black, with her face blackened, she knew the wolves wouldn't see her. She had covered her body with a concoction of leaves and wood smoke and secret ingredients known only to the elite were-hunters. The mixture blocked her human scent from the monsters she would meet.

A shuffling in the bushes set her senses on alert. With careful deliberation she slid her gun, loaded with silver bullets, from its holster and readied it. A group of five men, naked and grinning, stole into the clearing. Initiates, not yet able to transform without the fire and the ointments. She narrowed her eyes, trying to memorize their faces. Some were men she'd seen in the village, but Nick wasn't among them. She exhaled a relieved breath.

With leering grins, they set about lighting the fire. Each took an ingredient from a pot and threw it on the flames. Blue and green sparks shot from the fire. The men's manic laughter thickened the air.

The earth beneath her trembled and groaned. The hairs on her nape stood in warning. Something approached. She gripped her gun.

A huge gray wolf, eyes black as witch's brew, jumped over shrubs and landed next to the men. The wolf sat on its haunches and nodded at the others.

As if cued, the men began to dance around the leaping flames. The large wolf, ears cocked, watched. And waited.

Was he the alpha? Kyla's instincts told her no. Her heart pounded, the sound a drumbeat in her ears. When the men completed their transformation, the alpha would join them. Her mouth watered in anticipation and her nerves heightened. She held her gun steady. When she killed the alpha, the others would weaken. She carried enough bullets for each of them.

Dancing, the men began their chant.
"Hail, oh Magic Wolf,
Take my body,
Take my soul,
Give me power over young and old.
Give me flesh to eat
Give me blood to drink.
Send your Black Prince
To drive men to the brink."

They lifted their faces to the moon and howled. Chills swept up her spine and made the fine hairs on her arms stand up.

Soon. Kill or be killed.

Their bodies shaking, the men transformed into lean, hungry wolves. They snarled and snapped at each other as they continued their hellish dance around the fire. The large gray wolf tensed and took his attention from the creatures and the fire. He turned his large head toward her hiding place. Had he seen her or caught her scent? She aimed her gun.

A sudden wind blew through the trees, moaning and sighing like a soul in agony. The gray wolf let out an ear-shattering wail. The other wolves joined in until the entire woods rang with their foul cries. Night animals scurried by Kyla in their frenzy to escape.

A lump of fear formed in her throat. The noises were unlike anything she'd ever heard. Did they signal the black wolf, the most feared of all werewolves? Not a wolf at all, some said, but a demon.

That great black alpha was the stuff of legends, his stories passed down by hunters through the ages. The monster had destroyed the most skilled of the hunters sent after it. Its cunning and viciousness knew no bounds. Rumors swirled that it had been the black alpha that had killed her mother and bitten her father. It was also rumored to have killed Todd's parents. Anger—hot and red—obscured Kyla's vision.

She patted the dagger she'd slipped into the sheath strapped to her calf. If a silver bullet couldn't kill the monster, she'd plunge the knife into his heart, or use it on herself before she let him take her. She prayed she would at last avenge her parents and finally find the peace she craved.

Needing to keep her vision clear for the coming fight, she averted her eyes from the flames that leapt and danced to the sky. The other wolves were frenzied now, waiting for the alpha, waiting for the killing to begin.

The wind stilled to a deathly calm and the entire world seemed to hold its breath. The gray wolf turned toward the trees opposite Kyla.

A wolf, huge and powerful, ran from the trees to land before the fire. Kyla's heart beat a fierce staccato. The red-eyed wolf of her nightmares crouched in the circle. She'd known they would meet again. Eyes gleaming, the creature surveyed all around it, a monstrous prince in his kingdom. The thick black fur along its spine stood on end, signaling his power.

The beast's magnetism reached out to her as if it knew she watched. Bloodlust overtook her, sending spasms through her body. She held her gun with one hand and rubbed the crucifix around her neck with the other. Tonight the red-eyed monster would be hers.

The wolf aimed his red stare on the foliage near her. The leaves of the shrubs burned and dropped off. Drawn by his mesmerizing power, she gazed into the glittering lust-filled eyes. It wanted her. Her body swayed. She rubbed the pendant, praying for strength to fight the monster's pull.

She'd heard the tales of women who'd answered the powerful beast's call. Her own mother might have succumbed to the depravity. She was unlike her mother.

The other wolves stilled, sensing the tension and waiting for the alpha to attack. They sniffed the air. Had they found her too?

Desire for revenge coursed through her, setting steel into her spine. Holding her gun with both hands, she stood and locked gazes with the alpha.

The beast's intoxicating eyes, flashing colors of blue, green and gold, hypnotized her. She could not look away. As in a daze, she lowered her gun and moved toward the circle.

Nick's tortured face flashed before her, a vision cutting through her morbid fascination. In her head, she heard his voice calling to her, steadying her. His presence fused into her body and her mind, freeing her from the black wolf's unholy trap.

She lifted her gun and aimed.

A sudden, terrible wailing, borne of unspeakable

suffering, rent the air. Nick's face, contorted in agony, appeared again. He needed her.

The other wolves stiffened. The alpha stood at alert and turned his head in every direction, as if he recognized the sounds. Then the alpha and the other wolves pointed their snouts toward the moon and joined their howls with the wailing cries until the entire woods trembled.

The black wolf lowered his head and turned to her.

He sprang.

She fired.

* * * * *

Sunlight jabbed Kyla's eyes, forcing them open. She looked through a gently swaying canopy of leaves to a cloudless blue sky. She struggled to sit up. Pain shot through her head. Moaning, she lay still.

Taking sharp breaths, she slowly maneuvered to a sitting position. Massaging her aching head, she brushed leaves and dirt from her slacks. The memories of the night before flew at her. The black wolf. Howls and cries, then the quivering mass of fur had lunged at her. She'd fired her gun. The rest of her memory was gone, erased.

"I couldn't have missed again." The words tumbled from her. Despite her disbelief, no bloody body lay nearby. She blinked against the piercing pain in her head. She had no memory of the creature's body slamming into hers, yet something had knocked her unconscious. Did her attacker have the power to appear and disappear at will? If so, she dealt with something more powerful than any demon or werewolf she'd known.

The sunlight dappling through the trees hid the menace of last night. But she knew differently. With cautious deliberation, she examined her body. No slashes or bites.

She'd survived an attack by a very powerful werewolf, perhaps the demon wolf of legend, and it had let her live. It played a deadly game. And she was the prize.

She would win this game.

Nick pushed into her thoughts. She'd seen his tortured face before she fired. He couldn't be the black wolf, playing with her mind. He wasn't evil; her instincts could detect it. But her instincts were diminished in this place.

Holding onto a tree trunk, she levered herself up. Something glinted silver in her line of vision. Her gun. Relief washed over her and she bent to pick it up. A wave of dizziness overtook her and she leaned against the trunk. She checked the cylinders of the antique weapon. One bullet was gone.

Favoring her right ankle she'd somehow twisted in her attack, she cautiously neared the wolf clearing. The fire had burned out hours ago, leaving a charred hole. The area had been brushed and the ceramic pots taken away. She could almost believe she'd dreamed the whole incident.

She circled the space, looking for her spent bullet. Her foot knocked against an immobile object that sent her reeling. Her gun flew out of her hand. Feet tangled in a vine, she sprawled in the dirt. Her head pounded anew. She reached out to search the brush for her gun. Her hand connected with something cold and hard. Not her gun. Warning chills shot through her and she lurched up.

Her gun lay next to a deathly white hand protruding from the packed leaves. Heart hammering, she scooped up the gun and knelt to clear debris from the lifeless hand. With searching fingers, she felt for a pulse. Nothing. Swallowing bile, she swept dirt from the face. Neil's gaping, lifeless mouth greeted her. Flies swarmed in and out of the opening.

A deep, bloody gash on his neck had nearly ripped his head away. Her bullet hadn't done this.

Retching, she staggered to her feet. And knocked against something warm and hard. Weapon firmly in hand, she whirled. And met Dan Taylor's serious blue eyes.

"Hey, be careful," he said, eyeing the gun.

"Sorry." She lowered her gun.

He gripped her upper arms. "What are you doing here armed and dressed in black? Are you okay?"

His touch and the concern in his eyes should have comforted her, but uneasiness seized her instead. She freed herself from his grasp. His eyes hardened. She glanced down to his thick black boots. A memory triggered. She'd seen those boots before. When she looked at Dan again, his eyes were soft and gentle, making her wonder if she'd imagined their harshness a moment ago.

"The butcher's dead," she said.

"I know. I'm sorry you had to see that."

"How did you know?"

He shrugged. "He's my serial killer."

"Serial killer?" She took a step back. "Neil? The butcher-baker?"

He nodded. "Ironic, isn't it? Someone knocked him off. Whoever killed him did us all a favor."

She hugged herself against the sudden chill. "Someone did more than knock him off. His head is almost severed. What kind of monster would do that?"

His eyes darkened with barely concealed malice. "It's not your concern."

She stiffened and started to raise her gun.

"Put the gun away," he said. "I won't hurt you."

Lowering her gun again, she took a step back, prepared

to shoot if needed.

He frowned. "What's that black smeared on your face? And why are you skulking around here?"

Bristling, she notched her chin up. "Skulking? I'm doing research for my latest video game. Not that it's any of your business."

He raked fingers through his short hair. "I didn't mean to come on so strong. When I first saw you, I was afraid you were hurt. I wouldn't want anything to happen to you."

"I can take care of myself."

Desire sparked in his eyes. "A woman like you needs a man to take care of her. I'll see you home before you get into any more trouble."

She bit back her angry retort. Until she knew more about Dan Taylor, she would be very careful.

"Let's go," he said, gripping her elbow.

She shrugged free and began limping toward the narrow trail. He followed closely. Thoughts, dark and twisted like the vines tangled on the forest floor, scrambled in her mind. The butcher's body had been undisturbed when she found it. Yet Dan had known about Neil's murder.

CHAPTER SEVEN

"Damn it, Todd, I missed again. It's been two days since I saw the black wolf and found Neil's body and I still don't know what the hell is out there." Kyla slammed her coffee mug on the kitchen counter. Brown liquid sloshed over the sides onto the granite top, making a mess on the clean surface. Like the mess her life had become. Nerves tight, she paced the small room.

Todd grabbed her arm and pulled her to face him. "Hell, Kyla, settle down. I haven't seen you this agitated since that day in foster care when Stan—"

She put up a hand, cutting off his words, and jerked free of his grip. "Don't go there." Hurt and confusion settled in his blue eyes. With an effort, she relaxed. "I'm sorry. I don't mean to take out my frustrations on you."

He shrugged. "Hey, we're family." He studied her and his gaze softened. "You're the best were-hunter around. You'll get this werewolf. I know it."

She released a sigh and leaned against the nearest counter. Through the window she could see a neighborhood cat stalking a bird in the garden. Flapping its wings, the bird escaped to freedom. Escaped. Like the black wolf. She turned to Todd. "I had him in my sights, just like the Adirondacks. There was no way I could have missed. Yet I did."

He poured himself a mug of coffee and held the pot out

to her.

She shook her head.

"Are you sure it was the same wolf as that other time?" he asked as he set the pot on the counter.

"I can never forget those eyes. Somehow he manages to escape. I'm missing something." She looked out the window to where the cat stalked another bird. "It's almost as if the black wolf can fly."

Todd shuddered. "Quit talking like that. You're getting yourself riled up for nothing. He's just an ordinary werewolf."

"There's nothing ordinary about this creature. He could have killed me, but he didn't. Why?"

"Maybe something scared him off."

She frowned. "Maybe, but I wonder if he's toying with me."

"Your paranoia is giving this creature credit for being more cunning than he is. What if Neil was the black wolf and you got him after all?"

"My bullets don't sever necks."

"It was a thought. Don't bite *my* head off." He quickly drained his coffee and set the empty mugs in the kitchen sink. Grabbing a paper towel, he wiped the counter.

She tapped a finger to her chin. "I think Neil was the fat gray wolf."

Todd chuckled. "Fat man. Fat wolf." He threw his towel on the counter and looked at her, his brow furrowed. "I just thought of something. Maybe your bullet hit its mark."

She straightened. "What are you saying?"

"Could be that you didn't miss your target. You're just missing the obvious."

"What do you mean?"

"Maybe it's not a werewolf," he said. "But something

that takes the form of one. When we were kids, you scared the pants off me with those stories of shape-shifting demons that morphed into werewolves and couldn't be killed by silver bullets. How could you forget?"

"Why would you think of that now?"

His mouth set in a tight line. "My father told me stories too, trying to toughen me up to follow in the family were-hunting business." He shot her a wry smile. "It didn't work."

Sympathy welled in her and she touched his arm. "I didn't mean to bring that up." Todd, the son of elite were-hunters, had no stomach for hunting. Although his parents were killed when he was seven, Kyla knew he'd never forgiven himself for not living up to their legacy.

He waved Kyla away. "It's nothing. I'm over it. Do you think your black wolf could be a shape-shifting demon?"

She shook her head. "I don't know what the hell to think anymore. I never wanted to believe the stories about demons that shape shift into wolves. If the stories are true, then the tales of my mother seduced by a black wolf might be real." A tremor of disgust coursed through her. "Only the best demon hunters or a very powerful werewolf can kill such a creature. I almost fell under its spell."

"Settle down. You'll figure it out, but you need to rest now."

"I need to think. A demon." She chewed her lip and began pacing the small room again. She debated warning Hunter-Wolf and asking them to send their elite demon hunters.

"You're stubborn as always." Todd opened the dishwasher and began stacking dishes. "Have you heard from Nick?"

She stopped her pacing. Todd knew her too well. Thoughts of Nick were never far from her mind. She'd told Todd about her vision the other night that Nick had needed her. She couldn't shake the feeling that she'd failed him. She rubbed her temples against the twin pains of regret and self-doubt that pounded her head with the beginnings of a first-class headache.

"Antica intercepts my phone calls," she said. "I don't buy her story that Nick is out of the country. I'm heading to his place in a little while. I have to see him. Have to be sure he's okay."

Todd slammed the dishwasher door shut and faced her. "Maybe you were having some sort of weird dream and Nick really is out of the country. How can you know he was in trouble?"

"I felt it."

He grinned. "You have it bad for him."

"I do not."

"I think milady does."

Milady. The word jolted her, like a long-buried memory struggling for release.

"Will you be okay alone for a while?" He wiped his hands on a towel and grinned. "I wanted to check out that clothing store in town. There are some interesting items in the window."

"Go on. I'll finish up here." She gave him a little shove toward the door. "Maybe you can find out why the sheriff hasn't tried to question me, or at least call. I found Neil's body. A little strange I haven't heard from her, especially if the whole town's buzzing."

He turned from the doorway. "I'll try to find out what I can. Things get stranger around here all the time. Speaking of the phone, I'm tired of fielding calls from that detective who brought you home. I think he's got a thing for you."

She stiffened. "There's something about him I don't

trust. And he won't take the hint that I'm not interested."

"That's because you're hot for Radford."

"Enough of that," she said. The doorbell rang, making her jump.

"You're as nervous as a werewolf looking down a gun barrel full of silver bullets. I'll get the door."

"If its Dan, tell him I'm resting."

"I'm going to burn in Hell for all the lies I tell for you."

"If you burn in Hell, it won't be my fault." She reached for the dish detergent, moving slowly, favoring her right arm that bore bruises from her encounter in the woods two nights ago. She wished she could remember what happened and what game her attacker played. Thoughts cluttered her mind like puzzle pieces pounding against her skull.

"She's in the kitchen," she heard Todd say. "I'll leave you two alone." The front door slammed. She would kill Todd for leaving her with Dan. Plastering a smile on her face, she turned, expecting to see the tall detective.

Instead, a darkly handsome Nick filled the doorway. She sucked in a ragged breath. "You're here. You're all right."

His strength and power reached into the room, wrapping her in sensual heat so overwhelming she gripped the edge of the sink for support.

Wanting to reassure herself a flesh and blood Nick stood before her and that he was okay, she ran to him and brushed her hands up and down his arms. "I was worried about you."

"You've no need to worry about me." He cupped her shoulders and pulled her closer.

She studied him through narrowed eyes. Sunlight streamed through the windows and highlighted strands of white threaded lightly through his black mane. She'd never noticed the white before. Bruises and scratches marred the perfection of his features and he was pale beneath his tan.

"You *are* hurt. I knew it." She skimmed her finger over the small cuts on his face. "Nick, what happened?"

Taking her hand, he turned it over and placed a tender kiss on her wrist. Desire pulled low in her belly and she swayed toward him.

"Why did you worry about me?" he asked, his voice husky.

Their gazes locked. The heat shimmering in the golden depths of his eyes ignited a fireball deep inside her.

She placed her hand over his heart. "I had a dream you were in trouble." A dream or a vision? She no longer knew.

"Nothing can hurt me." The words, colored by pain, lingered in the still air. "You needed me and I couldn't get to you." He brushed a soft kiss on her temple.

She stepped back. "How did you know I needed you?"

"I just knew."

Her breath hitched. "But how?"

"It's not important." He swept fingers lightly along the bruises on her arm. "No one will ever hurt you again. I promise." He pulled her closer and bent to take her lips in a tender kiss that sealed his vow.

His kiss incited need deep inside her and dissolved her fears and misgivings. She could no longer deny what her body and spirit craved. Sighing, she looped her arms around his neck and pressed against his taut frame, feeling the evidence of his arousal. She deepened the kiss, releasing the pent-up yearning she couldn't voice.

He nibbled the edges of her lips and traced the contours of her mouth with the tip of his tongue, coaxing her body into willing submission. "I let you down." He trailed a fiery path of kisses along her neck, inflaming her hunger for him.

"But you're here now." Her words came out on a moan. "I need you." She barely recognized the hoarseness of her own voice. She took his face between her hands and flicked her tongue on the corners of his mouth and down his firm jaw line. The stubble of his beard teased her sensitized skin and his raw sensuality seared her. She savored his unique scent of pine and outdoors, and something else, something ancient and familiar that unleashed misty memories of passionate nights filled with soft words of love.

He kissed her with an urgency that matched hers. His kiss inflamed her until all rational thought fled. She knew only her intense desire to taste and feel more of him. He slid his tongue over her teeth, then dipped inside, joining her tongue in a slow, seductive dance.

Ravenous for him, she stroked his shoulders and slid her hands down his spine, reveling in the heat of his firm body and the feel of his muscles flexing under the smooth cashmere of his sweater. His low groans fueled her feminine power.

She would make love to Nick as no woman ever had. He would never forget her. She kissed his face and licked a path to his throat, nibbling his roughened skin and the jagged scar that marred his neck, tasting his faint hint of salt. Exotic, yet familiar, his scent and taste flowed over her like warm honey.

Wrapping his arms around her waist, he lifted her and turned her until her back was pressed against the unyielding surface of the kitchen wall. She slid slowly down his chest and felt the rush of arousal. His powerful body covered hers, trapping her in an erotic web she never wanted to escape.

Groaning her name, he cupped her buttocks and pulled her closer. His erection throbbed hard and hot against her stomach. Her breasts swelled and pushed against her thin shirt, eager for his touch. His warm breath whispered against her face, tantalizing and tempting.

Uttering small cries of need, she ground her hips against his, demanding more. Tangling her fingers in the thickness of his hair, his name ripped from her throat, the sound low and rough and filled with desire. The heated area between her thighs liquefied and burned. Her body needed Nick. Her soul hungered for him.

"I want to see you," he whispered. In one swift move, he pulled her T-shirt over her head, exposing her braless breasts to his hungry eyes.

His gaze worshipped her and he reached out to cradle her breasts in his large hands. A startled gasp escaped her, and she moaned. She leaned into him, raining kisses on the soft skin of his neck.

"Beautiful." His whispered word, filled with awe and desire, hovered between them. On fire for him, she pressed closer, needing Nick to fill her body and the empty places in her heart. He brushed the hard peaks of her nipples with his fingers and bent to suckle one hardened nub, then the other. He massaged and laved her aching, swollen breasts, the exquisite torture of his hands and mouth heating her to her core until she was a quivering puddle of need.

Crazed with desire, Kyla ran a trembling hand down his chest to his jeans. Unzipping them, she slid her hand inside to stroke his long shaft, gasping at his strength and fullness. "Nick," she breathed, rubbing her breasts against the softness of his sweater.

Taking her by the shoulders, he gently pushed away. She let out a small cry of protest and reached for him. With a wicked grin, he quickly shed his clothes until he stood before her, magnificently male, splendidly nude.

Her body clenched in anticipation. "You are a god."

With a soft laugh, he moved closer. The heat from his body drew her into his sensual sphere. Moistening her lips, she wrapped her hand around his cock and gently massaged. A guttural sound pushed from his throat, unleashing an answering ferocity in her. She sensed something savage in him, straining for release. Still massaging him, she stood on tiptoe and nipped his shoulder hard, wanting to taste him, wanting to meld her body with his.

He shuddered and she gazed up at him. A feral gleam lit his eyes. He took her hand from his shaft and knelt before her. "Let me love you."

His hands circled her waist and he pulled her close to kiss her feminine mound through the denim of her skirt. Her body felt languid and heavy. With small moans, she arched into him, winding her fingers in his hair, surrendering to him.

He lifted her skirt and rolled her panties slowly down her thighs, kissing a trail behind them. Trembling, she slid out of her sandals and kicked them away. Tossing her panties aside, he reached for her.

He slid his hands up her legs to her thighs, caressing and massaging until she groaned her pleasure. When he bit gently at the heated flesh of her inner thighs, she bucked against him, desperate for him to fill her. Releasing a harsh growl, he plunged two fingers inside her. She cried out at the sheer, aching pleasure, and dug her nails into his shoulders.

Her body on fire and her legs quivering, she clung to him. Vivid lights flickered and wavered before her. Pain stabbed her head. Unbidden, visions assailed her, a kaleidoscope of colors and scents.

Nicholas, his long black hair brushing her naked

breasts. Red silk bed hangings, soft and sensual, gliding over hot flesh. His scent of horseflesh and wood smoke and the heather that grew on ancient moors.

The strange vision cleared. Nick, very real and very hot, plunged his fingers deeper into her, possessing her, taking her to the peak of pleasure. The primal tang of musk and desire surrounded them.

* * * * *

Nick inhaled Kyla's sweet scent of lavender and woman. He kissed the trimmed black curls at her center and found her nub and massaged gently, lost in the heat of her responsive body. She was hot and slick, and so ready for him. A distant memory whispered through his consciousness. He knew Kyla's body, knew her touch and the feel of her hot skin. Knew her moans. He didn't understand it, but he knew instinctively how to please her.

Her unrestrained passion woke the Beast. It reared up, hungry to devour her. One bite and Kyla would be his for eternity. He forced the Beast back. It would not have her.

"Please," she begged.

Fire raged in his veins. He would possess her pliant, lush body and make her his, and only his. No other man would have her. He rubbed her core and stroked his fingers in and out, deeper and harder, sealing his possession. Her soft moans slid over him. Slipping his fingers from her, he pulled her closer and plunged his tongue into her satin wetness. She rocked against him, pulling at his hair and crying his name over and over, until her body shook and she screamed her release. Male pride surged in him, rousing the Beast again.

Struggling to control the Beast, Nick stood and pulled her trembling body close, burying his hands in the silkiness of her hair. "I want all of you. Now."

"Yes."

Desire bulleted through him and he growled her name. Unable to wait any longer, he grasped her bottom and lifted her up, bracing her against the wall. He entered her in one swift thrust. She locked her legs around his waist. Her moist, welcoming heat wrapped around him. Her muscles contracted, holding him tight. She was made for him. His mate. Abandoning all thought except his obsessive need for her, he held her firm bottom and thrust his cock deeper, wanting to meld their bodies until they were one.

A fierce possessiveness overtook him and he rode her hard and fast, as if his very life depended on pleasing her. Only Kyla could fill the hollow places of his soul. Wild and wanton, she met his every move, giving herself freely. When she pushed her tongue into his mouth, his body trembled, threatening his control. Growling his pleasure, he pumped harder and deeper, branding her.

Their bodies were meant for each other. Their souls knew each other.

She tasted of coffee and mint and female. Whimpering tiny sounds of pleasure, she wrapped her legs tighter around him as they rode the tempest together.

She shuddered with the force of her climax. Her screams reverberated through the room. He shook with his own climax and spilled into her. They held onto each other as passion rocked them. When his breathing slowed, Nick gently pushed away. She slid down his body, scenting him with her female essence.

He cupped her face between his hands. Something hot, raw, and untamed shimmered in the green of her eyes. He'd seen this same hunger before. The memory teased the edges of his mind.

Then she skimmed shaking fingers over his lips and the memory fled. He took her fingers into his mouth and sucked until she moaned softly.

"We're not finished." Sweeping her into his arms, he carried her through the house and up the stairs.

CHAPTER EIGHT

Kyla shivered against the chill and reached for the comforter. Instead of soft down-filled cotton, her hand encountered firm, warm flesh.

She jerked her eyes open. Nick, in naked glory, slept next to her on the bed. He lay on his back, one arm flung up to rest on his forehead. The red-gold rays of the setting sun angled across the harsh planes of his face and stroked a golden trail down his tanned, muscled body. His chest rose and fell with his even breathing.

Her gaze slid over him, as if studying a statue sculpted by a master. He was no marble sculpture, but an exciting, creative lover who ignited a flame in her that threatened to engulf her heart and soul.

She could lose herself in Nick. Fear fought with her overwhelming need for him. Memories of the magic he worked with his hands and mouth seared her. His unique outdoors' scent of pine and wood hue, joined with the musk of their lovemaking, covered her like a canopy of satin. Another scent, warm and familiar, wafted in the air for the space of a whisper. Cloves and sandalwood. An ancient scent, but one she knew. Craving Nick's heat, she reached out a hand. He stirred and she quickly withdrew. If she weren't careful, her growing feelings for him would allow him control over her. That couldn't happen.

She could almost believe he'd put a spell on her. In the kitchen, they'd taken each other like two people starved. Never before had she made love with such abandon, as if an alien force had invaded her body, fanning an insatiable hunger.

Later, in her room, they made love again, this time with a scorching passion overlaid with gentleness and yearning. She wanted him now, burned for his hands and lips to caress and kiss every part of her aching body. She wanted him deep inside her, wrapping her in heated sensuality that banished her private demons.

Nick wasn't like the other men she easily walked away from. She couldn't walk away from him. The thought terrified her. Slipping off the bed, she grabbed the comforter lying on the floor and wrapped it around her in a futile attempt to shield herself from her treacherous thoughts.

Her movements must have awakened him. He opened his incredible topaz eyes. His sensual, sleep-filled gaze roamed her body, and he held out a hand. "Come back to bed, beautiful." His low, smoky voice covered her like gossamer silk, promising sexual pleasures she knew so well.

His hard erection tented the sheet over him. Moistness pooled between her thighs. She had to fight her consuming desire for him or she would be lost.

"You have to go." Her mouth uttered the words, but her brain whispered *please stay*.

"Why?" Lips slanted in a sexy smile, he sat up and stretched his arms over his head. "I'm not ready to go." His chest muscles rippled with his movements.

Kyla's mouth went dry. She never allowed a man to stay long in her bed. But Nick was unlike the others.

He slid from the bed and stood before her. "Are you sure

you want me to leave?"

The fire in his eyes stoked a fierce desire in her to possess him again. Her gaze devoured his perfect body. Sensual beyond anything she could have imagined, his strength and stamina had sent her to heights she'd not thought possible. Her face burned and her nipples pebbled at the memory. He could not be of this world.

She had to resist his sensual pull, had to maintain control. Longing and desire weakened a person. Years ago, she'd learned that hard lesson. She raised her chin. "Your jeans are in the kitchen where we left them." Her voice came out a strangled whisper.

"Ah, the kitchen." He tossed her a sinful grin and moved closer, hooking a finger under her chin and tilting her face toward his. "You are one incredible lady."

He took her lips in a possessive kiss that branded her as his. Her traitorous body melted and she clung to him. The comforter brushed her sensitized skin as it slid down to settle in a heap by her feet. Her bare breasts pressed against his firm chest. She ached for him and the exquisite release only he could give. But he was dangerous to her heart.

Nick ran his hands slowly down her spine, peeling through the layers of her defenses. "I'll stay."

Fear of losing herself to him surged through her. But his hands and his body felt so good and she wanted him so badly. She shoved aside her uncertainties. She wouldn't allow herself to look beyond this moment.

"Stay," she whispered.

A long while later, Kyla opened her eyes and smiled, stretching languidly. Her whole body throbbed with satiated pleasure. She hurt in places she'd forgotten about. But none of that mattered. Nick had taken her again and again until she thought she could bear no more of the delicious torture, then he took her again. No man had ever given her such unselfish, no-holds-barred sensual delight. She wanted him again.

"Hello, beautiful," Nick whispered beside her. He turned to her and gathered her into his arms.

"Nick." It was all she could manage.

He brushed strands of hair back from her face and kissed her, a gentle kiss filled with promise. "You're insatiable." He laughed softly.

"So are you." She let out a contented sigh and glanced around the darkened room, then sat up quickly and looked at the illuminated face of her clock. It was late, too late.

Fear reared its ugly head again. Nick couldn't stay the night. She'd never trusted any man enough to allow him to spend the night in her bed.

"Kyla, what is it?"

She looked down at him. Oh, but she wanted him to stay, wanted to wake up again with him beside her. No. If she lost her heart to him she'd give him the chance to leave her. She was the one who always walked away.

With all the willpower she could muster, she scooted away from him. "You need to go."

His gaze speared her. "Why?"

"It's late. And Todd will be back soon."

He chuckled. "You know Bailey won't mind finding me here." He reached for her and pulled her down until she lay across him. Wrapping his arms around her, he asked, "What are you afraid of?"

"Nothing."

"I don't believe you." He nuzzled her neck, eliciting a shudder of raw need from her. With a resigned sigh, he brushed a kiss on her temple and released her. "But it is late, and I do need to get home. I'll find my clothes. Stay here." He rolled off the bed. She knelt on the mattress and hugged herself, missing his heat. Leaning close, he kissed her deeply, taking possession of her again. She gripped his shoulders, clinging to him.

"This isn't over between us," he said, straightening. He gave her a lingering look, then walked from the room.

She watched until his naked, perfect body was out of sight, then she grabbed the sheet and clutched it to her chest. *Don't leave me again, Nicholas.* The words, filled with an anguished and elusive memory, floated into her mind.

* * * * *

"Is it safe to come in?" Todd shouted from the living room two hours later.

"I'm in the kitchen," Kyla called back.

He sauntered in with a huge grin on his face.

She narrowed her eyes, trying to look stern. "What do you mean is it safe to come in?"

"I thought Radford might still be here." Laughing, he folded his arms across his chest and leaned against the doorframe. "I finally got to meet our mysterious neighbor." His gaze scanned her. "By the glow on your face, I think you and he had a real neighborly visit."

Ignoring him, she turned to stir her pot of soup.

He sniffed the air. "Is that your famous Italian wedding soup?"

Nodding, she reached for the grated cheese.

"I knew it," Todd said, a note of triumph in his voice.

"Knew what?" she asked, turning to him.

"You always make Italian wedding soup when you've had a good lay."

She snorted. "It's a cool night. Perfect for homemade

soup."

"Uh-huh." He walked to the refrigerator, pulled out a can of soda and yanked the tab open. Throwing the tab into the sink, he leaned against the counter next to her.

"So how was it?"

"How was what?" she asked, not looking at him.

He chuckled. "You know what I mean."

"That is none of your business."

"Something's different about you, Kyla." His voice softened. "This guy's gotten to you."

"I don't know what you're talking about." She stirred the soup, refusing to meet his gaze.

"Yes, you do."

She sighed. "You think you know me."

"We're family. I know your fears and I know what you really want even if you won't admit it. If Radford makes you happy, then go for it."

Todd set his can on the counter and took the wooden spoon out of her hand and laid it on the stove. With his arm around her waist, he guided her to one of the kitchen chairs. "Sit."

She sat across from him and met his concerned blue gaze. "I'm afraid." The words spilled out.

Shock registered on his face and he widened his eyes. "That's huge. I've known you since you were eight and I've never heard you admit that."

She twisted the hem of her T-shirt. "We made love. I let him stay." She chewed her bottom lip. "I never let anyone stay."

He shrugged. "Radford didn't stay overnight so you haven't broken your rule."

"You don't understand. I wanted him to stay." She looked

down at the table.

"That's huge. Kyla, you've got it bad."

She raised her gaze. "Don't be ridiculous."

He placed his hand over hers where it rested on the table. "You deserve happiness any way you can get it. If you're falling for Radford, go for it."

She stiffened. "Love controls people and weakens them. My father looked the other way when my mother took lovers. She played him and when she died, he killed himself. That's what love does."

He squeezed her hand. "Not all love is controlling. Your father chose to ignore your mom's affairs. What they had worked for them."

"My father didn't love me enough. He left me."

Todd let out an exasperated sigh and pulled his hand free. "For heaven's sake. Get this through your stubborn head. A powerful werewolf, or worse, attacked your parents. Your father killed himself because he knew the hell waiting for him as a werewolf." His gaze bore into hers. "He loved you too much to condemn you to a wretched existence."

She glanced toward the window. "His death threw me into a wretched childhood."

"Hey, you had me," he said. "How bad could it have been?"

Kyla turned to him and smiled. "Without you I wouldn't have survived." She bit down on her lip. "In my head I know you're right, but in my heart I feel betrayed. If my father truly loved me, he would have stayed. I've tried, but I can't get past that."

"You don't want to get past it because you've used that hurt and anger all these years as a barrier to keep everyone away. You even shut me out at times."

"When did you get your degree in psychology?"

"You know I love you."

"I know. I'm sorry. I don't mean to take my problems out on you."

"I'm your family. You can say anything to me."

"Thanks. We're a pair, aren't we? Both afraid of love. But at least your parents had a solid marriage so you know what a good relationship is. That's something I've never seen." Giving him a wry smile, she looked toward the window, then back to him.

"What am I going to do?" she asked. "I've never given any man the chance to hurt me. I always leave. But Nick's different. I don't know if I can walk away from him. What if I fall for him?" Too late. Nick had already captured her heart.

Todd grinned. "Fall in love or lust. Your choice. Either way, you'll have loads of fun."

"You're incorrigible. I'm glad to see my irreverent Todd is back." She swatted him on the hand. "Have some soup. I need air. I'm going for a drive."

* * * * *

Kyla backed her SUV out of the driveway and headed toward the scenic road, maneuvering away from the low stone wall that kept cars from plummeting off the cliffs into the churning sea below. On her left, the deep woods stood, silvered in the weak moonlight. Wind sighed through the trees, whispering melancholy and sadness, echoing her mood.

Soon she would leave this strange place—and Nick. But now, she had a job to do. So long as her quest remained unfulfilled, she had to stay here.

The mingled odors of balsam, fresh earth and salt wafted through the open window. The tranquility of her surroundings beckoned to her soul. She feared she'd never again know the peace and solace she'd lost that long ago day when her father killed himself.

Nick's mansion, like a silent guardian overlooking the ocean, seemed to watch her as she drove along the winding road. She and Nick shared a connection she couldn't explain. He could be her prey. The thought came unbidden. No. He couldn't be. But doubt remained. In this odd little village, anything was possible.

A car hurtling out of the darkness from the other direction headed straight for her. Heart pounding, she swerved toward the low wall and fought to stay on the road. The sea below crashed against rocks, mocking her with its power. She gripped the steering wheel.

The other car passed close enough to knock off her side mirror. She caught a glimpse of an unnaturally pale face and stringy black hair before the car disappeared from sight.

Shaking, Kyla pulled into one of the scenic cutouts carved into the road, rolled up her car window, and cut the engine. Leaning her head back on the seat, she tried to calm her racing heart.

Warning chills pricked her and the hair on her nape brushed against her jacket collar. She jerked her attention to the thick brush in front of her. A pair of red eyes, glowing with sinister cunning, watched from the deep foliage. Its dark power vibrated all around her. She grabbed her gun from the seat next to her.

Gun in hand, her gaze never leaving the evilness trained on her, she reached over to turn the key in the ignition, but the key wouldn't budge. Dread ratcheted to fear and her breath lumped in her chest. As if compelled, she stared into the spellbinding eyes, unable to look away. The eyes dimmed and a tall figure stood in the shadows. Man or woman? It was impossible to tell. The figure turned and faded into the light fog that had begun to form.

Foreboding shuddered through her. She quickly reached for the ignition and let out a small scream.

Four men, pale and gaunt, appeared like apparitions from the mist and surrounded the car. She hurriedly turned the key. Nothing. Self-preservation chased her fear and she gripped her gun, prepared for battle.

One of the men, tall and bony, dressed in fatigues, his features hidden by his low-slung hat, glided toward her. A slash of memory sliced through her, then was gone. Should she know him? The man pounded on the hood of her car. She glared at him through the windshield.

He lifted a flashlight and shone it in her face, blinding her. She put her hand up against the glare.

"Are you okay, miss?" he shouted. "We saw the car speeding down the road. Did it car clip you?" He lowered the flashlight.

The others, also dressed in fatigues, smiled and bobbed their heads.

Kyla relaxed slightly and shouted through the closed window. "I'm fine. Just minor damage to the car."

She turned the key again and the SUV purred to life. Blowing out a breath, she rolled down the window just enough to speak through.

"Glad to hear you're okay," he said, approaching her. "Name's John Vickers. These are my men. We didn't mean to frighten you."

John Vickers. A frisson of recognition, tinged with a hint of malice, curdled her blood. Recognition of what? "I don't frighten easily." She scanned the trio surrounding her car.

"Your men?"

He nodded. "I head a small marketing company in Portland. These are my top managers. Once a year we come to the wilderness for some relaxation and bonding." He smiled, showing sharp white teeth with lengthened incisors—teeth that could rip into her flesh.

"Thanks for your concern. Everything is okay." When she shifted into reverse, the men scattered. Tires squealing, she raced down the road to her house.

She would call Hunter-Wolf. Werewolves, witches and now vampires if her instincts about the four men were correct. And possibly a demon with gleaming red eyes. This was bigger and more serious than anything she'd battled before. Her superiors at Hunter-Wolf needed to know about this—and soon.

When she reached the cottage, she ran in and locked the door behind her. "Todd!" she called out, needing his comforting presence.

Silence greeted her. His jacket was flung over the dining room chair as always. She did a quick search of the house, calling his name. No Todd and no note. His bowl of soup sat unfinished. She ran outside. Night insects sang to each other, but Todd didn't answer her shouts. Sickening dread squeezed the air from her lungs and she doubled over with pain as her instincts kicked in.

Todd was in danger.

* * * * *

Nick fingered the stem of his wineglass and stared at the dying flames in the fireplace. The deep shadows of the darkened room mirrored his mood. He grabbed the wine bottle and refilled his glass. The bottle would soon be empty.

"You know who she is."

Antica's soft voice came from the doorway. He didn't look up. After five centuries, he was used to her gliding in and out of rooms.

"I know." His tortured visions of Kyla the night of the full moon had forced him to acknowledge what he'd tried to deny.

He took a swig of wine and slammed the glass on the table in front of him. Deep red liquid, the color of blood, sloshed down the sides onto the ancient wood of the floor.

"You are besotted with her," the old witch said. "She is dangerous."

"Dangerous," he whispered. Kyla had truly bewitched him. His body tightened at the memory of her lush body and her fiery responses to his lovemaking. But she was his enemy. Kyla was a hunter. What irony, or was it another cruel game played by the God who seemed to have deserted him? Regret slashed his gut with the sharpness of a sword.

"What will you do?" Antica had moved from the doorway to stand before him.

Nick shifted his position on the sofa and finished off his wine. He poured another glass and let the empty bottle drop to the floor. Empty like his life.

He gave Antica a wry smile. "I'll make love to her as often as I can until the next moon. After I've destroyed Montague, Kyla can kill me."

Antica's eyes widened and she clutched the crystal at her neck. "Take the pleasures she offers, but you cannot die. You have outsmarted the best hunters. You will escape this one. You must live. That which was prophesied will come to pass."

"You don't understand. I don't want to live."

Antica rubbed her crystal. "This Kyla is different from

the others." The witch's black eyes pierced him across the shadows. "Kyla is darker and more skillful. She is an old soul, one that has seen much tragedy. It has made her hard. I feel there is more, but something has fogged my gemstone and I cannot see clearly. Is she causing this? You would do well to avoid her until my visions clear."

"I can no more avoid Kyla than stop breathing." He let out a bitter laugh.

"Does she recognize the wolf in you?" Antica asked.

He shook his head. "I would know if she did. She may be a skilled hunter, but her powers are nothing against mine or Montague's." He drained the last of his wine and threw the glass into the fire. The delicate crystal exploded before being consumed by the heat. Consumed, as he was by Kyla Yaeger.

"Son, I beg of you to have faith. You will meet the one predicted all those years ago."

"Leave me," he said, with a sweep of his hand.

Antica floated from the room as quietly as she'd come.

Nick stared at the fading embers, a reminder of his own coming death. And what of Kyla? They would both get what they wanted. He would leave this world and she would be hailed as the greatest hunter of all for destroying him.

And his soul would ache for her through eternity.

CHAPTER NINE

The glow from the overhead light skimmed Todd's unconscious body sprawled on the stone floor. Montague waved his hands over the room, transforming it into Nick's living room, the tapestry of Diana dominating. If his victim woke up, the image of Diana would impress on his memory. His plans were falling into place better than he could have imagined. Twice he'd allowed the huntress bitch to get close, to narrowly miss wounding him.

He'd already sown seeds of doubt in her. Now he had stolen her companion, further plunging her into self-doubt. She couldn't protect her friend and she couldn't protect herself. Her anxieties would grow until she was incapable of killing Radford.

Radford was *his* to vanquish. Through the centuries, Montague's hatred and lust for power and revenge had festered. His time had finally come. The huntress bitch couldn't stop him. Nothing could stop him and his demons from fulfilling the plans set in motion by his master in Hell.

Todd stirred and Montague kicked him. Montague's insides vibrated with the hunger to kill. But he would wait. He had a bigger plan.

The woman's arrival in the village was an unexpected gift. The bitch had thrown him and his demons a powerful weapon. She'd distracted Radford, seducing him, weakening him.

Montague threw back his head and howled. He would have his revenge tenfold and take the woman as his prize.

* * * * *

Kyla screamed and jerked awake. Heart pounding, she pushed sweat-dampened hair from her face and blinked eyes raw from lack of sleep.

Panic surged, knotting her chest, squeezing air from her lungs. Disturbing images from her dream rushed her. Todd mutilated and left for dead. Wicked red eyes and maniacal laughter. Did a demon have Todd? The black wolf?

She pushed up from the sofa where she'd fallen, exhausted, into a fitful sleep. Pale sunlight crept through the lace curtains, cleansing all they touched with the promise of a new day and giving lie to the malignancy that infected this place.

Her phone rang. With a shaking hand, she grabbed it off the coffee table. James' number came up. She'd left a message for Hunter-Wolf's leader as soon as she'd found Todd missing.

"James, we've got problems."

"Sorry I couldn't call back earlier. We've got a few problems here, too. One of our best hunters went missing in Vienna. What's going on there?"

She could picture the one-hundred-year old leader, a demon who'd come into the Light, sitting straighter in his chair. "Todd is missing," she said. "I think he was abducted." Trying for calmness, she drew a deep breath. "There's more here than a werewolf. I'm almost sure we've got a demon, and maybe some vamps. There's a witch, too, but I don't think she's a problem. I need you to send demon and vamp slayers." She cleared her throat. "And there's something else. I've seen the black wolf again. And I missed him again. I suspect he may not be a werewolf at all, but a demon. And I'm afraid he may have taken Todd."

"The demon wolf of legend," James said with a sharp intake of breath. "It's possible. That explains a lot."

Kyla gripped the phone tighter. "When can you send help?"

A sigh from the other end, then James' frustrated voice. "We're stretched thin, my dear. We've lost our guy in Vienna, and we've got some of our best demon hunters in the UK. A particularly nasty creature is terrorizing a small village there. I'll send hunters to you as soon as they clear things in the UK. Our vamp slayers are spread thin also. There's turbulence in the supernatural world. Something big is about to happen. We're trying to find out what it is, but we've learned nothing yet. I can't promise when you'll get help."

She swallowed the dread that clogged her throat. "What about Todd?"

"I'm sorry, my dear."

"Then, I'm on my own?"

"For the time being," James said.

Resolve stiffened her spine and she stood straighter. She was a hunter, damn it. A good one. Nothing, not even the black wolf, could stop her. "You can depend on me, James."

"I know that." His voice had softened.

"There's one other thing," she said. "I need someone to check into a New York detective named Dan Taylor."

"I'll get my people working on that right away."

"Thanks. Good-by, James." She hung up, threw the phone on the couch, and put a hand to her stomach to stop its trembling.

Could she save Todd? She hadn't killed the black wolf.

And she hadn't protected Todd from whoever took him.

She needed help, but she feared the sheriff would dismiss Todd's disappearance as easily as she had that poor girl. Still, she had to let the sheriff know another person was missing. Maybe she'd help after all.

And Nick. He would help too. She reached for her phone and froze. She had to be careful not to let anyone, even Nick, know she suspected a demon had taken Todd.

* * * * *

"What brings you here so early in the day?" Giving Kyla a warm smile, Sally Weston put down the papers she held and rounded her desk.

"Have you seen Sheriff Sanders?" Kyla asked in as calm a voice as she could muster. "I called, but there was no answer and her office is closed." She'd called Nick too, but Antica said he was out. Frustration threatened to erupt, undermining the clear-headedness she needed to find Todd.

Sally studied her. "Max is an independent sort, especially lately. Don't know what's come over her. You look a mite agitated."

"Todd's missing."

"Missing? Maybe he was carried off by wolves." Sally chuckled.

"It's nothing to joke about. I see you can't help." Afraid her aggravation would cause her to lash out in a tirade against the elderly woman, Kyla turned on her heel and headed for the door.

"Didn't mean to offend, dear. I shouldn't have said that. Come back. Let's talk about it. Maybe we can figure out where he's gone."

Kyla stopped. She drew in deep, calming breaths before turning to face Sally.

"Your partner is a grown man," Sally said. "I know he's made friends with the young couple that own the antique shop. Maybe he's with them."

Biting down on her lip, Kyla shook her head. "I went out for a short while last night and when I came home, Todd was gone. He left his jacket and cell phone at the house. It's not like him to disappear without a word. I stopped at the antique shop before I came here, and they haven't seen him."

Sally reached over and patted her hand. "I'll get you some coffee, darlin' while you figure out what to do. I make the best java in town. You sit and relax. I'm sure your friend has a good explanation and he'll turn up soon."

Too wound up to relax, Kyla paced the crowded newspaper office. Papers were piled neatly on desks and the office smelled of fresh pine, as if recently cleaned.

A quick hit of pain knifed her, buckling her knees, signaling a vision. She sank into the nearest chair. As if a veil dropped over her eyes, the newspaper office wavered out of focus. Cobwebs covered the room. The odor of sulfur permeated everything. She heard Todd's cries in her mind. She pressed a hand to her aching forehead. What the hell was going on with her visions? She was friggin' tired of it all. She wanted answers, not more questions.

When the vision cleared, she gazed around an office that was clean and neat. Only the smells of paper and ink and pine cleaner remained.

"You look a little pale," Sally said, handing her a steaming mug of coffee.

Cradling the mug like a lifeline, Kyla said, "I was hoping the sheriff might help me. I don't know where to look."

Sally's eyes softened and she reached out to touch Kyla's hand. "I'm not sure Max will want to help. She's not much interested in the town anymore." She pushed her glasses farther up the bridge of her nose and jerked her head toward the window. "Here comes that good-looking detective. Maybe he'll help you."

Kyla turned to see Dan Taylor crossing High Street with determined strides. Her stomach plummeted. She had no appetite for flirtatious sparring with him.

Dan entered the shop and fixed his blue gaze on Kyla. "How are you feeling? I've called you for the last two days, but that guy at your place wouldn't let me talk to you."

Kyla flared her nostrils. "His name is Todd and he's missing."

"Missing? Are you sure? Maybe he's out with friends and forgot to tell you."

"Damn it! Todd wouldn't worry me like this." The words exploded from Kyla. "Something's happened to him and I intend to find him, with or without anyone's help."

Dan's eyes hardened to blue chips. "How do you know something's happened to him?"

The harshness in Dan's eyes shot warnings up her spine. She would tread carefully. Tamping down her annoyance, she said, "Just woman's intuition."

His condescending smile pumped renewed anger through her veins. "I need to look for Todd." She slammed her half-empty coffee mug on the nearest shelf and headed for the door.

"Wait," Dan said. "I'll help you search for him. I know something about missing persons."

The door opened and Sheriff Sanders strode in. A sudden draft of air swept through the room, unsettling papers and knocking a pen off the desk. The sheriff slammed the door shut and the wind inside died. Yet, outside all remained calm with no breeze rustling the leaves of the small trees that lined the street.

At the sheriff's arrival, a black cloud of doom seemed to settle over the room. Shaking off the feeling of darkness, Kyla gave a curt nod to the sheriff and turned to Dan. "Shouldn't you be heading back to New York? You found your serial killer." Agitation made her tone harsher than she'd intended. But she didn't want the detective's help and she no longer cared if anyone thought her rude.

"Detective Taylor is here on special assignment working for me," the sheriff said. "We're shorthanded." The iciness of her voice and her forced smile dared anyone to disagree.

Sally snorted. "Shorthanded? Then why did you fire your deputy?"

Frost seemed to cover the sheriff's eyes. "Since when has running my office been any of your business, Sally?"

Animosity arced between the women, chilling Kyla. She rubbed her arms, trying to rub warmth back into her body. Their problems weren't her concern. She only knew she had to find Todd.

"Sheriff," she said. "Todd is missing. Can you help?" She raised her chin. "If you won't help, I'll find him myself."

"Call me Max," the sheriff said with a cordial smile. "What's this about your friend?"

Kyla looked into Max's friendly eyes. She must have imagined the hard-edged sheriff of a minute ago. Her nerves were causing her imagination to run amok. "Todd has been missing since last night."

"The pretty boy's missing?"

"For God's sake, his name is Todd."

Max waved a hand. "He's probably shacking up somewhere. I wouldn't worry."

"That isn't like Todd." Kyla forced out the words through tight lips.

"Kyla." Dan reached out and touched her arm. "I told you I'll help." He glared at Max, who shrugged and looked away.

Kyla opened her mouth to reluctantly accept Dan's offer. Before she could say the words, her throat closed as if a hand gripped her neck, cutting off her breath. The urge to flee overtook her.

The screeching of tires tore through the silence. She yanked free of Dan. Outside, Nick's Jag pulled up to the curb. With the engine still running, he jumped out and ran toward the newspaper office. His gaze caught Kyla's and an understanding seemed to pass between them. Next to her, she heard Dan's sharp gasp.

Nick stopped just inside the door and stared at her. Electricity sparked between them like heat lightening in a summer sky. "Antica said you called. You weren't home. What's wrong?"

She was no longer alone. Nick would help. "Have you seen Todd?"

Apprehension flitted across Nick's rugged face. "He's missing?"

Tears formed and she nodded. Damn it! She would not cry. She never cried.

"The kid probably partied too much last night and is sleeping it off somewhere," Dan said.

Nick turned and the men sized each other up, two beasts preparing for battle. Antagonism pulsed between them. The air stilled and thickened.

Dan backed away and lowered his chin into the turtleneck of his sweater as if trying to disappear into the garment. A purple bruise Kyla hadn't noticed before colored his jaw, accentuating the paleness of his skin.

"You're new here." Nick's voice vibrated with challenge.

"Dan Taylor, NYPD. And I know exactly who you are." His lips curved in a sneer.

A dagger couldn't have cut the tension hovering in the room.

"Long way from home, aren't you?" Nick asked.

Max stared at Nick with barely concealed animosity. "He's here to help me," the sheriff said.

Nick held his body rigid and met the sheriff's gaze until she looked away.

Kyla glanced around the room, as if watching a stage play. Strange dynamics zinged among the others, but she cared only about Todd.

"We won't find Todd standing here. I'm leaving." She rushed toward the door.

"I'll go with you," Nick said.

Dan laughed, a scornful sound that hung in the room. "I'm a detective, Radford. She needs me more than some small-town novice."

Max snickered, eliciting a sharp glare from Sally.

Jaw tight and eyes flashing anger, Nick turned slowly toward Dan. Kyla pushed herself in front of Nick and turned to Dan with narrowed eyes. "If you want to help, question some of the merchants for me. I'm checking the woods."

Kyla's eyes raked the sheriff, communicating the disgust swirling through her. Then she turned and ran out of the newspaper office.

"I'm right behind you," Nick shouted. "I know those woods." He climbed into his car and followed Kyla's speeding SUV out of town.

* * * * *

Dread gripped Nick as he maneuvered the Jag over the winding road. He suspected Montague had taken Todd. He'd seen the bodies of the men and women his enemy had defiled through the centuries. If they found Todd alive, he might be an empty shell, his mind and spirit destroyed. He'd do all he could to find Todd before that happened.

Kyla pulled up to Nick's house and cut the engine, then dashed from her car and sprinted for the woods. Nick raced after her and grabbed her arm, pulling her back to face him. Green eyes fiery, her raven hair flying around her beautiful face, she was the most magnificent female he had ever seen. His gut tightened with longing and regret. If only he'd met her in another time and place.

"Where are you going, Kyla? My property stretches for miles. What makes you think Todd is here?"

The pain in her eyes cut straight to his heart. He'd move heaven and Earth to find her friend.

"He's here, Nick. A feeling came over me when we were at Sally's." She dug fingers into his arm. "Please don't ask me how I know. We haven't much time."

He nodded. "There are some abandoned hunting cabins deep in the woods. We'll start there."

The look of gratitude she shot him made him want to puff out his chest like a lovesick twelve-year-old. If he only had the time to know her, all of her, her wants and needs, her likes and dislikes. He'd never met anyone who affected him like Kyla, not even Catherine. But Kyla was his enemy, here to kill him. If she completed her mission, he'd get his wish. The Beast would die. He couldn't choose differently.

* * * * *

Kyla fought tears of frustration and balled her hands at

her sides. They'd searched the woods and two abandoned shacks, but no Todd. She knew he was close. She felt his pain. But they couldn't find him. Desolate, she'd trudged back to the mansion with Nick.

They stood in his driveway now. The old manor house loomed over them, silently watching. Unsure if her legs would hold her, she leaned against her car. Nick gathered her into his arms and pulled her close. She pillowed her head under his chin. The quiet beating of his heart helped steady her.

"We'll find him." He stroked her hair and placed gentle kisses on her temple.

She held onto the front of his shirt as fear snaked through her. She couldn't bear it if Todd was gone from her forever. Guilt knotted in her gut, shooting pain through her. She should have protected him.

"Could we have missed something?" she asked, looking up at Nick. "Are there any other cabins?"

He pulled her tighter against him. "I've heard stories of a large hunting lodge in the woods, but it must have been destroyed years ago. I've never found it."

"I hate to break up this touching scene."

At the sound of Dan's mocking voice, they jumped and pulled apart. The detective stood close, a sneering grin on his face. He'd snuck up on them silently, too silently.

Next to her, Nick tensed. "What are you doing here, Taylor?"

"I figured you might need help. But maybe you're more interested in playing hero to the lady than finding her friend."

Nick started toward Dan. Kyla put a hand on his arm, stopping him.

Averting his face from Nick, the detective looked at her.

"Do you want my help?"

She nodded. "I'll do anything to find Todd."

Triumph gleamed in Dan's eyes. "We need to search by grids. I'll show you."

* * * * *

Kyla and the men had searched acres of woods, in small grids as Dan directed. Her clothes were dirty, her boots were muddy and her hungry stomach rumbled a protest. But still no Todd.

She'd gotten back to her empty, silent house an hour ago, no closer to finding Todd than when she'd set out early this morning. Night had descended, bathing everything in a dark blue cover. There'd be no sleep for her.

A pounding on the door propelled her from her gloomy thoughts. She raced to the door and flung it open, hope in every bone of her body. Instead of Todd, Dan Taylor stood there.

Her shoulders sagged. "Have you found him?"

"I have to talk to you." His voice was grim.

Chills brushed over her arms. Forewarning or stress?

Once inside, he whirled to face her. "What do you know about Radford?"

"What do you mean?"

"I've heard things," he said.

She bristled. "I won't listen to gossip."

"I'm concerned about you, Kyla," he said in a smooth snake-like voice that sent a shudder through her.

"I'm not your concern."

His features softened and he moved closer until inches separated them. He hooked his finger under her chin and forced her to look into his eyes. "You are one beautiful and smart lady and I don't want you hurt."

She yanked free. "I can take care of myself."

"Radford has you suckered," he said. "Talk to some of the villagers. They'll tell you. The family is reclusive. No one really knows much about them. Radford disappears for long periods. The missing girl was found in his woods. I hear he's paying for her stay in a mental hospital. He's hiding something."

She couldn't listen to Dan's distortions, but his words incited doubts in her about Nick.

"And Neil was found dead on Nick's property," Dan continued. "I tried to question Radford, but that old hag he lives with wouldn't open the door for me."

His gaze impaled her and she looked away to hide the uncertainties she feared showed on her face. Did Nick have something to hide and why was he paying for the girl's hospital stay? Where had he been the night Neil died?

No, she wouldn't believe any of it. Nick wouldn't hurt the girl or kill Neil. And he didn't take Todd. But she didn't really know Nick Radford.

Shooting a glare at Dan, she asked, "If Nick were guilty, why would he commit crimes on his own property?"

Dan snickered. "To throw everyone off his trail."

Fierce pain shot through her, freezing her response. Todd's screams reverberated through her mind until she thought her head would explode. A vision flashed in her mind. She knew where he was. She grabbed her car keys and headed out the door. "Todd's at Nick's."

"I'll drive," Dan said.

When Dan pulled into Nick's circular drive, Kyla sprang out of the car without waiting for it to stop completely. A power she didn't understand urged her to the back of the house. As she raced, Dan's footsteps thudded behind her on the thick grass.

When she reached the backyard, she skidded in her tracks and gasped. Illuminated in the light from the back porch lantern, Nick knelt over Todd's still body draped in a blanket.

"What have you done to him?" she screamed.

Nick stood quickly and rubbed his hands down the sides of his jeans. "He's still alive. Help me get him into the house." He nodded toward Dan.

"Take him to my place," Kyla said, fighting tears. "I don't want him to stay here."

Nick gave her a startled look. She stared back, challenging him to disagree.

Pain flashed in his eyes before he shrugged and turned away.

The girl. Neil. Now Todd. All on Nick's property. Dan's words leapt into her mind. Either someone was setting Nick up or he was guilty.

CHAPTER TEN

"Take him upstairs." Heart pounding, Kyla raced into her house and up the stairs. She skidded into Todd's room and yanked down the bedcovers. Nick entered and deposited a moaning Todd gently on the bed.

"Thank God he's alive." Holding back tears, she covered Todd with the quilt, gathering it close under his chin.

Nick reached for her.

She flinched.

Hurt flared in his eyes and he dropped his hand. "I'll call the doctor."

"Nick." She put out her hand, but he'd already turned away. She didn't want to suspect Nick, but the doubts Dan had planted took root when she saw Nick leaning over Todd's still body.

"A doctor will ask too many questions," Dan said from his stand by the door.

Kyla frowned at him. "Why should you worry about that? You're a cop."

He shrugged and turned away.

She didn't want a doctor nosing around either, but she wouldn't sacrifice Todd.

"The doctor will keep quiet," Nick said, as if reading her thoughts. He pulled his cell phone from his pocket. "I'll make sure of it."

* * * * *

The doctor had come and gone. Todd slept peacefully, his breathing steady. His kidnapper had drugged him heavily, but the doctor had assured Kyla the drugs should have no lasting effect.

She sat on the bed and gathered the quilt closer around Todd. Smiling, she brushed a lock of blond hair back from his face.

"How is it he ended up on your lawn, Radford?" Dan's question cut through the silence.

Kyla started. She'd almost forgotten the men. When she turned toward Dan, he gave her a long look as if reminding her of their earlier conversation. Doubts assailed her anew. Todd had been kidnapped, drugged, then found, still drugged, on Nick's property. None of it made sense. She too wanted to know how Nick had found Todd. She shifted her attention to Nick.

His body rigid, Nick clenched and unclenched his hands at his sides and faced Dan. "He was dumped on my lawn by someone. What are you implying?"

"You know exactly what I'm implying, Radford."

Anger propelled Kyla from the bed. "Stop it, both of you. Todd is here and he's going to be okay. We'll sort the other things out later. Now Todd needs peace and quiet."

As if Fate mocked her need for peace, a cold wind gusted into the room from the open window. The wind slammed into her and threw her words back at her. She grabbed the bedpost for support.

Pain erupted behind Kyla's eyes and images swirled before her.

A beautiful young woman with curling red hair held a squalling infant. Terror twisted the woman's face and she backed away as long, bony hands grabbed for her. A young boy, scrawny and dirty, braced himself before the woman as if he could protect her from the evil threatening them. The woman and boy screamed.

Kyla's legs buckled and she collapsed.

"Kyla!" Nick's strong arms were around her, lifting her before she hit the wood floor. He held her to his chest. The rapid beating of his heart echoed the wild rhythm of hers.

He laid her gently on the bed. Panic clawed her like a wild beast fighting for freedom, sending her pulse rate soaring. Lashing her hands out at Nick, she tried to sit up.

More firmly this time, he captured her hands and pressed her against the mattress. "Stay there. The stress has been too much for you. You need to rest."

"I'm fine." The words came out on a ragged breath. With an effort, she sat up and pushed him away. Her throat burned, an aftermath of her vision.

"You have to leave," she said, looking from one man to the other, wondering if either of them had brought on the vision.

Dan raised an eyebrow but didn't move.

The pain that seared Nick's face pierced her with regret and brought a wisp of memory. Scenes played through her mind like snippets of a movie—the woman with the curling red hair, the malicious laughter. Then Nick, long hair framing his face, his eyes hollowed and stricken. She wrenched her gaze from his. Until she made some sense of her visions, she needed distance from him.

"Go, both of you." She forced out the words. God help her, she needed Nick. But he might have hurt Todd. Her heart refused to accept that. Nick was coming to mean too much to her. She really didn't know him. And yet she did.

"You heard the lady," Dan rasped.

A growl rumbled from deep in Nick's throat and he turned to Dan. Nick's movements exposed the large yellow bruise that discolored his jaw. She hadn't noticed that before.

Kyla clutched her forehead, trying to stop the dull ache, a signal of another vision. Nausea churned her insides. The men wavered out of focus. In their place, two wolves, one large and white, the other muscular and black, appeared, locked in bloody combat. Her heart pumped wildly and her throat clogged.

As quickly as they'd come, the wolves disappeared. The men stared at her.

"You're stark white," Nick said. "What's wrong?"

He headed toward her, but she held up a hand, stopping him.

"Please leave, both of you."

With a sneer at Nick, Dan turned and exited the room.

"I won't leave you alone," Nick said.

"Go," she said, pointing to the door.

His features tense, he studied her before he turned abruptly and followed Dan. When the front door rattled shut, she sighed with relief and sank onto the bed.

"So cold," Todd croaked.

With a small cry, she leaned over him and adjusted the quilt. "I'm right here, Todd. You're safe now." She could no longer fight the tears that streamed down her face.

"Thirsty," he said in a hoarse whisper.

She reached for the glass of water on the night table. Putting an arm around his shoulders, she helped him to a sitting position and held the glass for him to drink.

He took small sips, then pushed the glass away and lay back on the pillow.

She set the glass down and turned to him. "It's all over," she said, rubbing his hands. "I won't let anyone hurt you again."

He gave her a thin smile and focused heavy-lidded eyes on her. "Since my first day in foster care, you've always been there for me."

"We watch each other's backs." She placed a kiss on his cheek. His skin felt dry and fragile. "Hush now. You need to rest."

His body jerked and fear slashed his face.

Choking back tears, Kyla brushed a soothing hand over his brow. She had to be strong for him. "You're safe, love. It's okay."

"Stone floor," he whispered. "So cold. Diana. Wild boar. Golden arrow."

He was hallucinating. *Diana. Golden arrow*. Kyla's chest constricted. Diana at the hunt? The tapestry at Nick's house? Trepidation shot through her.

* * * * *

"Leave her alone. What are you doing?"

Todd's screams woke Kyla. She jerked up from her chair next to his bed and leaned over him. Sweat beaded on his forehead and he thrashed about, throwing his covers off.

"Wake up, Todd." She gripped his shoulders. He raged with fever. Panic lodged in her chest, stifling her breathing. She raced into his bathroom and wet a small washcloth with cold water.

When she returned to the bedroom, his hands were balled into fists and he flailed wildly at the air. "Stop it, Stan," he screamed. "You're hurting her."

Kyla bit back a cry as memories slammed into her. She saw that long ago day clearly. She was twelve, and Todd

127

eleven. Their foster father Stan had accosted her and thrown her on the floor, pinning her under him. She'd felt his hard cock and retched at his fetid breath in her face. He'd fumbled with her panties.

Suddenly, a strangled scream and Todd was in the room. He threw himself on Stan. The older man flung Todd aside like a piece of garbage, and he lay whimpering on the floor, his arm at an odd angle. With Stan distracted by Todd, Kyla had rolled away and sprung to her feet. Fury had whipped her into a frenzy and she had found her strength that day. She wouldn't let anyone hurt Todd. She'd kicked Stan in the groin, then clawed his face, sending him sprawling. Screaming, he'd put his hands up to ward off more blows, but she'd jumped on his chest and began pounding him. It took two of the older kids to pull her off.

The police wouldn't believe a young girl could maim a grown man. She and Todd were removed from the house the same day. Their protectors at Hunter-Wolf, Ltd., had intervened and sent her and Todd to a safer house.

She shrugged away the painful memories and laid the cool cloth on Todd's forehead. Unbidden, the scrawny boy of her vision flashed before her. He'd tried to protect the terrified woman and baby much like Todd had tried to protect her that day. What did it mean and what had triggered Todd's memory?

For close to an hour, she kept cold compresses on Todd's brow. He tossed and shivered and tried to throw off his covers and escape the bed. It took all her strength to hold him down. Maybe she shouldn't have sent Nick home after all.

Nick. Anxiety formed a tight knot in her stomach. *Please, God, don't let Nick be the one who hurt Todd. I couldn't bear it.*

At last Todd opened cloudy blue eyes and stared at her. "What happened?"

She skimmed fingers over his face. His skin was cool to the touch. Shoulders sagging with relief, she sank down on the bed.

"You need to drink this." She held out a goblet of water, then helped him sit. He drank greedily, handed the empty glass to her, and lay back on the pillow.

"Rest now," she said. "We'll talk later."

Giving her a weak smile, he closed his eyes.

Much later she brought Todd a bowl of warm soup. He'd slept all day and now shadows invaded the room. When he saw her, he sat up and smiled.

She laughed. "Now you look like the Todd I love."

"Food always cheers me up, especially your wedding soup." He grabbed for the bowl.

"Take it easy. You've had a trauma."

He tackled the soup, making loud sounds of enjoyment. "Nothing ever tasted so good." When he finished, he set the empty bowl on the night table.

Kyla straightened in her chair and clasped her hands on her lap. "Do you feel like talking? Tell me what you remember of what happened."

"It's like a dream. There was a knock at the door. When I answered it, some strange creature with long black hair and the whitest face I've ever seen stood on the porch."

Kyla shivered. A pale creature with long black hair had almost knocked her off the road.

"What's wrong?" he asked.

"Go on."

"My memories are foggy after that. I was lying on a stone floor. It was so cold. I felt a presence but couldn't see anyone." He frowned and settled onto the bed.

"Take your time."

"I remember something."

"What?" She leaned closer.

His eyes widened. "Laughter. Horrible, chilling laughter, like something out of a horror movie. And then I opened my eyes to Nick."

CHAPTER ELEVEN

Like a bullet, Todd's words pierced Kyla's heart. "Nick found you. That's why you remember him." Her words sounded hollow. She wanted to believe someone dumped Todd in Nick's yard, but the truth could be much more sinister.

Todd dropped back, mumbling, as sleep overtook him again. Kyla watched for long minutes before she staggered from his room, reeling from the impact of what he'd said.

Gulping deep breaths, she leaned against the wall for support. Had Todd seen the tapestry from Nick's house? Doubts about Nick drummed through her, and she fought a wave of nausea.

* * * * *

"What are you doing?" Three days after his ordeal, Kyla found Todd at her computer in the dining room, staring intently at the screen.

He turned startled eyes to her. "Don't sneak up on me like that."

She patted his shoulder, then pulled up a chair. Her gaze swept him. Outwardly, he appeared the same boyishly handsome Todd. But his haunted eyes sent a different message. Fury formed a tight ball in her stomach and she fought to transform her anger into strength. She would destroy the person or monster that had done this to him.

"Why are you out of bed?"

"I was tired of lying around, so I thought I'd do some work on the video game. Look what came over from Hunter-Wolf." She peered at the computer. A picture of a smiling Dan Taylor filled the screen. "I asked James to check him out. What does it say?"

"On the NYPD force twelve years," Todd read. "Highly decorated. Widower. Wife killed by armed robbers in a home invasion." He looked at her. "Sounds like a fine, upstanding man."

"He does."

"But what?" he asked. "There's a 'but' in there somewhere."

She rubbed a hand over her eyes. "There's something about him. I can't figure him out."

"Maybe he's just a lonely guy interested in you."

She shrugged.

He studied her from narrowed eyes. "You're falling in love with Nick."

"Love?" She gave a bitter laugh. "Don't be silly. You know how I feel about love."

He frowned. "And you know how I feel about the walls you've set up around yourself. Lighten up."

She placed her hand over his. "How can I let my guard down after what happened to you? And what if Nick was somehow involved?" Just saying the words punctured her with sadness.

"You can't believe that," he said.

"I'm not sure what to believe any more."

"Me neither." He closed his eyes. When he opened them again, his gaze was haunted.

She bit her lip, fighting her anger and sorrow. Guilt

rushed at her, twisting her insides. She should have protected him.

"I wish I knew who did this to me, but the drugs were powerful and I hallucinated a lot," he said in a flat voice. "Maybe it was all an illusion. Nothing makes sense."

Kyla gave his hand a quick squeeze, then released him.

He shuddered. "One minute I was lying on a stone floor and the next Nick was standing over me." He reached for her hand. "I just remembered something else."

"Go on," she said, nodding encouragement.

His features tightened and he glanced away. "After I opened the door to the weird creature with the white face and stringy hair, I blacked out, as if the thing had cast a spell on me. But for a second, I had the impression the creature wasn't alone. A little later, I woke up and realized two people, or whatever, were carrying me. I couldn't see them, but I twisted around and punched one before I went out again. I think I got him in the jaw. Maybe I gave one of my assailants a bruise."

"A bruise?" Dan and Nick each sported a bruised jaw. But hadn't she seen Nick's bruise before Todd was taken? She wasn't sure. Trying to keep the worry from her face, she patted Todd's arm. "We might find your attackers yet."

His expression closed. He pushed his chair back and stood. "This place is too strange. Let's go home. Back to Manhattan where the only things I have to worry about are the coffee shop getting my order wrong and badly-dressed tourists."

Smiling slightly, she shook her head. "You know I have to stay. I've never run and I won't start now."

The fear in his eyes wrenched her. She stood and grabbed him in a fierce hug. "I'll send you to Hunter-Wolf's headquarters. They'll protect you."

"What aren't you telling me?" he asked, pulling back.

"Trust me. I don't want to scare you."

"Like I'm not already frightened out of my tightie whities."

"You're starting to sound like the Todd I love."

He sagged back into his chair. "I've traveled all over the world with you as you hunted smelly beasts, and I don't know if I can take it anymore." He gave her a weak smile. "Forget I said that. I don't know what I would have done all these years if I didn't have you."

"I don't know what I would have done without you, either."

She looked toward the window, but instead of the garden, she saw the day of her eighteenth birthday. "I've wished many times Hunter-Wolf hadn't contacted me."

Representatives of Hunter-Wolf, Ltd., had appeared at her new apartment and told her the time had come to claim her birthright. They'd hidden her and Todd in foster care all those years to protect them from whatever killed their parents. They offered to pay for college for them both and train her to hunt. It had appeared a fair deal, but they'd extracted their proverbial pound of flesh in the ten years since.

"I don't mean to be a whiner," Todd said. "Hunting were-creatures is what you do. I wouldn't have it any other way." He stood up and grabbed her in another quick hug. "I'm staying here with you. We watch each other's backs, remember?"

She gave him a gentle punch on the arm. "I'm serious about wanting you to go to the group's headquarters. I'm not sure I can protect you. Please, Todd."

He shook his head. "I'm staying. If my kidnapper wanted

to kill me, he would have. He was sending a message. You won't run and neither will I."

Sending a message. Nick didn't need to send her a message. He'd already gotten close to her. She let out a resigned sigh and met Todd's gaze. "We may be dealing with an extremely cunning monster."

"I don't care. You've looked out for me all these years. I won't abandon you."

"Stay close. Let me know where you are at all times." She touched his arm. "If things get really bad, you go. Agreed?"

He nodded.

She glanced down at the computer screen and Dan's smiling image. He seemed an ordinary guy, yet somehow she knew he wasn't. The fine hairs on her arms stood at attention. An omen? She shook herself and closed the laptop's cover.

* * * * *

In the midnight quiet, Kyla leaned her hip against the kitchen counter and gripped her mug of tea. She'd heard nothing from Nick since they'd found Todd four days ago. She knew she had hurt him, and she missed him.

True to his word, Hunter-Wolf's leader James sent vampire slayers and they were now housed in a B&B in town. No demon hunters were available yet, and she hoped it wouldn't be too late.

Todd tried to stay clear of the vampire slayers, saying their hypnotic eyes and tight, pale bodies creeped him out. What would he say if he knew she suspected a powerful demon had kidnapped him?

Through the opened curtains she could see the half-moon suspended in a black sky. Todd slept upstairs and the house was tightly closed against the spring air and whatever danger lurked. She had nothing to fear, yet foreboding shivered through her, giving lie to her thoughts.

A sound reached her ears and she jerked her head up, listening. Strange music, haunting and seductive, wafted through the room, its hypnotic notes luring her. Mesmerized, she set down her mug as she heard her name whispered. As if soft hands pulled at her, she walked through the kitchen and out the back door, her body liquid and pliant, unable to fight the strange allure.

The crisp Maine night wrapped around her, but she barely felt the coolness. She glided down the steps, her bare feet seeming to float above the wood. She crossed the yard and kept walking, drawn by the spellbinding music. Far below, the ocean pounded the rocks in a savage rhythm, and above her Radford Manor loomed, watching.

She ignored everything but the promise of unearthly delights that hung heavy in the fog-shrouded air and wove through the exotic music. Red eyes glittered at her from the copse of trees. A deep voice rasped her name, calling her closer. Lust trembled through her and she curved her lips in a smile. In a sensual haze, she walked toward the red glow.

Out of the mist, pale creatures approached and surrounded her. Their sunken eyes stared at her with hunger. Their claw-like hands reached for her breasts. Trancelike, she swayed toward them, wanting the debauchery they offered.

Maniacal laughter rang through the trees. *You will do what I command. Your power is nothing against mine.* The words repeated over and over in her mind.

From somewhere deep inside Kyla, fire coalesced, spreading through her body to her heart. She jerked her head up as strength burned through her, heating every muscle and joint, and releasing her from the odd hypnotic pull. Herself again, she assumed a fight stance and whirled to face the creatures surrounding her.

Howling, they dissipated into black mists, swirling at her feet, before disappearing.

She turned to the glittering eyes and sent a silent message. *You won't take me.* Power pulsing through her veins, she sprang at the thing lurking in the brush.

Laughing hysterically, the creature, his body a misshapen lump, feinted to the left. The red eyes dimmed and her fist punched air. Wind whistled through the trees, an ominous sound that echoed in the darkness. Then the wind stilled and Kyla knew she was alone.

Fear stung her. Todd! She sprinted home.

She lurched through the opened back door and up the stairs to Todd's room. He slept peacefully. All was quiet. She had fought the devil and won. This time.

* * * * *

The game just got more interesting. Montague licked his lips and felt himself harden. He had underestimated the bitch's willpower. He chuckled. Breaking her would be more enjoyable than he'd anticipated. Maybe he'd keep Radford alive long enough to witness the depravity he would inflict on the huntress.

She would bow before him. Calling her out tonight proved that. He had weakened her. He had taken the boy. She knew he could do it again. He'd lost Catherine, but the huntress bitch was his.

CHAPTER TWELVE

The seductive song of the haunting music flowed over the red-haired woman. As if in a trance, she clutched the baby to her bosom and walked slowly out a heavy wooden door and down stone steps to the mist-shrouded woods beyond. The hem of her gown dragged along the rutted forest floor and her hair curled around her face in wild disarray.

"My lady, where do you go?" a small, ragged boy called as he ran after her to tug on her sleeve. His face was shrouded in shadow, but through the fog his eyes, large with fright, shone clearly. "The master charged me to protect you and the babe."

Clearly annoyed, the woman jerked free of the boy's grasp. "The master did not charge you to watch us, Aiden. You know that. Go to bed and do not worry for me."

The boy followed closely on her heels, but she barely gave him or the whimpering baby notice as she continued her walk through the woods. The music grew louder as she approached a copse of trees surrounded by bushes. The woman hurried toward the sound, the hem of her gown snagging on vines and branches. Red eyes gleamed through the dense brush, following her progress. Sexual energy pulsated around her.

"Stop, my lady." The boy grabbed the woman's arm and pulled her to face him. Love and fear flickered from his eyes

and seemed to bring a semblance of calm to her. A voice, pledging sins of the flesh that would fulfill her like no other, floated on the wind, calling her back to the watching red eyes. The boy tugged on her sleeve, urgent now. The baby in her arms wailed. She shuddered and gasped, then crossed herself.

Still clutching the woman's arm, the boy dragged her and the baby away. Howling, heinous and ferocious, rang through the forest. The boy trembled and released the woman. They turned toward the sound. The woman screamed.

Kyla's scream tore from her throat, an eerie echo of the dream woman's. She shot up in bed, fully awake now. Sunlight filtered through the open shades, reflecting on the sweat that covered her body and made her silk nightgown cling to her. She brushed hair back from her face with a shaking hand and glanced at the bedside clock. Ten. She never slept this late.

Filled with dread, she leapt out of bed and pulled on her robe. The music she dreamt was the same seductive sound that had called to her at midnight, the witching hour. Shivering, she padded to the bathroom and glanced at herself in the mirror. Ravaged. Her hair was wet and plastered to her head, dark smudges shadowed her eyes and her face was as pale as the strange vampire-like creatures that haunted her dreams and the forest.

The remnants of her dream cut through her mind with the sharpness of a knife. She gripped the edge of the sink to steady herself. The woman's cries had matched her own and she knew death would claim the woman, the boy, and the infant. Kyla touched her throat, feeling long, bony hands squeezing the life from her. She retched. The face of the woman had been shaded in fog, but she knew it was the red-haired woman of her visions.

Nick intruded into her mind, and she saw his eyes, dark and suffering. Where was he? Like a starving woman reaching for sustenance that was just out of reach, she craved him. But she'd sent him away.

Hand shaking, she pulled open the medicine chest and snatched the aspirin bottle. She had the feeling it would be a very long day.

Her scream hadn't woken Todd. She dropped the aspirin bottle and raced to his room. He slept safely in his bed, snoring lightly. She let out a sigh and leaned against the wall.

* * * * *

The furious pounding on her front door set Kyla's nerves on high alert and triggered the headache that had finally begun to subside. She picked up her gun, lying on the table where she worked at her computer, and made her way into the living room.

"Who is it?" she shouted at the closed door. She cocked her gun and glanced at Todd who'd crept down the stairs.

"Nick."

She slid her gaze to Todd.

"I'll be in my room if you need me." He bounded back up the stairs.

She disabled the gun and opened the door. Nick slid through and she locked the door, then leaned against it and faced him. Joy bubbled up in her as she scanned him. The bruises and scratches that had spoiled the perfection of his features the day they made love had faded. Only his mesmerizing, seductive beauty remained.

He glanced at the gun she held. "We've met like this before."

At the reminder of their almost-kiss in the woods that

first day, some of the tension and doubt left her. Her gaze on his, she set the gun on the nearest table. They stared at each other. His nearness and his heat made warmth seep into her belly.

She moved away, unsure if she could trust herself not to rush into his arms.

"How's Todd?" he asked.

"Better. He's upstairs working on our video game."

He let out a relieved sigh. "I'm glad." Frustration etched his features, drawing fine lines around his mouth. "You sent me away. You know I had nothing to do with Todd's kidnapping."

He reached out and took her hand, pulling her to him. "I'll make sure Todd's abductor is found. Trust me."

"I want to trust you, Nick." Blowing out a breath, she pulled free and strode into the living room. He followed.

She whirled to face him. "Todd saw something that might be your tapestry of Diana when he was held prisoner. How could that be?"

He moved closer and gripped her arms. His hard, unwavering gaze locked onto hers. "Things are not always what they seem. There are forces that can make a person see or believe what's not there."

"Who are you, Nick?"

"You know me."

She shook her head. "No." The lie lodged in her throat. In her deepest soul, she knew him. She wouldn't admit that to him, not until she understood it herself.

He stepped back. "I was out of the country on business the last few days or I would have been here sooner." The pain in his eyes seared into her heart. "I missed you, and I need you to trust me."

141

She searched his unwavering gaze and found the answer she'd sought. She wanted to take a chance on him, and she would. "I do trust you, Nick."

His throat moved as he swallowed, then he breathed a sigh of relief. "Thanks for that. I would never hurt you or anyone you loved."

"I know that now." The air between them thickened. Her gaze went to the jagged scar on his throat. She imagined herself nibbling him there. She tilted her head to meet his eyes, gleaming gold, drawing her under his spell.

Her heart opened to him, welcoming him, accepting the truth of his words. "Nick."

He brushed his hands down her arms. His touch sent heat tingling through her. Spanning her waist with his hands, he pulled her closer. "I don't know how or why, but there's something between us that transcends this world. And you feel it too."

"Yes." Despite her suspicion that he held dark secrets, she sensed honor and goodness in him. If he were evil, she couldn't want him with this raw passion that ate at her soul.

He bent and captured her lips in a fierce kiss that ignited her hunger for him, a hunger that grew stronger every time she saw him. Needing to taste and possess him, she dipped her tongue into his mouth, stroking the moist contours, reveling in his heat and strength.

Moaning, he cupped her bottom and pressed her close until she felt his hard arousal. A feral wildness rose up in her and she shuddered with a volatile mix of lust and need. She swept her tongue over his lips, tasting coffee and mint and Nick. She couldn't think beyond the smooth feel of his skin, the power of his muscled chest, and her consuming desire for him. A low growl rumbled from his chest, the sound rough and seductive.

Their tongues locked together in an ancient ritual that sent erotic excitement through her. Her blood on fire, she ran her hands along the strong muscles of his back to curve around the hard contours of his buttocks, telling him with her body that she wanted all of him.

Nick left her mouth to nip tiny love bites along her neck. Wetness pooled in her private parts and she ground her hips against his, seeking release. A force, dark and untamed, pulsed from him, inciting an answering wildness in her. She wanted his lips on her breasts, tugging at the hard nipples. She wanted his body over hers, wanted him filling her, spilling himself into her. Only Nick could chase away the demons of her soul. Frantic with desire, she clutched his shoulders. "Please," she groaned.

He pulled away to stare down at her. She shivered at the savagery shining from his eyes. She threw back her head, exposing her throat, inviting his kisses, inviting his possession.

He bent toward her, then abruptly pulled away. She fell back and reached out her arms to him.

"I won't hurt you." He turned and strode to the door, yanking it open, then hurried from the house.

CHAPTER THIRTEEN

Nick clasped the stem of his wine glass and stared into the flickering fire, barely noticing the flames groping the chimney or the sparks falling on the stone hearth. Spread out on the low table in front of him were papers from his various accounts and holdings, all needing his attention, but he'd been unable to concentrate.

This afternoon, consumed by loneliness, despair and lust, he'd almost committed the grievous sin that would condemn his wretched soul to Hell, if it weren't already. One strategic bite to Kyla's soft neck, and she would be his wolf mate for eternity. Like the demon before him, he had the power to curse her to a life as a werewolf.

His chest knotted with a desperate rope of need and regret. Images rose unbidden. He and Kyla, in wolf form, running through the woods, wind ruffling their fur, the scent of balsam surrounding them, pine needles digging into their paws, their bloodlust stirring as they stalked prey. As the full moon rode the sky, he would mount her. She would carry his mark and his seed forever.

"Damn it all to hell!"

The words exploded from him. He dropped the empty glass onto the floor and leaned back on the couch, closing his eyes as if he could shut away the futility of his life. In all the long damning centuries, he'd never wanted to make a mortal woman his wolf mate. Not even Julia.

His mind tumbled back in time to New York in the 1890's. They now called it the Gilded Age, but to him it was an age of unbridled freedom where any man with brains, ambition, and few scruples could make or lose great fortunes with no restrictions and no recriminations. Friend to robber barons and honest men alike, he'd increased his fortune by whatever means necessary. He'd belonged in that barbarous world.

His bitter laugh echoed around him. He'd spent the last century atoning for his greed in that time. And there was Julia.

Her memory scorched him with wrenching guilt. She'd loved him and she'd died for it. Beautiful, willful, spoiled Julia, the daughter of one of the wealthiest and most ruthless of the robber barons. A virgin when they'd met, he'd initiated her into the ways of lovemaking. A willing student, she'd taken to sex with an enthusiasm unmatched by any woman he'd known, until Kyla.

Truly her father's daughter, Julia's sexual appetite and lust for adventure knew no bounds. When she'd pledged her love, he'd proposed marriage, sure he'd met the woman who would fulfill the prophecy handed to Antica centuries before. If his love for Julia wasn't as deep as hers for him, so be it. Ignoring Antica's warnings, he'd told Julia his horrific secret.

The terror in her eyes that day imprinted on his mind forever. He heard her screams in his head as if it had happened yesterday. His throat thickened with the memory. Calling him all manner of vile names, she'd retched and run from his house, out to the street, half-dressed, hysterical and shrieking.

And Montague had been waiting for her. Nick had tracked them to the most notorious house in New York, an opium den and place of iniquity that had no equal. He'd found Julia's broken body, throat slit, sprawled in a pool of blood. She'd been sexually mutilated. Charles Ashbrook, the Earl of Montague, had stood over her.

In a purple haze of rage, Nick had pulled out his dagger and leapt at Montague. But his grief over Julia had weakened him. Instead of the demon, he'd grabbed air. Montague had vanished, but his hideous laugh had echoed through the blood-soaked hallway. Nick vowed that the next time they met, he would have his final vengeance on his old enemy. He'd not seen Montague since that terrible day.

Along with Antica and her brood, he'd escaped New York that same night, minutes before Julia's father and brothers, accompanied by a lynch mob, had stormed Nick's Fifth Avenue mansion. He'd lost all hope then that Antica's prophecy would be fulfilled.

He opened his eyes now to the flames in the hearth. Flames of Hell waiting to devour him.

Had Kyla provoked thoughts of Julia? His desire for Julia couldn't match the soul-deep connection and longing he felt for Kyla. She was his enemy, sworn to kill him. Yet that didn't matter. The yawning emptiness of an eternity without her filled him with incredible sadness.

"No!" He swept his hand over the papers strewn on the table. The papers spread over the rug, a tangled mess. Like his damned, cursed life.

* * * * *

Swaying in the gentle breeze, hundreds of brightly colored Japanese lanterns ringed High Street. Loud rock music blared from the pavilion at the end of the street. Nick watched from the shadows as revelers, most of them in various stages of drunkenness, celebrated the small town's tri-centennial. The unseasonable heat dampened his forehead with sweat. It seemed the weather wanted to partake of the merriment too.

The villagers would string him up for sure if they knew he had once roamed this land when it was a densely wooded Indian hunting ground. His pulse quickened at the memory of being chased by a fierce band of warriors, arrows slinging toward him. In wolf form, he'd brought down a young deer they were tracking and they were determined to destroy him. One of the arrows pierced his wolf shoulder, slowing his trip back to Montreal and his ship waiting at port to take him and Antica's family to Barbados. Sadness nipped him like that long-ago arrow. Barbados would always hold tragic memories for Antica. Better for them all had he died at the Indians' hands.

Despite the dangers hidden in the forest that long ago time, Nick had learned to love the wildness and sanctuary of this corner of Maine. He'd moved Radford Manor here, hoping for some semblance of peace. But that tenuous calm was shattered now. Montague was here.

Nick lifted his face, sniffing the air. The salt tang of the ocean carried the scent of evil. The Beast stirred. His insides shook with the effort to control it.

Inebriated, laughing town folk strolled the streets, and couples exchanged kisses in darkened alleys, all unaware of the demon forces that surrounded them. He hoped Kyla wasn't part of this madness. He hadn't seen her since yesterday, but she had filled his dreams last night. Afraid of his own dark cravings, he'd walked away from her. He wanted her for eternity, but it couldn't be. He would protect her from the monsters that lurked here, protect her until it was time for her to fulfill her vows.

A movement caught his eye and the hairs on his nape stiffened in warning. The stealthy figure of a man, thin, his tall frame bent, slithered close to the buildings. Recognition punched Nick like a fist to the chest. He bit his lip against his scream of fury.

Moving cautiously, he followed the lone figure to a dark side street. The man heard Nick's steps and looked back. Apprehension morphed to horror as the man recognized him. He began running. Nick gave chase.

They wound through the narrow streets. The Beast struggled for release. Nick lifted his face to the three-quarter moon. Soon he would give the Beast the blood it craved. He ran harder and faster. His lungs filled with the sea air and the scents of stale liquor and animal waste. He heard the frantic scurrying of the vermin who lived in the sewers and knew they acknowledged the Beast in him and ran in terror. His heartbeat matched the sound of his leather soles on the hard pavement. He threw back his head and laughed as the joy of the hunt thrummed over his nerve endings.

The other man, not as powerfully built, finally stumbled against the brick wall of a building, chest heaving and eyes bugged out with exertion and fear. Wincing, he shielded his face with his arm when Nick approached.

Nick grabbed the man's arm and bent it behind his back. The other man screamed. "You always were a coward, Vickers," Nick spat out. "Look me in the face, you fucking piece of garbage, and be a man for once."

"Don't hurt me, milord." Trembling, Vickers tried to pull away, but Nick tightened his grip.

"Where is he?" Nick growled the words. "What form has

he taken? We'll be done with this thing once and for all."

Vickers's thin lips curled in a sly smile. "Who do you mean?"

Nick twisted Vickers's arm tighter until the other man shrieked. "You fucking son-of-a-bitch. Where is Montague?"

Vickers sneered. "You'll never find him. He's too clever for you. He always was."

Nick put his hands around Vickers's throat and threw him against the wall. "Tell me in what lair Montague hides and cowers from me."

Vickers gagged. With a force of will, Nick released him. The time to kill had not yet come. The other man fell to the ground and stared up at Nick with frightened defiance.

"You won't win this time, Radford. He'll kill you and take the woman." He cackled and rubbed bony hands together. "She's a sweet piece of ass, like Lady Catherine, and my Lord Montague knows how to make her cry for mercy. Like he did with your wife. You'll go to Hell with the image of my master breaking your woman."

Rage released hate so powerful that Nick's veins throbbed and his heart pumped with the need to kill. Howling, he lunged at Vickers. Crying out, the other man put up his hands to deflect the blows. Nick pushed the hands away as if they were feathers.

He punched a hard right to Vickers's face. Blood spurted from a cut on the man's lip. "That was for the night you betrayed me to Montague." Nick pounded harder. A crunch of bones told him he'd broken Vickers's nose. "That's for my Catherine and the other poor women you defiled through the centuries." He punched again until Vickers's face was a bloody pulp. "And that's for my son, my Jonathan."

Emboldened by the smell of blood, the Beast fought to

escape. Grunting with the effort to control the Beast, Nick forced it back where it belonged. Grabbing Vickers by the neck, he pulled him up and slammed his head against the wall. Blood splattered onto the dirty brick.

He squeezed his hands around Vickers's throat. The other man's eyes goggled and Nick squeezed harder. He would kill him now and take his revenge for that long-ago, horror-filled night. Despite Vickers's immortality, given him by Montague, his powers were weak. Nick could extinguish the other man with one sharp blow to his neck.

Antica's image intruded into Nick's mind. Her eyes implored him. It wasn't time yet.

"You're not worth it." He threw Vickers away from him.

Rubbing his throat, the other man stumbled, then righted himself. Whimpering, Vickers stared at Nick with his one good eye. "Please, milord, don't kill me. I can work for you."

"You think I would trust a cowering bag of scum like you?" Nick rasped. "You betrayed me once. You won't get the chance again." He grabbed the other man by the collar of his shirt and pulled him closer. "I allow you to live so you can carry my message to Montague. He won't have the woman. I'll see him in Hell first."

Nick threw Vickers from him and strode away, back to the music and the revelry and his everlasting despair.

* * * * *

"You're sure you'll be okay?" Kyla asked.

Todd nodded. "I'm fine. I can take care of myself." He glanced toward the mob of villagers clogging the sidewalks and streets in celebration of the town's tri-centennial. "Look at all the people. Nothing can happen. Are you sure you don't want to come with me? The people I'm meeting are cool." He chuckled. "Who would have thought there were so many hipsters in this little backwater town?"

Kyla laughed and relaxed her stance. "Coolness follows you wherever you go. Be careful, please."

"I will, Kyla, don't worry. You be careful too." He headed into one of the bars that lined High Street. Shouts and raucous music from inside spilled out onto the sidewalk.

A small knot of self-pity worked its way through Kyla's chest. Shaking it off, she strolled down the street, smiling at passersby and stopping to peer into shop windows. Thoughts of Nick invaded her mind. She missed him. She could no longer pretend to herself that he meant nothing to her. He'd walked out on her yesterday. And she wondered why.

A sudden wave of dizziness overtook her. Another vision? Gulping deep breaths, she leaned her forehead against a dusty shop window, not seeing the items on display.

The dizziness passed with no vision. She turned toward the street. All seemed normal, yet she knew differently. What a strange village, she mused.

"Come in, dearie, and let me tell your future."

Kyla started. A tiny gypsy woman stood at her elbow. The gypsy's large gold hoop earrings caught the light from the street lamps; gaudy necklaces adorned her ample chest and gold bracelets jangled from both arms.

"No," Kyla said, backing away. "I don't want my fortune told."

The woman grabbed Kyla's arm. Her small fingers pressed into Kyla's flesh. "What are you afraid of, dearie?" Her eyes clouded with a faraway look and she kept a firm grip on Kyla. "Two men want you," she said. "Dark men with stains on their souls. You alone have the power to save one. You must choose wisely."

A rushing noise filled Kyla's head and her heart pumped

wildly. Frozen in place, she stared down at the odd little gypsy.

"Come inside, dearie, and I'll tell you more." Loosening her hold, the woman crooked a finger, signaling Kyla to follow.

As in a trance, Kyla went with her into the shop. She noticed the sign on the door as she entered. *Madame Cassandra, Psychic.*

The pungent odor of incense burned Kyla's eyes and formed a cloud over the small, close room. The scent took her back in time to Sunday Mass with her parents, before the evil destroyed them. She had not been to church since. Blinking her eyes to dislodge the painful memories, she scanned the room. Blood red curtains hung from the windows and plump pillows in a riot of colors and patterns were strewn haphazardly over red velvet couches. A glass-beaded curtain, shimmering in shades of gold and green, beckoned her to the deeper recesses of another room.

The click of the front door locking filled her with dread and she turned quickly, ready to escape.

"Don't be afraid, my pretty," Madame Cassandra said. "Come."

With a lingering look at the door and freedom, Kyla followed the gypsy through the glass curtain. The beads swayed and jangled as if protesting the intrusion. Or perhaps it was a warning.

"Sit," Madame Cassandra said, pointing to a straight-backed chair next to a small table covered in black velvet. A large crystal ball rested on the table.

Kyla laughed. "A crystal ball. Of course." Her tension eased and she sat in the chair. Despite her theatrics, Madame Cassandra was no more than an ordinary woman out to scam a few dollars from gullible citizens. Kyla had time on her hands. She'd play the woman's game.

With a flurry of red-tipped fingers and satin skirt, Madame sat in the chair opposite her and stared at Kyla with fathomless black eyes. "You think I am a scammer out to make a few bucks." She shrugged. "With some people that is what I am. But not with you."

Foreboding shrieked along Kyla's nerve endings. She glanced quickly around. Trapped.

Madame leaned forward and rubbed ringed fingers over the large crystal. The gold and colorful gems of her rings flashed in the light from a small lamp and reflected on the red walls.

"You can't really see anything in there," Kyla said.

Madame appeared not to hear her, but continued rubbing the crystal, her attention focused on the now-cloudy ball. "Your parents were taken from you cruelly at a young age," the gypsy said.

Ice settled in Kyla's stomach.

"The one who took your parents is near," Madame continued. She then looked at Kyla.

Kyla gasped and touched a hand to her throat. Madame Cassandra's pupils were dilated with barely any white showing. She seemed to look straight through Kyla.

"The devil who killed your parents wants you," Madame intoned in a sing-song voice. "He seeks revenge for ancient wrongs. You are not powerful enough to vanquish him on your own. There is another who will join with you. Together you can destroy the monster. But only if you open your heart and take the leap of faith that was preordained long ago. If you do not heed my warning, prepare for a living hell."

Breath whooshed from Kyla on an angry exhale. She

pushed up from the chair. It toppled to the wood floor with a crash. "I won't listen to your fear-mongering."

Madame gave a desperate shake of her head and focused on Kyla. "You must believe me."

Without a backward glance, Kyla ran from the room. The glass beads of the curtain tinkled furiously, mocking her. With shaking fingers, she unlocked the front door and slid outside. She breathed in the humid air, willing calmness into her body. Ocean scent mingled with the smell of alcohol and marijuana drifting by with the crowd.

"Kyla."

Strong hands gripped her arms. She whirled.

"Dan."

CHAPTER FOURTEEN

"Odd little woman," Dan said with a frown. He focused on something behind Kyla.

She looked back to see Madame Cassandra peeking out from a slit in the lace curtains. Madame slid a furtive glance at Dan and her features twisted in surprise and terror. She gave Kyla a pleading look, then crossed herself before closing the curtains. Kyla shivered.

"You don't believe in those swindlers, do you?" Smiling, Dan stepped closer and ran his hand lightly up Kyla's arm.

Revulsion, like slimy worms, crawled over her skin, and she pulled free of him. "Madame seems a harmless old woman."

With a flirtatious grin, he leaned forward to whisper in her ear. "You don't need her. I can tell your future."

She wrinkled her nose at the smell of alcohol emanating from him, and glanced at the half-empty plastic cup he held. "You're drunk."

He shrugged. "I've had a few." His gaze made a leisurely sweep of her body. Licking his lips, his gaze lingered on her breasts before meeting her eyes again.

A sea-drenched breeze had hardened her nipples under her thin tank top. She should have worn a bra. Resisting the urge to fold her arms across her chest, she turned to walk away.

Dan grabbed her hand, pulling her to face him. He gave her a wolfish grin. "I know your future. You're having a drink with me tonight." His leering gaze locked on her breasts again. "Then I'll show you what a real man can do for you."

"Let go of me." She snatched her hand back.

Her scalp tingled. Someone watched her. She whirled around. Madame Cassandra peered from behind the curtains again. Her eyes caught Kyla's. *Choose wisely.* The gypsy's words whispered in her head. In a swirl of curtain, the gypsy disappeared.

"Come on, just one drink," Dan said in a silky voice that made Kyla think of the snake in the Garden of Eden.

Shaking her head, she turned away and began walking down the street, away from him. Possibly Dan was just a lonely man who'd had too much to drink. Her instincts warned her to guard against him. Except she could no longer trust her instincts.

She strode along the sidewalk, scanning the boisterous crowds, hoping to see Nick.

"Enjoying yourself?" Sheriff Sanders sauntered by and stopped her. Despite the warm temperature, the sheriff wore her usual thick turtleneck.

"Sheriff." Kyla glanced around. "Looks like everyone's having a good time. Maybe too good a time." She nodded toward a group of teens who were laughing and harassing passing pedestrians.

Max shrugged. "Just kids letting off steam. Nothing to worry about."

A smiling Dan, still holding his paper cup, strolled up to them. He stood close to Kyla. She refused to look at him.

"Nice night," Dan said.

"Sure is." The sheriff and Dan nodded to each other.

As Kyla looked from one to the other, coldness streaked down her spine. She shivered.

"You two have a good time." Max touched the brim of her hat and moved on.

Kyla turned to Dan. "Stop following me."

Loud yells from farther down the street snagged her attention. Two men, both very drunk, began a shouting and shoving match on the sidewalk. A large crowd quickly gathered, urging the men to fight, but the sheriff walked by them without a glance.

Kyla whirled on Dan. "Shouldn't the sheriff be doing something? And shouldn't you be helping her?"

He took a sip of his drink. "Max can handle things on her own."

Red-hot anger boiled in Kyla's gut, spilling over until her control slipped. She reached to snatch the cup from him. Instead, she drew her hand back and balled it at her side, digging her nails into her palm. "Handle things on her own? It doesn't seem as if Max does much of anything. She sure didn't help us find Todd."

Rage flared in his eyes and his lips stretched in a forced smile. "Keep out of it. We know what we're doing."

We? she thought.

He smiled. "Forgive me, Kyla. I didn't mean to take my frustrations out on you. The sheriff moves too slowly for me too at times."

With a wave of disgust, she turned away. The two fighters, followed by the chanting crowd, had taken their argument into the street. And Sheriff Sanders had disappeared.

This was one weird town.

Dan still followed her. At first, he'd seemed a drunken nuisance, but he'd moved onto stalking. Well, not for long.

She wished Nick were here, then shrugged the thought away. She could handle Dan Taylor.

Like an apparition she'd conjured up, Nick appeared out of the crowd and strode to her. He touched her arm, stopping her. "Kyla, I've been looking for you."

Joy loosened the knot of tension in her stomach. "You were looking for me? You walked out on me the other day."

"Forgive me."

She nodded and placed her hand over his where it rested on her arm. His skin was warm and smooth, the muscles taut.

"Radford." Dan stood so close his alcohol-laced breath whispered along her cheek. Anger vibrated from him, dampening her happiness. Stiffening, she moved away and thrust out her chin, daring him to cause trouble.

He shrugged and took a swig from his cup.

Nick slanted a look at the other man and his features tightened. "Taylor."

Dan's face twisted in a sneer that reminded Kyla of the gargoyles at Radford Manor. "The lady and I have plans, Radford. Plans that don't include you."

She stepped closer to Nick and met Dan's glare. "We never had any plans."

Dan's eyes darkened to the color of storm clouds off the Maine coast. "My mistake." Switching his gaze to Nick, he said, "This is just the beginning, Radford." Dan turned on his heel, tossed the plastic cup onto the sidewalk and strode quickly away, pushing aside anyone in his path and ignoring the epithets they shouted after him.

"Bastard," Nick said.

"Thanks for the rescue."

With a short laugh, he turned to her. "You don't need rescuing. You can hold your own." He cupped her shoulders and pulled her close.

His eyes smoldered and that rich topaz enticed her with the memory of the day they'd made love. Desire burned straight through her to liquefy in a hot rush between her legs.

"I'd hoped to find you," he said.

"Why?" she asked on a throaty whisper.

"I need you."

Consumed by the fire in his gaze, she couldn't move, could barely think.

Nick gently ran his hands up and down her bare arms, his eyes never leaving hers. Awareness shuddered through her as his scent of male and outdoors filled her.

"Why did you walk out like that the other day, Nick?"

He blew out a breath. "I was afraid I would hurt you, but I can't stay away from you."

"You'll only hurt me if I let you."

He sobered. "I won't hurt you." He cocked his head as if listening to something, then turned back to her. "Dance with me?"

She heard the music coming from the pavilion for the first time and smiled. Her spirit longed for the intimacy of Nick's body, but a warning whispered to her. Intimacy led to hurt.

Ignoring the warning, she placed her hand in his. "Sure."

They walked toward the music. As drunken festival-goers bumped them, Nick pulled her closer and his muscular thigh pressed against her hip. Her body responded to his closeness with an answering heat.

When they reached the music pavilion, a raucous salsa tune started. Nick turned to her with a sexy smile. "Can you dance to this?"

"Of course."

His scorching gaze sent a thrill of anticipation through her. He put his hand on the small of her back and led her up the stairs to the wooden deck. Couples danced and shimmied all around them. A few bolder ones ground their hips together.

Nick swayed to the music and she picked up the tempo, moving her body in time to the pulsing beat. Grinning, he followed her lead. The Latin rhythm thrummed through her, transporting her to an exotic place of light and love. The gold blazing from Nick's eyes seared her with carnal want, and she let out a low groan.

He put his hands on her waist and pulled her closer until they were hip to hip. His touch scorched her through the thin fabric of her clothes. The driving beat of the music echoed the rapid beat of her heart. The swing of her hair as it whipped around her face and down her back enhanced the torrid need coursing through her veins.

With a smile, Nick twirled her around, catching her in his arms, and twirling her again. She separated from him and spun around, never missing a step. He took her in his arms and pulled her against him. Breathless, they clung to each other, swaying to the sensuous rhythm. The music ended, but they continued holding each other.

"We're good together, Nick."

"Are you surprised?" He pushed aside her hair to expose her neck and placed a gentle kiss on her nape. His tender touch incited a riot of need deep inside her, a need she knew only he could satisfy. Others stared at them, but she didn't care.

The sea-laced breeze, scented with lilac, caressed her sweat-sheened skin and she sighed. Nick pulled her tighter against him.

"Come home with me." His lips brushed her temple.

"Yes."

After the short drive along the coastline, Nick pulled his Jag to the front of his house and cut the engine. He turned to her and traced a finger along her bottom lip.

"You're sure?" he asked.

He provoked yearnings in her she didn't understand, yearnings that frightened and excited her. She should leave. She couldn't.

"I'm sure."

With his arm around her waist, he guided her up the cracked stone steps of the old manor house. Inside, a welcoming fire glowed in the living room hearth, illuminating the tapestry of Diana at the hunt. She stared at the image and froze. Had Todd seen this very tapestry? No, she didn't believe it, and she would trust Nick.

He pressed his hand against her back. "Is everything okay?"

She turned. The fire of his gaze evaporated any lingering doubts. Smiling, she stood on tiptoe to sweep a kiss along his firm lips.

A soft laugh escaped him and he took her hand and led her to the staircase tucked into an alcove. She followed him up the narrow stairs. The quietness of the house closed around them. Where was Antica with her dark looks? Kyla glanced at Nick. She wouldn't ask.

They paused at the landing, then Nick guided her onto a faded Oriental rug that stretched the length of the long hallway lined with paneled wooden doors. Portraits hung from walls covered in pale green watered silk from France.

Watered silk? France? How did she know that? Kyla stopped, suddenly unable to move. Waves of dizziness rippled through her and she grabbed Nick's arm. Visions assaulted her, spiking pain in her head.

"Kyla." His voice came from very far away.

Servants dressed in drab medieval garb carried trays laden with food into the various rooms. Sweet rosemary mingled with the scents of cooked meat, spiced wine, and unwashed bodies.

"Kyla." Nick clutched her shoulders. The visions disappeared.

She blinked and focused on his face. She was safe.

"What is it?" he asked. "You turned so white. Do you want me to take you home?"

"It's nothing." She walked into his arms and pressed against him. "I want to be here with you."

He planted a feather soft kiss on her brow. Taking her hand again, he drew her to a door at the end of the hall and opened it, gesturing for her to enter.

Kyla walked over the threshold and gasped. She'd awakened in this room the morning after her attack, but she'd been so upset and in such a hurry to leave she'd not noticed the treasures it held.

Furnished in ancient grandeur, Nick's bedroom was nearly as large as the living room, but warmer, with stone walls painted the color of burnished copper, and muted tapestries hanging from velvet-covered rods. She hesitated to walk on the richly colored wool rugs she was sure were worth more than the national income of some small countries.

She entered the room slowly, almost reverently, and reached out to run her fingers over the smooth wood of an intricately carved walnut chest. A Venetian vase in vibrant yellows rested on it. She'd seen its mate in a museum in Venice.

She looked at Nick. "I hadn't noticed before. This room

is exquisite."

"Thank you," he said, giving her a small bow. A light breeze touched her, as if a gentle spirit breathed on her neck. Nick belonged here. An image of him dressed in silks and satins, with a black cape draped over his broad shoulders, and bowing over her hand, flashed in her mind.

Smiling at the fanciful picture, she turned to explore the rest of the room. The fire in the huge marble-mantled fireplace lent a glow to the gold velvet drapes and the gleaming walnut of the chests and armoires along the walls.

She walked to the bookcase next to the floor-to-ceiling windows and ran her hands lovingly over the books. Modern spy novels rested next to leather-bound tomes that looked hundreds of years old.

A large bible with gilt lettering rested on its own stand. An ancient book. She touched the smooth leather and felt a tingle of recognition. She hesitated, then slowly opened the heavy cover. Flowery script met her gaze. She read the names—Nicholas of Radford and Catherine of Somerset. Deep pain seemed to flow from the book, burning her fingers. She quickly drew back. The cover snapped shut.

She heard a movement behind her, then Nick reached for her, pulling her against his hard chest. All thoughts of the strange book with the pain pulsing from its pages fled in the warmth of his touch.

When she leaned against him, he wrapped his arms around her waist. Her head fit under his chin. She glanced at the nearby window. Their reflections looked back at her. Nick, tall and powerfully built, towered over her slim form. Somehow she knew she had nothing to fear from him. He smiled and her heart pounded.

"You're beautiful," he said.

"So are you," she whispered.

Turning in his arms, she took his face between her hands and brushed her fingers over his chiseled planes, lingering on the full curve of his lips. "Let me make love to you tonight."

She slid her glance to the high four-poster covered in golden velvet bedclothes and topped with a fringed canopy. Just for tonight, she would lose herself in Nick and use all he offered to ease the ache of loneliness that lived deep inside her. She took his hand and led him to the waiting bed.

Nick touched her shoulder and pulled her around to face him. Something dark glimmered in his eyes, sending a tremor of longing through her. She needed this man.

Placing her hands on his shoulders, she stood on her toes to reach his mouth and traced her tongue languidly over his lips, savoring his heat. His hands spanned her waist, his touch shooting fire through her veins.

Secure in the circle of his embrace, she leaned back and skimmed a finger over his high cheekbones. The heat in his eyes burned through to her heart. Hypnotized, she searched their smoky depths for the answers she sought.

As if in response, the image of a white wolf appeared. The creature's eyes glowed with something hot and wild, rousing a primal need deep inside her. Desperation like nothing she'd ever known clawed her. Craving Nick's taste, his body, his soul, she cupped his jaw and licked a trail along his neck, nipping and tasting the smooth skin and inhaling his scent of aroused male.

A low growl rumbled from him. An answering wildness tore through her and she swayed into him. "Nick." The word ripped from her. She raised her head, giving him her trust. She needed his lips on her burning skin, needed him to possess her.

With a groan, he stiffened and pushed her away. The wolf image disappeared, leaving his eyes tortured. "You don't know what you ask." He rasped the words on a pain-filled breath.

Confused, and wanting to take away his pain, she pulled him to her and kissed him, testing the fullness of his mouth and telling him with her body she wanted only to please him. He softened against her and she eased her tongue between his lips. Moaning, he opened for her, taking her trust, giving her his. She rolled her tongue over his teeth and the moist contours of his mouth. He tasted of wine and desire. Moving back, she gently eased his hands away. "No touching now. I'm in charge."

She lowered her head to press a tender line of kisses down his neck to his collarbone. Delicious anticipation simmered in her, boiling to a frenzied desire that threatened to overwhelm her senses. She wanted to make him forget for a time whatever nightmares shadowed him. For a little while, she wanted to forget her own nightmares.

With deliberate slowness, Kyla unbuttoned his shirt, licking and nibbling her way down his chest covered in fine black hair. She tasted the salt of his skin and the freshness of the soap he'd used. His soft cries of pleasure pierced her with a hunger for something unnamed that would cleanse and complete her.

Desperate to see and touch all of him, she tugged his shirt from his jeans and slipped it off, brushing her fingers over the flexed muscles of his arms. His skin was smooth, hot, and inviting. A sigh quivered through her and she knelt in front of him to take off his shoes and fling them aside. She ran trembling hands up his denim-clad thighs to the evidence of his arousal pressing against his jeans. Groaning, he tightened his hands at his sides and she knew he fought the urge to touch her.

A fierce need to please him shot through her, blinding her to all other thoughts. With her gaze on his, she unzipped his pants and slipped them down his long, muscular legs. She discarded the jeans and his underwear and stood slowly, sliding her body against his nakedness. His scent of male and musk filled her and his hard erection pressed against her belly.

A strangled-sounding moan wrenched from him and she pressed against him, stroking her hands over his shoulders, tracing his biceps, and grazing her fingers over his muscled arms to take his hands in hers. His heat wrapped around her, turning her insides to fire.

His eyes, molten gold, captured her in their flame. Struggling to harness her raging need, she released his hands to trail her fingers along his long, shapely thighs. He tensed and released a growl. Emboldened by her sexual power over him, she slid down to kneel in front of him again.

"Kyla." His whispered word, filled with aching desire, caressed her.

She drew in a shuddering breath. She would give Nick all she had, telling him with her body what she couldn't voice.

Her insides clenched and she cupped his firm buttocks, massaging the smooth curves with her fingers. His strength incited a wanton need in her to capture all of him, body and soul, and never let go. The firestorm inside her surged and she reached out a hand to test the hard, full length of him. When he trembled, she reeled with feminine pride.

"Woman, do you know what you do to me?" His smoky voice blanketed her in sensual need.

Flicking out her tongue, she licked his cock. His body

jerked and a low moan escaped him. Running her hands and tongue slowly and deliberately over him, she took him into her mouth. With a low growl, he buried his fingers in her hair.

She wanted to devour him until their bodies melded. She'd never wanted any man the way she wanted Nick, with a soul-shattering obsession that frightened her. Cupping his buttocks, she sucked on his cock and swirled her tongue over his hardness, licking the beads of liquid at his tip. He shuddered and cried out, and she knew he was on the brink of climax.

The juncture between her thighs throbbed, and her whole body threatened to spin out of control. With an effort she pulled away and stood on trembling legs. "Not yet," she whispered, raking her gaze over his powerful body. "Beautiful." The word escaped on a breath.

Gripping her shoulders, he pulled her tight against him and bent to take her lips in a bruising kiss.

"Get undressed," he growled.

Her pulse pounded in her ears. With every ounce of will she possessed, she backed away. "No. You get on the bed."

He arched an eyebrow.

"Now," she said.

He hesitated, then turned and strode to the bed. With violent force, he yanked the velvet covers and silk sheets back and slid onto the bed. The mattress shifted under his weight. The gleam in his eyes sent her a challenge, a challenge she would meet.

She searched the room, pulling open armoire doors until she found what she wanted. Holding up two silk neckties, she approached the bed.

"I will have you, Nick."

Realization dawned on his face. "You'll use those against me?"

She climbed onto the bed and straddled him. "Not against you, but to give you pleasure."

"Pretty sure of yourself," he rasped.

"Always."

"I'll let you have your way—for a while."

Savagery flashed over his features. With unsteady fingers, she secured his wrists to the bed posts with the silk ties. She smoothed a hand over his chest and heard his quick intake of breath. Running her hands down his thighs, she climbed off the bed to stand before him.

"I want to see you," he said.

The fire between her legs became unbearable. She swayed her hips, desperate for release. With unsteady hands, she slipped off her tank top, freeing her breasts to Nick's hot gaze. He tensed and his eyes devoured her. Her nipples puckered and her breasts swelled, their hardened peaks straining toward Nick, begging him to suckle them.

Her gaze locked with his and she cradled her breasts, testing their heaviness. She licked her finger, then swirled the tip over her pebbled nipples. The bedposts groaned as Nick struggled against the silk holding him.

Rubbing her breasts, she walked to the low chest at the end of the bed. She put her leg on the chest, and with deliberate slowness peeled off one high-heeled boot. Then the other. Nick's velvety gaze followed her every move. He moaned. Wetness surged at the juncture of her thighs.

She unzipped her slacks and kicked them off. Clad in only a red thong, she moved closer to Nick's squirming body. His thick cock invited her to take him.

When their gazes locked, something primitive and raw

passed between them. "Not yet," she whispered.

Forcing herself away from the bed, she lifted her arms over her head. Gyrating in an ancient sensual dance, she stroked a lazy trail with her fingers down her body. She flicked her tongue over her lips in invitation and was rewarded with Nick's tortured cry. Her gaze never leaving his, she slipped one hand under her panties and pressed against her throbbing center, finding her nub. With her other hand she caressed and massaged her swollen breasts, rolling the nipples between her fingers.

Passion glazed his eyes. "Sorceress."

"Only for you."

Kyla closed her eyes, imagining Nick inside her, spilling his hot seed into her. His harsh breathing reverberated through the room and fanned the fire in her. Her climax built into a raging crescendo and she cried out.

Shaking, she opened her eyes to Nick's scalding gaze. "I need you, Nick. Now."

She tugged off her thong and threw it aside, then hurried to the bed, needing to touch him, naked flesh to naked flesh. Bracing her body over his, she positioned herself between his spread legs. He thrust his hips upward, rubbing his hard erection against her wet, pulsing center. She moaned her pleasure.

She bent closer until her breasts, full and heavy, touched his chest. Nick lifted his head and flicked his tongue over one firm nipple, then took it into his mouth, sucking until she threw back her head and cried out.

"Nick." His name tore from her. Kneeling, she reached her hand out to trace the contours of his face, a face that was becoming more beloved every day. She feathered her fingers over his long, thick eyelashes, strong nose, and high cheekbones. He strained toward her.

She'd told herself she could walk away from him like the others. Now she knew she couldn't. The thought scared her to death. She needed him too much. "What have you done to me?"

"You're the one who has bewitched me," he whispered.

"Have I?" She lingered over his full lips, dipping her finger in and out of his mouth. He sucked on her, sending spasms of pleasure through her.

She wanted to touch and kiss and nibble every inch of his magnificent body, to savor every part of him. Reveling in Nick's strength and beauty, and her consuming need for him, Kyla kissed his jaw, rough with his days-old stubble of dark beard. The feel of his roughened skin along her sensitized lips further inflamed her.

With her fingertips, she skimmed a path down the firm muscles of his chest to circle his hard nipples. She darted her tongue back and forth over them, tasting the faint muskiness of his skin and provoking a low rumble from him. Sliding her tongue over the muscular contours of his chest, she blew gently on the areas she moistened. His breathing ragged, he whispered her name.

Holding onto what little restraint she still possessed, she nibbled a path to his navel, blowing small huffs of air on his firm skin as she went, kissing her way down his belly to his throbbing cock. He writhed under her. The scent of his desire surrounded her, threatening to send her spiraling over the precipice. Her breathing shallow, she wrapped her hand around his hard, thick cock and stared into his passion-filled eyes.

"Magnificent." She bent to take him into her mouth again. Nick bucked against her. She massaged him with her hand and tongue, taking as much of him into her as she could. Fiery need burned through her defenses. He was her addiction.

Nick and the room suddenly wavered and darkened as if a curtain dropped down. An ache started in her head. Visions formed in her mind.

A dark, stifling room, lit by candles. Nick moving over her, love burning from his eyes, his long unbound hair sweeping her naked, straining breasts.

She squeezed her eyes shut until the vision dissolved. Anxious to dislodge whatever demons possessed her, she sucked and massaged Nick harder and harder until only his groans of ecstasy filled her mind.

With a loud roar, Nick broke free of his bonds and grabbed her, flipping her over. He leaned over her, his eyes glazed with raw need. She shuddered.

"I will touch you now."

"Yes." Uttering tiny cries, she surrendered to him, spreading her legs. He thrust into her. She screamed as he rode her, higher and faster, taking her and making her his, telling her she belonged to him and only him. She curled her legs around his waist and met his fierceness with a reckless abandonment that overtook her until she no longer knew where she ended and he began.

She held onto him, scraping his back with her nails, and cried out his name over and over. Tears sprang to her eyes. They belonged together, locked in this passionate embrace forever. Then spasms shook her and all thought fled as bright lights exploded around her. Her climax ripped through her, over and over, never-ending. She clutched Nick tighter and rode the storm with him.

He let out a howl as his body shook with the jolt of his

own climax. He spilled into her, hot and wet. Joy mingled with carnal satisfaction. She and Nick were one.

They clung to each other, their breathing jagged. Sweat moistened Nick's powerful body, joining with her own wetness. Kyla's pulse rate finally slowed, and she let out a contented sigh. Nick gave her a quick kiss and rolled off her, taking her with him to hold her in the curve of his arm.

"Liked that, did you?" he whispered, with a hint of amusement.

"What do you think?" Smiling, she leaned over him. Her hair brushed his chest and he reached out to wind a long strand around his finger.

"I think you are a sorceress who has taken control of my body and my heart."

"Not a sorceress, but an ordinary woman."

"Extraordinary." He kissed her temple and pulled her closer.

Sighing, she snuggled into his arms and inhaled his male scent mixed with the musk of their lovemaking. She hadn't felt this safe or this happy in a very long time. She refused to question why or allow herself to look beyond this moment. The stillness and quiet surrounded them, as if the old house approved of their coupling. She smiled at her silly thoughts and snuggled closer.

"Are you cold, love?" Nick reached down to draw the covers over them, tucking the sheet under her chin and cocooning her in security and warmth.

Love. He'd never called her that before, yet the word, tinged with his British accent, and the tenderness of his touch, elicited a fleeting memory. The memory dissipated, leaving her feeling vaguely sad.

She placed a kiss on the soft skin of his neck. Contentment

made her eyes grow heavy and she felt herself drifting into sleep.

The scent of burning wax perfumed them. Nick leaned over her, his eyes filled with desire and love. His long hair teased her face. She twined her arms around him, kissing him deeply, running her tongue along his soft lips. The sudden roar of a fierce wind filled the room. The candles sputtered, then went out. Something tore her from Nick's arms. He screamed, his face contorted with fear and rage. She was thrown down a deep, dark abyss. She tumbled over and over into darkness, cold and absolute.

Kyla jerked upright, heart hammering. Sweat formed on her hands. Disoriented, she stared around the strange room. A small lamp in the far corner threw shadows on stone walls. Nick's room. Familiar. Yet strange.

"What is it?" Nick sat up and gathered her to him.

"I had a dream." She shivered, despite his closeness.

"You're safe, love. Stay with me tonight."

His words sent apprehension shooting through her. She pushed away from him. "Stay?"

The dream had been so vivid, her pain so wrenching, and Nick's fear and rage so frightening in their intensity. A warning? Every minute she spent with him she lost a little bit more of her soul. Her need for him weakened her. She couldn't allow that. To be dependent on a man wasn't who she was. She needed no one.

"I can't." She jumped from the bed and reached down to retrieve her clothes. He followed and pulled her around to face him.

"What are you doing?" Confusion replaced the satiated softness of his face.

"Please let me go."

Hurt washed over his features and he released her.

Not looking at him, she dressed quickly and fled from the room. On shaky legs she ran down the stairs. The truth hit her like a giant snake reaching out and squeezing her heart. She loved Nick Radford.

This could not be happening.

Tears streamed down her face. She tripped on a step and reached out to grab the railing, shifting her gaze to the bottom of the stairs.

Black eyes, obsidian beads in a wrinkled face, stared at her.

She screamed.

CHAPTER FIFTEEN

Antica moved out of the shadows. Her black eyes seemed to look right through Kyla.

Gripping the stair railing, Kyla returned Antica's glare. The crone would not intimidate her.

Antica's features relaxed slightly and she drew an audible breath, as if awakening from a dream, or a vision. She rubbed the crystal pendant at her chest. "I know," she whispered in a thin, high voice.

Intimidation be damned. Kyla wanted out. She brushed past Antica and pulled open the heavy front door. Footsteps sounded behind her and she turned to see Nick, fully clothed, running down the stairs.

"I'll drive you. We left your car in town." His features were tight and closed. She'd hurt him.

Antica touched Nick's arm. "I know what the crystal tells me." A note of desperation had crept into her voice.

The urge to flee overwhelmed Kyla. She turned and ran down the stone steps, Nick close behind.

"Come back," Antica shouted. She rushed after them. "I know the answer."

"Later," Nick called over his shoulder.

Kyla jumped into the Jag. Without glancing at her, Nick got into the driver's seat and started the engine.

* * * * *

175

From behind the thick trunk of an ancient oak, Montague watched them speed off. Stepping out of the shadows, he approached the old hag who stood on the landing. Leaves crunched under his feet. With a startled cry, she turned toward the sound.

"Who goes there?"

"Don't you know me, witch?" Montague gathered his cape around him and bowed.

Her mouth formed a circle as recognition hit her. She turned to run into the house, but he sprang onto the landing and blocked her way. He grabbed her by the throat, stifling her scream, and pressed her against the stone façade. The red glow of his eyes reflected on her shocked face. He laughed.

Antica gagged and he released his hold on her throat, but gripped her arms and held her against the house. She hissed at him. Hate blazed from her eyes, but not fear. He liked that. He would enjoy killing her.

"He knows you are here," she rasped.

He laughed. "But he doesn't know my form."

Her gaze fixed on the scar at his throat. "He will see the scar."

He sneered and tightened his grip on her arms. "I have kept my identity well-hidden from him. When the time is right I will reveal myself."

"Kill me if you must, but it will not stop him. He will destroy you." She touched the pendant at her neck. "Your powers are no match for his."

"You have eluded me all these centuries, hag, but my powers have grown stronger than you could imagine. That crystal no longer protects you and him." With a flash of hand, he tore the necklace from her. Gripping the pendant between his fingers, he let the thick gold chain slide off to land on the steps. He kicked the chain into the bushes and waved the pendant in front of Antica.

With a cry, she reached for the crystal. Grinning, he slipped the gem into his pocket.

"You will not win." Her voice was strong despite the fear he knew must now course through her.

"Tell me what you know about the woman," he growled.

"She is a huntress."

He laughed. "Think you can fool me? She and I have met before. She cannot kill me. But there is something else, something you are desperate for Radford to know." He shook her. "Tell me."

"Never." She spat in his face.

Fury pumped through his veins. He slapped her hard. Her head hit the stone and she moaned.

He pressed closer. "You and your whelp of a son saved Radford that night. You counseled Catherine to refuse my hand. You started me on my damning path."

Antica straightened and her jaw firmed in defiance. "You were set on your evil path well before my lady refused your suit. Even then, rumors abounded that you'd made a pact with the devil. 'Twas your lust for power and favor at court that damned you."

He curled his lips in a snarl. "I loved Catherine like no other. I would have given her all my treasure, but she chose Radford and died for it along with his brat." He aimed the red of his eyes onto Antica's shoulder. A hole formed, burning her flesh. She let out a high-pitched wail.

He wrapped his hands around her throat again. "Radford spied for Clement." He choked out the Pope's name. "I sought to kill Radford and bring his body to my king. But for you, Henry would have given me whatever I desired. You saved Radford and hid him. Your powers and that crystal have protected him all these centuries. No more. You'll join Radford in Hell."

Her defiance gave way to fear that clouded her eyes and twisted her mouth. A triumphant laugh spilled from him.

"I have waited almost five hundred years to see you dead. I will have my revenge." Releasing her, he lifted his hand in a sweeping gesture. His magic propelled Antica through the air to hit the hard ground. With a groan, she quieted and lay still.

His creatures, pale and gaunt, materialized from the bushes. "Take her," Montague commanded. "She is not yet dead. I will deal with her later." They picked up Antica's limp body and carried her toward the forest.

Montague reached into his pocket to bring out the crystal, holding it up to the lantern light. The facets glowed black and silver with tinges of red and orange. Growling low in his throat, he grinned. The crystal's power belonged to him now. His fingers closed around it. A soft hum came from the stone and heat pulsed from it. The heat built at a rapid rate, burning his flesh. He yelped, flinging the stone to the ground. With death near, the witch thought to defeat him. She would suffer. Radford could not save her. No one could.

He kicked the pendant under the bush to join the chain. Laughing, he held up his arms to the black sky, calling forth the powers of Hell. Red light shimmered around him. His bones stretched and muscles contracted, shifting into the human form he'd taken. The light dimmed and he let out a breath. He would soon shed this pathetic body and become himself again, the powerful Charles Ashbrook, Earl of Montague, once the favorite of Henry's court.

* * * * *

Kyla and Nick rode back to town in strained silence. The moon, hanging low in the sky, followed them. She could almost imagine the orb laughing at her. Soon it would be full and this time she wouldn't fail. She'd track her prey, kill him and leave this place. And Nick. Loss, pointed and sharp as a blade, stabbed her heart. She would handle her grief.

The lie stuck in her throat.

Sudden foreboding shivered over her, a warning of something dark and dangerous, of tragedy. "Something's wrong, Nick," she said, breaking the silence. "I feel it."

He slowed the car and turned to her. His face was pale in the soft moonlight. "I agree. Something's wrong between us." He turned his attention to the road, negotiating carefully around drunken festival-goers walking away from town.

"That's not what I mean," she said. "I've got a bad feeling that has nothing to do with us."

He gripped the steering wheel, not looking at her. "It's been a long night."

Kyla studied his strong profile. Something was very wrong. He felt it too. She'd seen the look of dread on his face before he masked it.

The Japanese lanterns still swung in the breeze and music and raucous laughter filled the square when they arrived. But something evil resided here, covering the village like a giant web, sucking the life from all it touched.

Nick pulled up behind her SUV. "Be careful," he said, turning to her. "There are too many drunks around. Get in your car, lock the door, and drive out of here as fast as you can." The firm set of his mouth and the tension in every line of his body told her he feared something much worse than drunken villagers.

She stiffened. "Drunks don't scare me and you know it.

There's more than that going on here."

Pain slashed across his rough-hewn features. She held herself rigid, fighting her need to reach out and caress his pain away.

"The only thing going on is that you've turned on me. What happened, Kyla?"

"I don't know what you're talking about." She grabbed the door handle, but he reached out and stopped her.

"Yes, you do," he said. "The sex was incredible. If that's all there is between us, I could let you go. But I can't. And you feel the same way."

Unable to meet his gaze, she pulled free. "Don't make anything more of it than what it was. Sex. Amazing sex."

"Liar," he said softly. "Look at me."

She stared into his eyes, dark and velvety in the dim light from the street lamps. And she was lost. "What do you want from me?"

He cupped her face between his hands. "Perhaps I want more than you're willing to give, more than is good for either of us."

She gave him one last lingering look, committing his face to memory for all the lonely days and nights ahead. Then she exited the car and left him sitting there with only the unanswered questions between them for company.

* * * * *

What the hell was wrong with him? Five centuries on Earth and hope still lived in him. Nick pounded the steering wheel as he drove out of town. He'd lost control. He knew better than to dream. But he needed Kyla in his bed and in his life. A laugh escaped him, a bitter sound that cut him like sharp wire. His life? A life of hell.

His body stirred, remembering Kyla's lovemaking.

Beautiful, passionate, and generous, she provoked a desire and longing in him unlike any he'd ever felt. But it was too late. If he didn't leave this world soon, he would become more Beast than man.

His destiny was to destroy Montague. And Kyla had her own destiny. Fate had put them here together. For what? A cruel attempt to plunge the blade of his hellish existence deeper into his heart? Whatever the reason, things were as they were meant to be. He couldn't change them.

His heart heavy, he slowed the car to let a group of rowdy teens pass. On the sidewalk, a man and woman clung together, hips gyrating. Disgust welled up in him. Sleepy little Heavensent had been a refuge to his wounded soul for more than a century. All goodness had been wiped out now. Montague's work. He'd cast a malevolent spell over the village and its inhabitants. His old enemy had destroyed other small villages and towns through the ages.

The demon's hand was evident in the chaos that ran rampant over whole countries. Unless stopped, the planet would soon belong to Montague and the forces of Hell. Fury and determination churned in Nick's soul. This would be the last place that would ever know Montague's depravity.

Montague wanted Kyla. Her were-hunting powers wouldn't help her against the demon. Nick hadn't saved Catherine or Julia, but he would save Kyla. Then he would die in peace.

Dark thoughts, unbidden, penetrated his mind. He had the power to make Kyla his forever with one bite on her neck. Once he destroyed Montague he and Kyla would roam Earth together, for all time.

"No!" He raised a fist to the mocking moon, pale now in the first light of the dawn sky. Kyla was duty-bound to kill him. He wouldn't condemn her to a hell without end or rob her of her legacy. He loved her too much.

He loved Kyla.

The thought caused him to lose control of the car and it swerved to the side of the road. He fought to keep it from plunging over the low wall into the water below. Heart pumping, he finally gained command and slammed on the brakes. The car nicked the stone wall before coming to a halt.

He looked at the moon, almost obscured by scudding clouds. A roar yanked from the recesses of his despair and he shook his fist at the heavens. "Why, God? Why have you done this to me? Weren't you content to damn me for eternity?"

Spent, he rested his head on the steering wheel and laughed. What irony. He loved the woman sent to destroy him.

Warnings curled through him, cutting into his self-pity. He raised his head. Wavering green lights shone through the trees opposite the road. Ghostlike figures floated in and out of the dense foliage. The Beast roused, sensing danger. Other forces haunted this night.

Nick pulled his keys from the ignition and slipped out of the car. Treading carefully, using skills he'd sharpened through the centuries, he crossed to the forest, going from tree to tree, hiding as he drew closer to the ghostly creatures. They entered a small clearing and he could see they carried something wrapped in a white cloth. Soft moans came from the thing they carried. Nick drew in a tense breath. A person, and still alive. He wouldn't allow another murder. Keeping to the trees, he hurried after them.

The creatures seemed to sense his presence and began

to move more quickly. Forgetting all caution, Nick sprinted.

A brilliant green light exploded before him, tossing him backwards. A red-eyed demon, bloody fangs bared, floated out of the mist. Memories of that horror-filled night long ago when Montague had cursed him assaulted Nick. He struggled to sit up.

The demon's wicked laugh rang through the forest before the image disappeared. All was quiet again, but the creatures carrying the moaning body had disappeared.

Nick brushed leaves and twigs from his clothes and headed deeper into the woods.

His breathing shallow, he ran a jagged course through the trees. Underbrush clawed him, slashing at his jeans. Branches and leaves whipped his face. He ignored them. He saw the wavering green light again and sped up.

He gained on the light and the ghostly figures still carrying their strange bundle. Strength coursed through him, infusing him with new energy.

Suddenly the air around him filled with horrific screeching. Demons in the form of ancient Native Americans, long hair flowing and eyes shooting fire, flew through the air toward him. Their fingers curved into talons, ready to rip him apart like the warriors from that long-ago hunt when he'd been so badly injured. Nick put up his hands against their onslaught and parried, diving away from the monsters. Roaring like guardians of Hell, their colorless lips twisted in malignant grins, exposing long fangs.

Fury pummeled Nick. Montague thought to weaken him for the final battle. Montague's army of demons wouldn't defeat him. Not now. Not ever. His rage woke the Beast and he released howls of fury. The sounds echoed through the deep woods, shaking the tree branches and sending dry leaves scattering along the forest floor.

The night when Montague cursed him flashed in his mind. He reached for the sword he'd kept in his scabbard. His hand came up empty. The sword and scabbard had disappeared centuries ago.

But he had powers now he hadn't possessed then, powers strengthened through the centuries. He'd used them once before and almost paid with his life. He was stronger now, but he didn't know if his body could withstand the physical toll. He saw Kyla's clear green eyes before him. He must try. For her. For the world. He assumed a battle stance and prepared to kill.

The largest of the demons attacked first. Nick quickly sidestepped. The monster disappeared into the thick air. The other creatures, hate swirling like a fog around them, charged him. With a fierce cry born of centuries of anguish, Nick lifted his hands toward the sky and summoned the spirits that lived in the trees and deep in the ground.

The air around him crackled. Thunder rumbled and lightening streaked across the brightening sky. Fire fell from the heavens, lethal weapons bent on destruction. The fire scorched nearby trees and shrubs and sent the monsters shrieking away in terror. Nick's body burned from the force of his channeling. Strength, like a turbulent river, rushed through his veins.

Visions pounded him. Catherine. The babe she'd borne for him. Their bodies twisted in death. Montague's face distorted with evil. And Kyla, holding out her hands, giving him courage and hope. With one last cry, he flung out his arms toward the remaining monsters. Flames sparked from his fingers, vaporizing the screaming creatures. He collapsed.

CHAPTER SIXTEEN

Dawn streaked red and purple across the sky. Birds warbled a greeting to the morning. Kyla, huddled in her wool blanket on the cold porch, her mood as black as the night that had just passed, ignored the beauty of the awakening day.

Nick dominated her thoughts. She rubbed hands over her sensitive breasts, remembering his body and the heat of his lovemaking. She wanted more. So much more, of his body, of him. She clutched the blanket closer.

Loving Nick gave him power over her. Love meant hurt and betrayal.

She'd known Nick a short time, but she trusted him. Surely, she reminded herself, he would never have committed those deeds literally in his own backyard. He would never have been so stupid as to attack the young girl and Todd. The girl, Emily, would have recognized him if he'd been her attacker. Nick had rescued the traumatized girl. And someone or something had dumped Todd on Nick's property. Someone was framing Nick. That had to be the answer.

A car pulled up to the curb in front of the house. She stiffened, ready for flight or fight. Todd swaggered from the front seat and turned to wave goodbye to a young woman behind the wheel. Grinning, he ambled up the walk and stopped when he spotted Kyla.

"You're up early," he said. "I didn't get much sleep last

night. I'm ready for a nap."

"I haven't been to bed yet."

The teasing glint left his eyes. "Kyla, what's wrong? Are those tears?" He sat in the chair next to her and took her hand in one of his.

"I love him, Todd."

"Radford?"

She nodded. Fresh tears started and he brushed them away from her cheek.

"And that's bad?" he asked. "Why?"

"I can't love him. I can't love any man, not that way. I walk away from men. It's what I do."

"Kyla, darling, you deserve love, just like everyone. Maybe more than most. Does Radford feel the same way?"

"I don't know."

His gaze softened. "Tell him how you feel."

"I can't."

"Don't let this one get away."

"What do I really know about him?" She pulled her hand free. "I'm good at what I do because I always focus on the mission and never let down my guard. With Nick, it's different. He's distracting me from my job. I think about him all the time and I trust him, but my instincts don't work well here. For the first time since Hunter-Wolf contacted me when I was eighteen, I've begun to question my vows and my legacy."

"Don't beat up on yourself." He touched her chin, tilting her face toward his. "You'll figure it out. You always do."

She laughed softly and reached over to ruffle his hair, then kissed him on the cheek. "Thanks."

The screeching of brakes jolted their attention to the driveway. A large black sedan pulled into the drive and rumbled to a stop. The car windows were darkened, hiding the occupants from view.

Kyla stood up. The wool blanket slipped off to pool at her feet. She reached for her gun in her shoulder holster and slowly drew it out. With her body tensed for a fight, she watched the car.

The four vampire slayers from Hunter-Wolf, Ltd., slowly exited the vehicle and approached the porch. She released a breath and holstered her gun.

"Those people give me the creeps," Todd said. "They're all yours. I'm outta here." He turned and disappeared into the house.

She waited on the porch for the slayers. Their faces looked grimmer than normal. "What's wrong, Liam?" she said to the oldest of them, the leader, when they reached her.

Liam faced her while the others flanked him. "It's bad," he said in his thick Scottish accent.

Chills chased over her skin. "What do you mean?"

"There are no vampires here."

Kyla looked at the woods surrounding them and felt sinister forces stirring and watching. "Come inside."

They followed her, four black-clad figures that bore a striking resemblance to the Grim Reaper. No wonder they made Todd nervous.

Once inside, she and Liam sat in chairs across from each other. His companions kept watch at the door.

"What's going on?" she asked.

"The creatures you saw are meant to look and act like vampires," he said. "But they're demons, controlled by the devil's most powerful servant, a mighty demon who's caused untold suffering all over the Earth. They do his bidding."

She'd been right about the menace here. A demon? The

black wolf? "How do you know this?"

His pale face turned ashen. "Rumors have been flying."

"I've heard them," she said.

"An apocalyptic showdown."

Dread washed over her, and she knew. "It's here, isn't it?" She released a nervous laugh. "Here in tiny Heavensent. How appropriate. When will it happen?" "We're not sure. Most probably at the full moon."

She glanced through the window and saw the faint image of the waxing moon in the dawn sky.

"James has alerted demon hunters from around the world to gather here," Liam said.

"When can I expect them?" she asked.

"You won't be here. Everyone, except the demon hunters, has been ordered back to headquarters."

She straightened. "I can't leave. I have a werewolf to slaughter."

He stood and looked down at her. "We don't know if what you hunt is a werewolf or something worse. If you stay, it will be at your own peril.

She stood and faced him. "I won't leave until I've completed my mission."

Sadness flitted over Liam's gaunt features. He reached out a hand to touch her shoulder. "You're sure?"

Kyla cringed at the coldness of his flesh, a chill she felt through her shirt. She nodded.

He dropped his hand. "I knew your parents. Be careful, my dear."

Then he and the others left, gliding slowly out of the house.

"Wait!" she called.

Liam looked back. The others continued to the car.

"Take Todd with you," she said. "He can't stay here."

"What's going on?" Todd asked from behind her.

Kyla turned to him. "Pack a bag quickly and go with them."

"No."

She grabbed his arm. "You have to. I want you safe."

She recognized the stubborn look on Todd's face. Anxiety threaded through her. "Please listen to me. You have to go. I may not be able to protect you."

"You saved me more than once when we were growing up. I won't leave you now."

Love and fear tightened a knot in Kyla's chest. "Todd, I can't let anything happen to you."

"I know what I'm doing. You're the only family I have. I'm not leaving." He turned to Liam. "Go."

With a shrug the vampire slayer joined the others and the sedan pulled away, a sleek black snake abandoning her and Todd to their fate.

She turned to him. "You should have gone."

He shook his head. "We live together or we die together."

* * * * *

Sudden pain shot through Kyla's head. Driven by the ferocious pounding in her head, she jumped up from the sofa where she'd tried to sleep after Liam and the other slayers left. Something terrible was about to happen, or had already happened. She'd felt this same hammering pain and dread the day her parents were attacked and her mother killed. Recognizing the omens then, she'd begged them to send another hunter to slay the werewolf. They'd laughed and shrugged off her fears. She never saw her mother alive again.

She ran to Todd's room and flung open the door, slamming it against the wall. He roused from sleep and sat up, staring at her with startled eyes.

"What's wrong?"

"You're okay." Pressing a hand to her trembling midsection, she leaned against the doorframe.

He frowned. "Why wouldn't I be?"

She forced a smile. "Go back to sleep."

Shaking his head, he lay down. Nerves on edge, she quietly closed the door. Less than two weeks before the full moon. The demon hunters might get here too late.

She was alone.

Evil, greater than she'd ever known, mobilized all around her. She felt it, could almost taste it. Anger rose in her, cutting off her breath. She inhaled deeply, filling her lungs. The monsters wouldn't win.

Pain, swift and hard, lanced her again and she doubled over. Nick's face swam before her. He needed her. This time she wouldn't fail him. Resolve pushed through her anger. She raced to her room to gather her weapons.

A gentle breeze blew over her, stopping her just inside the doorway. *Black Fox*. The ancient Navajo had sent spirits to comfort her and set her on the right path. Their presence wrapped around Kyla and their warm breaths whispered on her neck. All doubts fled. She knew what she had to do.

Minutes later, dressed in warm clothes, she stood on the porch. She would find Nick. Black Fox's spirits had departed, but their energy remained. Todd would be safe; whatever was out there wanted her. It wouldn't come for Todd now, but it had Nick. Maybe it was a trap, luring her. She had to take that chance.

She parked her SUV at the old logging trail and jumped out. Urgent foreboding pressed her forward and she took off at a trot, sure-footed as she ignored the wet leaves and leapt over fallen branches. Pushed by a power she couldn't explain, she ran harder. Nick needed her. She wouldn't question how she knew.

The banging of her heart was the only sound in the ominous quiet that had settled over the woods. A shaft of early sunlight opened before her, pointing a path. The still form of a man lay on the forest floor.

With a small cry, she ran to Nick. He was pale and lifeless. Scratches slashed his face and burn marks reddened his palms. Kneeling beside him, she lifted his head onto her lap and felt for the pulse at his neck. "Don't you dare die." His pulse was faint but steady. A tear slid down her cheek and she raised her head to the heavens. "Please, God."

Nick stirred and opened pain-filled eyes. "Kyla. I saw you."

She stroked his roughened cheek.

With a heavy sigh, he closed his eyes and lay back. She brushed a lock of hair from his forehead and traced her fingers along his full lips. She loved him. She was lost.

Small creatures scurried among the leaves and the wind picked up, blowing through the trees. Someone or something watched. "Nick." She gently shook him. "We have to go. Can you stand?"

He opened his eyes and struggled to sit. She pushed up from the ground and reached down to grab his hand, helping him stand on unsteady legs. "Lean on me," she said. He draped an arm around her shoulders. Holding onto him, she walked as swiftly as his weight would allow.

Shrieks suddenly blasted around them, vibrating through the thick air. She froze and looked at Nick. His jaw tightened and his mouth set in a grim line. He pulled away and glanced up, his body tense, as if poised for a fight. What did he expect to materialize from the sky? She put her hands over her ears, trying to block out the deafening noise. As suddenly as it had started, the shrieks stopped and all was quiet again.

Nick's breathing was labored and a growl rumbled from deep in his chest.

"What the hell was that?" She turned to him and gripped his shoulders.

"I thought they were coming back," he said. "Something turned them away, or maybe they can't fight the two of us."

"What are you talking about? Who was coming back?"

His eyes darkened and he winced with pain. Freeing himself from her grip, he stepped back. "You need to leave Heavensent. Now. You and Todd get away while you still can."

She raised her chin. "No."

His gaze, golden and filled with grief, implored her. "You don't know what's here."

"Tell me what's here."

His jaw set in a stubborn line. "You have to leave."

"I'll take you home now." She put her arm around his waist.

"Obstinate, aren't you?"

She nodded. "As obstinate as you."

"Stubbornness can kill you," he said.

Determination stiffened her spine. "Only if we let it."

He tripped on the roots of a large tree and she held tighter to him. "I'm not leaving, Nick. Don't ask again."

He shook his head, but kept quiet.

They continued walking, their pace as fast as Nick's injuries allowed. The tree branches rustled in the faint wind. The soft cries of a wounded creature carried to them. Next to her, Nick stiffened. They stared at each other. Death pulsed around them. The stricken look on Nick's face told her he felt it too.

"What's happening?" she whispered.

"Let's get the hell out of here," he said.

When they reached his house, he turned to her. "If you won't leave the village, stay with me, at least through this day and night. I'll protect you."

"I can take care of myself." She looked down at the ground. "I'll stay for a while, only until I'm sure you're okay."

"You refuse to run from the danger here, but you won't stay with me?" He touched her chin and tilted her face until their gazes met. "You're afraid of me."

"I'm not."

"Prove it."

Challenge and desire glowed from his eyes. For the space of a heartbeat, wolf eyes flashed in the topaz depths, then they were gone. Her exhaustion made her see things that weren't there.

She was so tired of fighting her need for Nick. "I can't leave Todd alone."

His gaze gentled. "I'll send one of Antica's sons to watch over him. He'll be safe."

She chewed her lip. "You're sure?"

"I'm sure." He gave her a smile tinged with sadness. "Let's enjoy what little time we have."

Fear for Nick knifed her gut. "Little time? What do you mean?"

He shifted his gaze away. "I leave early tomorrow for Geneva, Switzerland. I don't know when I'll be back."

"You're leaving?" Her whispered words hung between them. Another word hovered in her mind. Geneva.

Werewolves had been reported there, but she hadn't found any. Nick was no werewolf. And yet… She let the thought drift off.

"I have no choice," he said. "I have obligations."

He bent and kissed her lightly on the lips. Warmth and longing mixed a heated brew in her stomach, weakening her resolve. She needed this man, but her need for him could be her destruction.

* * * * *

"Witch, would that I had killed you centuries ago." Montague kicked the unconscious Antica sprawled on the stone floor. "Where's your magic crystal to protect you now?"

Moaning, she stirred and opened bruised and swollen eyes. She struggled to a sitting position and spit at his black boots. "Kill me if you must, but you will never defeat Nicholas."

Montague roared and grabbed her by the neck, yanking her to her feet. He fisted his hand on her blouse and pulled her to him. "You will pay for what you've done." He pushed her against the wall.

Despite her trembling, her eyes flashed and her defiant gaze scanned him. "So this is the human form you've chosen. My Nicholas will find you."

"Radford will know me when I deem it so. You will die this day and take my secret to your grave. My powers are too great for you."

"A curse on your powers."

He slapped her hard across the face, splitting her lip. Blood dripped down her chin.

The door flew open and John Vickers rushed into the room. "Is all as it should be, master?"

Montague sneered. "You think this old hag can best me?"

"You!" Antica cried. Wiping blood from her mouth, she charged Vickers. Laughing, he grabbed her and held her at arm's length.

"You betrayed my Nicholas," she screamed. "But for your betrayal, he would have lived a goodly life and died at the appointed time."

Vickers shoved her away. "Radford could not promise the powers and immortality of my lord and master." He bowed toward Montague.

Montague threw back his head and laughed. "And now my demon forces converge on this small, insignificant place. We will have our revenge. Radford will be destroyed and the world will be ours."

Hate blazed from Antica's eyes. "You will lose. And my Nicholas will be whole again, granted the future you tore from him so brutally."

"Shut up, hag." Montague slapped her across the face again and sent her reeling. The heat in his eyes told him they glowed red. He lasered a burning beam at her face. She clutched at her cheek and shrieked in agony.

"I will kill you today, but first you will tell me what you know of the woman." He moved closer and grabbed her face between his fingers. "Tell me now and your torture will be lessened."

Fear contorted the old witch's battered face, but she jerked free of him. "Torture me as you wish. I tell you nothing."

The old crone still had fight in her. Montague grinned. Torturing her would bring more pleasure.

He turned to Vickers. "Leave us."

With a leer, Vickers backed out of the room. When he

opened the door, the sounds of anguish and torment reached Montague. He smiled. The young women he and his demons had captured were meeting their fates in a variety of cruel and sadistic ways.

He would force the old hag's secret out of her, then he would destroy her and seek his sexual release in the torture of a young, innocent woman.

He leveled his gaze on the defiant Antica and grabbed her by her long gray hair, pulling until she cried out. "Tell me what you know about the huntress."

"Never."

He pushed her. She stumbled and fell into a heap before him. "Bitch!" he yelled, dragging her up by her hair. "You saved Radford and protected him all these years."

She raised her bloodied face and jerked free. Then she lifted shaking arms to the ceiling and began a low keening chant.

"Your spirits have no power against me," he screeched. "Who protects Radford? Is it the huntress? What do you know about the woman? Tell me before I send you to Hell." He waved his hands and she flew across the room, hitting the wall. She slid slowly down, a broken, battered, useless crone. With a smile, she closed her eyes. Lilting music filled the room.

Howling his rage, Montague ran to her and felt for a pulse. "No!" He wasn't finished with her yet.

A shaft of white light appeared over Antica. Her spirit rose into the light. He covered his eyes against the brightness and the goodness. The light disappeared and the room darkened. Her empty shell of a body lay before him.

She would take her secret to the grave, but he had other ways of finding what she knew about the huntress. He looked down at his boots, covered with the witch's blood. He would need a new pair.

He raised his arms. Black and gray mist swirled around him. When the mist cleared, he was once again the proud Charles Ashbrook, Earl of Montague.

* * * * *

Nick woke to a throbbing headache. Something was very wrong. The room was gray and shadowed in the early morning, increasing his feeling of uneasiness. He looked down at Kyla, sleeping soundly next to him. A fierce urge to protect her welled up in him.

Had a dream or a premonition woken him? He kissed Kyla's temple and settled next to her, trying to ignore the dread pressing against his chest.

Needing to hold her, he took her into his arms. She shifted but didn't waken. She'd stayed with him through the night. Holding her close, he stared at the velvet canopy above his bed. Despite his weakness, they'd made love, hungrily, as if she too knew this could be their last time. He'd cherish the memory of their lovemaking for eternity. She'd fallen asleep in his arms, but sleep had eluded him for hours before it briefly claimed him.

Pain seized his head again and he moaned. He knew instinctively that Montague had slaughtered another victim. Antica? Her name jutted into Nick's consciousness. He hadn't seen her when he and Kyla came in yesterday. Antica always waited for him, fearing for his safety. He'd sent one of her sons to guard Todd, and consumed by Kyla, he'd not given Antica another thought.

Fear, powerful and intense, flowed over him. He rolled from the bed and walked to the window. The brightening sky mocked him. It wasn't a new day for him, but the beginning of the end. Soon the moon would be full.

The hammering in his head worsened. He threw on jeans, and with a last look at Kyla, left the room. Spurred by ominous warning chills that tingled over his skin, Nick sprinted down the long hallway and threw open the door to Antica's sparsely furnished room. Her small bed was neat and tidy. Either she'd awakened very early or she'd never slept in it.

Nick raced down the stairs, his heart thumping in time with the pounding of his feet. He ran into the kitchen. The room was clean and undisturbed. He stood in the empty room and raked impatient fingers through his hair.

Footsteps sounded behind him and he spun around to face Luka, Antica's eldest son. "Where is your mother?"

Luka rubbed a hand over his sleep-filled eyes and shook his head. "Don't you know?"

Nick tamped down dread. "I haven't seen her. Her bed doesn't look slept in."

Luka's broad face paled. "I assumed she went to gather her special herbs. The moon is nearly full, the best time to gather them. I thought she must have told you."

Shaking his head, Nick leaned against the counter. Antica frequently disappeared for days to search the woods for her healing herbs, but she never went without telling him or her sons. He locked his gaze with Luka's and saw the panic forming in the other man's eyes.

CHAPTER SEVENTEEN

Together you and Nicholas have the power to defeat the devil.

The whispered words, the voice eerie and familiar, jerked Kyla awake. Antica? Kyla's skin crawled. She slid from the bed and grabbed her clothes off the floor, then swept her gaze through Nick's room in a panicked inventory. She expected the witch to slide from under the closet door or slither from an armoire. The room remained empty. Completely empty.

Where was Nick? After their frenzied lovemaking, she'd fallen asleep in his arms. Being with him had filled her with peace, a peace she'd not known for most of her life. Even now, having just awakened, she missed him.

The bright sunlight slanting through the velvet curtains told her it was mid-morning. She hadn't meant to sleep so late. She gathered up the rest of the clothes she'd hastily discarded the night before.

The memory of his lovemaking made heat spiral through her. She flicked her tongue over her lips, still puffy from his kisses. She could spend a lifetime in Nick's arms.

That was the problem. Pressing a palm to her midriff, she struggled to breathe. Love hurt. She'd loved her father, but his suicide had plunged her into a wretchedly lonely childhood. She was no longer a child, but an adult with adult wants and needs, and adult pain. Losing Nick would bring heartache unlike any she'd ever experienced. She couldn't allow another man the power to hurt her like that.

Too many thoughts and emotions crowded in her head. All her senses told her Nick hid dark secrets, but her obsession for him blotted out her doubts. She needed time to sort it through. She dressed hurriedly and raked fingers through her tangled hair, catching a quick glimpse of herself in the large dresser mirror. Her face looked different, softer, like a woman well-loved. Well-loved. Fear and joy mingled in her, coiling a tight knot in her stomach.

Together you will defeat the evil one.

"Stop it!" she said to the empty room. Now Antica was in her head. She must be going mad. It would soon be a full moon. She was alone to fight whatever wickedness possessed this strange little village. What had the whispered words meant? *Only together could she and Nick defeat the devil.* All she needed were her weapons and her fighting skills. Or at least that was all she had.

She yanked open the door and ran into the hall. The stairs and escape beckoned. She raced along the ancient Oriental rug and slid to a stop. Nick faced her at the end of the hall. She'd heard no door opening or steps creaking.

Despite her apprehensions, her gaze devoured him. His hair was ruffled, softening the harsh planes of his face. The heat blazing from his eyes awakened need deep inside her.

"What's wrong?" Nick was at her side in an instant. "You look like you've seen a ghost, or worse." He gripped her shoulders and pulled her tight against his hard chest. "Your heart is thundering. Did something frighten you?"

She wanted to trust him, but she couldn't tell him she'd run from Antica's voice.

And from the truth—that she'd lost her heart to him.

"I don't scare easily." She should pull away, but her traitorous body melted against his firm contours.

He pressed her closer. "I'm sorry I wasn't in the room when you woke up, but something's happened."

She pulled away and looked up at him. Tension etched fine lines around his eyes and mouth. "What's wrong?"

"We can't find Antica."

She placed her hand on his chest. "I'm sorry. First Todd, and now Antica may be missing. Can I help?"

"It's probably nothing. Her son Luka is out looking for her."

Nick put his hand over hers. "Antica frequently gathers herbs before…before the full moon. Sometimes she loses track of the time."

She'd felt his heart rate speed up.

He pushed gently away. "We'll find Antica. I'm sure she's okay."

The note of panic in his voice notched up Kyla's own fears. "I hope you find her soon. I'll help any way I can." She chewed her lip. "I need to get home to Todd. What if something's happened to him too?"

"Todd is fine. Antica's son Lycan is watching over him."

Lycan? Wolf?

She shivered. "You're sure he's okay?"

"I'm sure. What else is bothering you?"

Kyla opened her mouth to tell him about the whispered words, but the tightness of his features silenced her. "Nothing," she lied. "I was worried about Todd, that was all."

"Go on home, Kyla. I'll call you when we find Antica." He took her hand and placed a gentle kiss on her palm, then closed her fingers over it as if he wanted her to hold onto his kiss. "I need to go away. A business trip I can't postpone. I don't want to leave until we find Antica, but I have no choice."

He dropped her hand and cupped her shoulders. "I fly to Geneva for a few days. That's all."

Somehow she knew it was much more than that. "But you'll be back."

He nodded. "I'll call you when I get back. We need to talk."

She planted a soft kiss on his lips. "Okay. Have a safe trip." Turning on her heel, she headed down the stairs. He wanted to talk. Apprehension sliced through her. She wasn't sure she wanted to hear what he had to say.

* * * * *

Nick glanced at his watch. Time was moving too swiftly. He needed to get to the small airfield and his private jet. He didn't want to leave until Luka found Antica, but he couldn't delay. The flight plan had been filed. His pilot was waiting, and his lawyers in Geneva needed him to finalize the arrangements that would insure the continuation of the Foundation. When he returned, the moon would be close to full. Soon it would all be over.

Regret covered him like mist from a rain cloud. Antica knew his plans for Geneva. She should have been here to see him off. She'd been anxious to tell him something the other night, but he'd been too obsessed by Kyla to listen. Guilt coiled in his stomach. He should have stopped to listen to Antica. He hoped it wasn't too late.

* * * * *

Thirty-six hours later, back from Switzerland, Nick had tried to sleep, but instead tossed in his bed, restless in the dark, heart pounding, listening, waiting, for what he didn't know. The trip had been frustrating and stressful, but he'd left with the knowledge that the good work he'd started would go on. Antica and her sons would be taken care of and protected through however many years they would be on Earth.

He'd not seen Antica when he'd arrived home exhausted two hours ago. Luka said she hadn't returned from her herb gathering. The worry on Luka's face had mirrored the dread in Nick's heart. Antica had never stayed away this long before, but he needed rest before he started to search for her.

As he lay in bed now, visions flickered before him. Catherine. Montague. Vickers. Antica. And finally Kyla.

Suddenly, a presence surrounded him, comforting and warm. His heart calmed. A soft draft of air brushed by him, caressing his cheek and bringing whispered words that floated through his mind. *The beach. Kyla.*

Prompted by an overwhelming urge he didn't understand, he bolted from the bed and dressed quickly in jeans and a T-shirt, then left the house at a run. He sprinted along the treacherous path that led to the beach below.

The three-quarter moon lit his way. A shudder ran through him. Within days the Beast would demand revenge and this time he would grant it.

When he reached the beach, he stopped and looked around. What had compelled him to this place? Rugged cliffs, black and forbidding, rose around him, framing the dark sea. Foaming white-capped waves glowed in the moonlight, violent in their beauty, as they crashed onto the rocks and the cool sand, the sound soothing in its rhythm and furious in its intensity. He lifted his head and inhaled the fresh scent of salt and sand. He would soon leave this Earth he loved so much. Had he made atonement or would he burn in Hell for his sins?

The small hairs on his arms stood in warning and he knew he wasn't alone. Muffled footsteps sounded behind him and he spun around.

Kyla, black hair blowing softly around her perfect oval face, glided toward him. She looked like a sea sprite come to life. The moonlight outlined her lush body under the filmy nightgown she wore. The pale silver fabric shimmered around her, moonbeams sent from Heaven.

"Kyla." His voice carried on the gentle breeze. He walked quickly to meet her, afraid she would disappear like his long-ago vision of Catherine on that fateful night five hundred years before.

Kyla was a vision in her beauty, but she was no dream. She was alive, real and vibrant.

"Nick." She touched his arm.

Need and longing shot through him.

"A voice called me here," she said. "What strange magic is this?"

"The magic of you and me together." He cupped her shoulders and looked into her eyes. The light of the moon was reflected in their depths, awakening something hidden deep inside him where hope once lived.

She studied him, as if trying to see into his soul.

He brushed a kiss on her temple. "Tonight is ours."

Desire darkened her eyes and she parted her lips. "Love me, Nick."

He took her face between his hands and kissed her waiting lips. He wouldn't question the powers that drew them together. For tonight, he would forget everything and find satisfaction and release in the curves and valleys of her body.

She tasted of mint and passion and the essence that was Kyla. Desire arrowed to his groin and he parted her lips with his tongue, testing the silkiness of her mouth, tormented by her beauty and softness. This might be the last time he possessed her. He pushed the thought aside. He had an eternity to grieve.

"You belong to me," he whispered against her mouth. Drawing away, he stroked his fingers over the smooth, supple contours of her face and slid his hands over her shoulders to push aside the thin straps holding her silk gown.

The gown slid off her, exposing her creamy skin and lush curves. She wore nothing underneath. The moonlight glimmered gold on her body. Surely she stepped down from Mt. Olympus to tempt him.

"A goddess," he said on a shaky breath.

Her eyes softened to green velvet and she reached out to run a finger over his lips. "Not a goddess," she said. "Just a real woman with a woman's needs."

Taking her by the shoulders, he gently turned her toward the ocean and pulled her against him until her buttocks pressed against his erection.

Circling his arms around her waist, he said, "Look how the moonlight touches your beautiful breasts." Following the moon's path, he ran his hands down her full breasts, massaging the nipples until soft cries escaped her. "So beautiful."

She rubbed against him, a temptress he would love forever.

Tremors of pleasure, shot with yearning, washed over him. "Touch yourself," he whispered.

"Yes." She followed his hands with her own, stroking her fingers over her breasts and moaning softly.

He trailed his fingers slowly down her body, reveling in the velvet heat of her skin and the flatness of her stomach. He would give his soul to see her swell with his child. It couldn't be. He willed his regret away. Tonight he would think of nothing but pleasing her.

When he stroked her curls, she bucked against him. "Easy, love," he said. "We have all night."

She leaned her head against his shoulder. "I want you so badly."

"And you'll have me." He pressed his hand against her mound and rubbed her until her moans joined the sounds of the surf breaking onto the shore. His body on fire, he slipped fingers into her heated wetness, finding that special spot that would drive her over the precipice. Uttering tiny sounds of pleasure, she writhed and ground her hips into his.

He slid his fingers in and out, watching the moon's light play on her body. She wrapped her hand around his arm, begging him with her body and her urgent, rasping pleas, to take more, to give more. He stroked faster and harder, wanting only to please her, to possess her, to make her his. With a tortured cry, she screamed her release and collapsed against him.

He held tightly to her until she stopped shaking, then he gently lifted her away and turned her to face him. Smiling, she reached out and touched his mouth. "We're not done yet." Her words drifted over them into the cool night air.

As if worshipping a goddess, he knelt in front of her and pulled her gently toward him. He kissed her firm stomach, laving the tender flesh, and dipped his tongue into her navel, swirling and sucking, hungry for her and all she could give him, hungry for salvation. But it was too late for salvation.

Forcing aside his dark thoughts, he concentrated on

Kyla, and only her. She tasted of lavender and salt and the untamed ocean. Licking, caressing, and nibbling, he wound a trail down her luscious body to the sultry heat between her legs. Crying out his name, she curved her fingers into his hair.

He parted her slick folds and delved into her with his tongue. She gasped and pulled on his hair. His body burned for her. The Beast stirred and shook with its desire to escape and render the bite that would brand Kyla his mate forever. Temptation reared up, goading him to give in to the Beast.

Moaning softly, Kyla whispered his name. It echoed around him, filling him with love and longing. He couldn't condemn her to live as he did. He loved her too much. With every ounce of will he possessed, he fought the Beast until it quieted.

She gripped his shoulders, digging her nails into his flesh, and threw her head back, surrendering to the invasion of his tongue. She was liquid fire in his hands. A heady sense of power overcame him and he thrust his tongue deeper into her softness, tasting her, devouring her. She was his tonight.

Her climax shuddered through her. Her loud cries filled the empty beach. He plunged his tongue deeper and deeper, pushing her to the edge and back. Her body shook and her knees gave out. He held onto her hips and kissed her soft curls until she stilled.

Holding her, he moved slowly up her body, kissing every sweet inch of her that he touched. Her breathing grew shallow and ragged and she clung to him, trembling.

When he reached her mouth, he took her lips in a rough kiss that told her she belonged to him, and only him. Melting against him, she returned his kiss with the same urgency. Their tongues danced and mated in a timeless lovers' ritual.

Her musky scent of aroused woman and her eager responses to his possession strained his self-control. He left her mouth to nibble and lick a hot trail down her throat. The Beast inside growled, desperate for freedom, desperate to mate with her. Wild, fierce desire overtook him and he cupped her buttocks, pressing her against his hard cock.

"Nick," she whispered. "I want you inside me."

He quickly slipped off his clothes, and with a flourish, laid the T-shirt on the packed sand and placed her on it.

"Need you." Kyla held out her arms, a goddess made for love. Her lips were swollen and red from his kisses and her eyes burned with passion. He'd never seen anyone more beautiful in all the centuries he'd roamed Earth, had never loved anyone more.

He positioned himself over her. She opened for him, inviting him, giving herself to him. With a strangled moan, he slid into her waiting softness. She let out a cry and clutched his shoulders, wrapping her legs around his waist.

Her full breasts, silky, hot, pressed against his chest. He thrust harder and deeper. She met his every move, her body urging him to take the pleasures she so freely offered.

Harder. Faster.

Her heat seared him. Every nerve end burned and he felt his control slip. He threw back his head. Low, guttural sounds of pleasure escaped him until the air was thick with the sounds of their lovemaking.

Together they rode the tide, rocking and grinding until their bodies became one with each other and with the ocean that seethed behind them. In the distance thunder rumbled and flashes of lightening streaked the sky, igniting the storm raging between them.

Kyla raked her nails over his back. The slight pain

roused the Beast again. A soft growl rumbled from Nick and he nipped the enticing flesh of her neck, careful not to draw blood. She cried out and wound her legs tighter around his waist. He pumped into her, claiming her. She was his mate. She would always be his mate.

They climaxed together, drowning in a swirling, consuming ecstasy.

Nick collapsed against her and nuzzled her neck, inhaling her woman scent mingled with the salt air. He tightened his hold on her as if he could forestall time.

"Nick, I love you."

Her words tore into his heart, splitting it. Her love condemned her. He pulled slowly away, bracing himself on his hands, and looked down at her. "You don't know what you're saying."

Tears glistened in her eyes and she reached out to stroke his face. Because he'd never loved her more than at that moment, he would let her go.

He hardened his features and stood. "I'll take you home." He held a hand out to help her stand.

The hurt on her beautiful face drove despair deep into his soul. "It's better this way, Kyla. Please believe me."

She stood, refusing his hand, and slipped on her nightgown. Without a word, she walked quickly away over the packed sand, ethereal and otherworldly, like Venus come to life.

Nick watched her until she disappeared from sight. Lightning lit the sky, a heavenly reminder of the hopelessness of an eternity without her.

* * * * *

From his hiding place deep in the shrubs and twisted driftwood that rimmed the beach, Montague let out a low growl. His eyes, burning red, followed the bitch as she walked away from Radford. The huntress's lush body and her passionate responses to Radford had incited spasms of pleasure that had rocked him until he found his own release. The couple on the beach had been too involved with each other to hear him. As his own climax surged, he'd shifted to his true form. Had either of them noticed, they would have seen the real Montague, a proud Earl of Henry's Court, the man he'd been before Catherine's rejection sent him on his damning spiral. Catherine had escaped him through death. The huntress would not be so lucky.

CHAPTER EIGHTEEN

"I'm a damn fool!"

Kyla could no longer bear the sight of her reddened eyes, shadowed by dark circles, staring solemnly back at her from the mirror. She bent over the bathroom sink and splashed cold water on her face, then grabbed a towel, averting her gaze from the accusing glass.

Tears clogged her throat, but she refused to cry. She'd lost control and allowed herself to fall in love with Nick. Worse, she'd told him she loved him. And he'd rejected her. Her heart felt ready to shatter into a million pieces.

Straightening, she dried her face and threw the towel on the floor, then stalked into the bedroom. She may have fallen in love with Nick, but she would not let his rejection destroy her. Or distract her. She had a mission to accomplish.

The grayness of the outside between the closed curtains and touched the corners of the room. There would be no sunlight today. Like her life, drab with all hope gone.

"For God's sake, get a grip." Her words hung in the cool air. She flung herself on the bed and pulled the heavy comforter over her, knowing she would get no rest.

What power had pulled her from deep sleep a few hours ago and whispered for her to drive to the beach clothed only in a thin nightgown? Somehow she'd known Nick would be waiting. His lovemaking, gentle and passionate, had been bittersweet, as if he knew that would be their last time together.

A snippet of memory brushed her, one too strange to believe, but she couldn't ignore it. She sat up, clutching the comforter to her chest. Once before, as they had hours ago, she and Nick had made love with the same fierce passion on a moonlit beach, the surf pounding behind them. Where and when? She'd only just met him. Or had she? An explanation surfaced, swimming up through her thoughts. No, it wasn't possible. She lay down and grabbed her pillow, wrapping it around her head. It couldn't silence the whispers in her mind.

* * * * *

Nick roamed his quiet house. The floorboards in the cavernous dining room squeaked a protest with his heavy footsteps. No other noises disturbed the hushed calmness, as if the house waited with breath held, for he knew not what. He ran fingers over the polished walnut of the huge table, trying to find solace. But the cool, smooth wood and the surrounding stillness wouldn't bring him peace.

Thoughts crowded him, making sleep impossible. He headed for the living room, gripping the half-empty wine bottle he held. The liquor couldn't still his pounding heart or drown his despair. Nothing could.

Except Kyla.

Her name sighed through the room. The hurt in her eyes when she'd fled the beach hours ago pierced him with new guilt. The moon would soon be full. Once she knew the truth, she would understand why he'd sent her away. The truth would make it so much easier for her to kill him.

"Damn!" The word roared from him. He set down his wine bottle and grabbed a glass paperweight from the desk, ready to fling it against the wall in frustration. Flames from the fire in the hearth reflected on the red rose imprisoned inside. Like the rose, he was a prisoner too, of Montague's curse. That awful night so long ago ran through his mind. He slammed the paperweight back on the desk. Antica should have let him die.

Apprehension whipped through him, churning dread. Where was Antica?

"Master Nicholas."

Nick whirled to face Luka and Lycan. For such large men, Antica's sons moved with quiet, cat-like grace.

"Have you found her?" Nick asked.

The tears streaming down the gentle giants' red-rimmed eyes knifed Nick with dark premonition. Luka held out his hand. Antica's crystal, white lights glowing, rested on his palm.

Tears formed in Nick's eyes. Without the crystal Antica's powers were diminished. He knew the truth. She was gone, dead at Montague's hands. "We have to bring her home," Nick said through his tears. "The crystal will lead us to her."

Wordlessly, he, Luka and Lycan took off for the nearby woods. Tension seemed to drip from the dark trees and a pall hung over the dense foliage, as if the world waited for them to find Antica's body.

They finally found her, broken and bloodied, in a thick copse of trees. Her sons' wails ricocheted through the air. Nick clutched the precious crystal to his heart and sank to his knees. Tears flowed from his eyes.

He picked up Antica's beloved body and held her against his chest until Luka took her from him.

* * * * *

The white wolf ran toward her, powerful muscles rippling with his movements. His yellow eyes flashed gold, mesmerizing and seducing. She lifted her gun and fired. The wolf fell. Mist covered him. When the mist cleared, Nick lay there, a bullet through his chest, his white shirt stained with his blood.

Kyla's eyes flew open. Heart racing, she sat up quickly. The living room swayed around her. She gripped the arm of the sofa, where she'd drifted off to sleep, until the dizziness left.

"No!" Fear knotted her chest, strangling her. She closed her eyes and saw the white wolf again. The truth battered her, demanding she listen. Her heart cried.

Noises from the kitchen brought her from the sofa. Todd. Fighting nausea, she ran into the kitchen to find him stacking dishes in the cabinet, such an ordinary task on such an extraordinary day. Grabbing his arm, she pulled him around to face her. A dish fell out of his hand and shattered on the floor. She didn't care.

"What the hell?" he asked.

"You're leaving. Now. No arguments." She gripped his arm.

A muscle ticked in his jaw. He shook his head and pulled free. "The full moon is in three days. You need me. You know how you are after a hunt. I won't leave you."

"You will, Todd. This hunt will be different from the others." Swallowing, she looked away from him. "I may not survive."

"Kyla, don't talk like that." He touched her shoulders and forced her to look at him. "We're a team. I couldn't live if anything happened to you."

Kyla stroked a hand down his arm. "Something more powerful than anything I've ever faced is waiting for me. Don't ask how I know, I just do. I have to fight it. It's my duty. But I couldn't bear knowing you might die."

"You're talking crazy." Rubbing a hand over his hair, he backed away. "There's nothing more here than your garden-variety werewolf."

"It's lots more than that," she said. "Please, do as I say. If anything happens to me, whatever is out there will come for you. They took you once. They can do it again. Go to Hunter-Wolf headquarters. They'll protect you."

He studied her. "This isn't like you. I've never seen you so fatalistic. What's happened? You've acted strange the past week."

The small room closed in on her. She bit down on her lip and turned away to head into the living room, wishing she could walk away from her troubles as easily. Todd followed close behind.

When she reached the windows, she stopped to stare out. Spring blossomed all around. Tulips and hyacinths poked from the young grass. New birth. And death was so close.

"I had a dream. Oh, God." Her shoulders shook.

"What's wrong?"

"My dream. I saw the white wolf."

"So? You always have wolf dreams before a hunt."

She stared into his eyes. "This wolf morphed into Nick. And then I knew."

Todd's eyes widened. "You can't be saying?"

"Nick is my prey. One I have to kill."

CHAPTER NINETEEN

His last transformation. The time had come. In three days the moon would be full. Already white strands threaded through the blackness of Nick's hair and the yellow eyes staring back at him from the mirror bore the mark of the wolf.

And Antica was gone. Sadness twisted in his chest like a sharp dagger he couldn't dislodge. He missed her love and her comforting presence. Maybe it was better this way. She wouldn't witness his death. The woman she'd prophesied had never appeared. So be it. He knew what he had to do.

The sounds of weeping drifted from downstairs, pushing the dagger deeper into his heart. Antica's sons. In a rage, they'd searched the woods for Montague. He knew they would never stop grieving for their mother. He'd arranged for them to live in a castle in the Balkans, where they would be safe. Radford Manor would belong to the Foundation, to do with as they saw fit. The important thing was that the Foundation would continue the good work he'd started. They were on the verge of a major breakthrough that could forever cure malaria. He'd done some good with the cruel turn his life had taken.

He looked again at his face, still human, but shadowed by the wolf he would become. Despite himself, his pulse accelerated and adrenaline pumped through his veins. Soon he would be free to roam the woods and fields again, to feel the wind in his fur, the earth under his paws, and to howl at the cursed moon for the last time. Then he would destroy Montague and face his own death.

And there was Kyla. Anger boiled through him, heating his blood. A low growl escaped. Montague would not have her.

Unable to look at himself any longer, he turned away. He had made his decision. He grabbed his cell phone and punched in Kyla's number.

* * * * *

Nausea churned Kyla's stomach and she choked back bile. Her hand shook as she lifted the wolf's head knocker on Nick's door. She'd come at his call, compelled to learn the truth, yet not sure she wanted to know.

The door flung open before she released the knocker. She almost lost her balance and quickly straightened. And looked into Nick's yellow eyes. Wolf eyes. The white strands that lightened his black hair and the fine lines that fingered his mouth and his eyes confirmed what she dreaded. Until this moment, she'd held out hope her instincts were wrong.

"No!" She ran back down the steps, away from the nightmare before her. He was her enemy. She loved him. She had to kill him.

"Kyla, stop." He chased her and grabbed her arm, pulling her to face him.

She yanked free and rubbed her arm where he'd gripped. Huffing out a ragged breath, she stared at him.

"Come into the house," he said. "We have to talk."

"Why are you showing yourself to me?" His silence screamed a reality she didn't want to hear. She swallowed around the dryness in her throat. "You know who I am."

He nodded.

"When?" she asked.

"Almost from the beginning."

"And yet, you—we, oh, God."

He pulled her to him. "I'm still a man, Kyla, and I love you as a man loves a woman."

With a cry, she jerked free. "Don't say that. You know what I have to do."

"Yes."

She felt hollowness in her heart, as if all feeling were scooped out by a cold hand. "Why?"

His wolf eyes darkened in pain and he tensed. She dug her nails into her palms, fighting her need to smooth the lines of anguish from his face.

"Come in, Kyla. Please."

She turned and followed him up the steps. The wooden door yawned open, waiting for her. Heart heavy, she stumbled into the house.

Nick grabbed her and held her tight against his firm chest, brushing a kiss on the top of her head. "My love."

"Don't call me that." Tears sprang to her eyes, but she blinked them away and pushed free of him. She was the best were- hunter at Hunter-Wolf and she'd fallen in love with her prey. A short, bitter laugh erupted from deep inside her.

"Come," Nick said in a voice laced with torment. He took her by the elbow to guide her into the large living room. A fire burned in the great hearth, taking the spring chill from the room. But it couldn't melt the bitterness and sorrow that held her heart in an icy grip.

"Sit down," he said, pointing to the red sofa.

"I'll stand."

His yellow eyes dulled. From sadness? She wasn't sure.

He shrugged and strode to the heavy carved desk in the corner. Lifting a decanter of ruby wine, Nick poured two generous glasses.

"Here, you might need this." With a small smile, he handed her one of the goblets, then walked back to the desk and leaned against the edge.

She lifted the glass and drank greedily, as if the alcohol could dispel the dread that pressed in on her. Finally, she would get her answers. "Geneva, Switzerland. Two full moons ago. That was you."

He nodded. "Antica's sons hid me before the hunters found me." He leveled his gaze at her. "I know who you are. And you know who I am."

She filled her lungs with air and steeled herself. "Yes."

"Don't be afraid. I won't hurt you. I would never hurt you."

"I'm not afraid," she said, lifting her chin. "I've never feared werewolves." *And I've never loved one before.*

"I've been expecting you for centuries," he said.

"What?"

He finished off his wine and poured himself another glass, holding the decanter out to her. She nodded. What the hell? More alcohol might dull her senses, for a time at least. He walked toward her, his mouth tilted in a wry smile, and refilled her glass. She gripped the stem so hard she feared the glass would break.

He stood close, too close. She inhaled his unique scent, spicy and woodsy, seductive and tempting. She backed away, putting distance between them.

Sorrow darted over his face. He strode to the desk and set the near-empty decanter down with a thump. "I knew someday I'd meet the hunter who would destroy me," he said, his back to her. "I didn't figure to fall in love with her."

"Don't talk of love," she said on a tortured breath. Her hand shook. Red wine splashed onto her jeans. "Did you kill my parents?" The words slipped out. She needed the truth.

He whirled to face her. "No."

Somehow she believed him. Relief flooded her. She stared into the ruby liquid, then back at him. "Are you the white wolf I've seen in my visions?"

"Probably."

Her gaze locked with his. "Is it true white werewolves with yellow eyes have never killed a human?"

He shrugged. "I've never killed a human so maybe the story is true."

Drawing a shaky breath, she walked to the sofa and sank down, unsure if her legs could hold her. "I knew you couldn't be evil."

"I'm no saint," he said. "I've wanted to kill, many times. I've lived a long time and done things I'm ashamed of."

She gripped her wine glass. She couldn't love him if he were truly wicked. "Why did you call me here tonight?"

"To be sure you killed me."

Her glass slipped out of her hand to land on the marble-topped table. The crystal shattered, sending red wine dripping onto the floor. Red, like blood. His blood. Her breath came in short gasps.

He quickly set down his own glass and was at her side in an instant. Kneeling in front of her, he grasped both her hands between one of his large ones. "You have your orders. I won't ask you to break your vows. If you kill me, we'll both get what we want. Let me kill Montague first. That's all I ask." Montague. The name provoked a shudder. "Who is Montague?"

Hate pulsed from Nick, a living force that chilled her. He stood. "Montague is the demon shapeshifter who did this to me."

The truth punched her with such force she fell back on the sofa. "The black wolf with the red eyes," she whispered. "A demon." And she knew. "*He* killed my parents."

Nick nodded. "Probably. He's slaughtered thousands through the centuries, including Antica. And my wife and baby."

The pain in his eyes arrowed to her heart. She put a hand to her chest. "Antica is dead? I'm sorry, Nick, for all you've lost."

Then anger slammed into her, sudden and crushing. She jumped up. "I'll kill the demon. I have to avenge my parents."

Nick grabbed her by the arms and held her tight. "No! Your silver bullets are useless against a demon."

"I'll find another way. I have to kill him."

"Stop it, Kyla."

She knew he was right. Her shoulders sagged. "I've seen him. Twice. I couldn't believe my shots missed him. Now I know why. My bullets couldn't kill him."

Hopelessness overwhelmed her, squeezing the air from her. She stared at Nick. She couldn't kill the demon, but she could kill Nick. The irony made a bittersweet laugh bubble from her. She wanted to curse something, anything—God, Fate, whatever—at the unfairness of it all.

Nick studied her, then released her and strode to the desk to pour her another glass of wine. His mouth tight, he handed her the fresh glass. "I'll avenge your parents and everyone else Montague has tormented and killed through the centuries."

His gaze bore into hers. "And you know what you have to do."

She had her orders. She closed her eyes against the ache. When she opened them again, Nick was staring at her with love, sadness and despair in his eyes—wolf eyes.

"Tell me your story, Nick." The next time they met, she would have to kill him, but she would learn all she could about him while there was time. Holding her wine goblet as tightly as a lifeline, she slid onto the sofa.

His gaze swept her and he tensed. Then, as if he'd made up his mind about something, he turned abruptly and stalked to the fireplace. With his back to her, he leaned his hands on the marble mantle and stared into the flickering flames. "He cursed me in 1530, but my story begins a few years earlier." The muscles of his back flexed under his sweater. Once he was transformed to a wolf he would rip the sweater to shreds.

She twined her fingers around the stem of the glass and waited for him to continue.

"Charles Ashbrook, the Earl of Montague, was my friend and neighbor in the last Henry's time, until Catherine came between us."

"Catherine?" The name triggered a fleeting memory in Kyla that disappeared as quickly as it had come.

He turned to her then. "My wife. Catherine's father promised her to Montague. Even then, rumors swirled at Henry's court that Montague dabbled in the dark arts. My friend Cardinal Wolsey warned me against him. I didn't believe the rumors, but Catherine did and she was afraid of Montague. Catherine and I loved each other deeply. She went against her father's wishes and chose me."

He gave her a wry smile. "Fortunately, Catherine was an only child and her father quickly forgave her. But Montague never forgave us. When I married Catherine, I gained her lands, which were extensive, and also Henry's favor at court."

His gaze riveted on a spot above Kyla and she knew he was seeing that time and the love he'd lost. With a sigh of resignation, he looked at her again. "Catherine's father was one of Henry's staunchest supporters. Neither ever guessed that my loyalties lay with Rome and our Pope. When Montague discovered I spied for Pope Clement, he went to Henry and vowed to kill me and bring Henry my head."

"But he didn't kill you," she said softly.

"Antica saved me. And after all these years has died for her effort." Grief swept over Nick's face and his voice vibrated with rage. "Montague killed Catherine and our infant son, Jonathan. I can still see their bruised bodies, and little Aiden, too, the servant boy who tried to save them. But it wasn't until long after Montague cursed me when I'd already fled England that I learned he'd murdered them." He balled his hands at his sides and a muscle worked in his jaw. "Had I known before then, I would have put my sword through his dark heart."

Kyla pressed a hand to her stomach. The red-haired woman, the servant boy, and the baby, all in her visions. Catherine, Aiden, and Nick's child.

Trying to gather her thoughts and unable to bear the hurt slashing Nick's features, she looked away to study one of the muted tapestries that adorned the walls. Ancient tapestries. Now she understood. She turned to him. She had to ask the question, but she already knew the answer. "Did Catherine have red curly hair?"

She heard Nick's sharp intake of breath. "How would you know that?"

"I saw them, Nick."

"What?"

"I saw them in visions and dreams. The infant Jonathan and Aiden, the servant boy. And Catherine. Strange visions made stranger by the fact they wore medieval clothes." Kyla widened her eyes. "Catherine's been trying to tell me something, but I don't know what it is."

He frowned. "Tell me."

Gripping the stem of her glass, she described her dreams.

He paled. "Do you have the second sight?"

"Never like this." Fighting for calmness, she sipped her wine and stared at him over the rim of the glass. "How did the Earl of Montague become a demon shapeshifter?"

He raked a hand through his hair. "He lusted for power and treasure. After Catherine rejected him, his hatred for me became an obsession. His crops failed and he blamed me, saying I'd put a spell on them. He fell out of favor at court and grew increasingly dark. I think that was when he made his pact with the devil. He bartered his soul for immortality and power. His evil has grown over the centuries. Look around you at world events—at the chaos, greed, and wars—and see Montague's hand. If I don't stop him, the world will belong to him."

She set her drink onto the table and stood, no longer able to remain still. "The upheaval in the demon world. That explains it. Hunter-Wolf is right. The epicenter is here."

"Hunter-Wolf? I've wondered which group you work for."

"My parents worked for them, too. And Todd's parents."

"Yet he's not a hunter."

She tried to smile. "Todd prefers to do his hunting in video games."

Sadness darkened Nick's eyes. "You have your legacy, Kyla. You know what you have to do."

Tears threatened and she turned away to study one of the tapestries up close. Grief for his loss and hers throbbed through her, stiffening her resolve. She went to him and skimmed her fingers over the sharp planes of his face, already shadowed with the look of the wolf. "Montague took those we loved the most. I'll help you kill him."

His eyes blazed with a fury that sent shivers up her spine. "I told you I'd take care of Montague. You'll have your revenge. Trust me."

He cupped her shoulders. "Montague's powers are legendary. He'll crush you. But my powers are strong enough to take him."

His face hardened. "At the full moon, stay away from the wolf circle. When it's over, I'll come to you. When you see the white wolf, shoot me."

Tears stung her eyes and she yanked free and turned from him. "No, no."

He grabbed her arms and pulled her around to face him. "Don't make this any harder. There is no other way. Go now."

She gripped his sweater, bunching the fabric in her fists. "It can't end like this."

"This ending was written centuries ago. We're all pawns in a much bigger game. You and I and Montague were meant to be here. We have to play this out."

He pushed her away. "Go." He wheeled around and stalked from the room.

Kyla started after him, then stopped. The set of his jaw and the rigid lines of his body told her she couldn't dissuade him.

She'd taken a vow to destroy all were-creatures. She

couldn't give up her heritage. Perhaps this moment had been preordained at her birth. Fighting her despair, she grabbed the wine glass from the small table and threw it into the heat of the fire. The wine burst into flames and the crystal shattered into small pieces. Just like her heart.

* * * * *

The quietness of her small house suffocated Kyla. When she'd come home from Nick's yesterday, she'd insisted Todd go to New York and Hunter-Wolf's protection. Something in her face must have convinced him because he hadn't argued. She missed Todd already. Would she ever see him again? Heaviness pressed against her chest.

To honor her vows and keep her skills she had to kill the man she loved. If she gave up her legacy, what then? What future would she and Nick have?

She needed guidance. Black Fox. She ran up the stairs, stripping off her clothes as she went.

Kyla sank slowly into the warm, soapy water. The calming scents of gardenia and lavender from the candles that ringed the tub wafted over her. She closed her eyes, but pictures of Nick and the white wolf intruded. With every ounce of will she possessed, she cleared her mind and waited for Black Fox.

Soon the familiar bright lights swirled before her. Out of the shadows she saw the beloved figure of her Spirit Guide.

"Little one, you are troubled."

"Dear sister, you know what is in my heart."

The old Navajo rubbed the large silver disc that hung from her neck and studied Kyla with concern shining from her eyes. *"You want that which is forbidden."*

"Tell me what do to, sister."

Black Fox gave her a smile filled with love. *"Only you*

can decide."

Kyla shook her head. "*I can't.*"

"*You can and you must.*"

"*Madame Cassandra said I must choose between two men, one good and one evil. I know in my heart that Nick isn't evil, yet I'm sworn to kill him. Who is Montague? I can destroy him and fulfill my vow.*"

"*You will know what to do when the time comes.*"

"*Help me now.*"

"*The decision must come from your heart, and your heart alone.*" Her dark gaze bore into Kyla. "*I leave you with these words: The power of two will succeed where one cannot.*"

She was gone the way she had come, in a swirl of flashing lights.

Kyla opened her eyes. Cold fingers of fear and sadness squeezed her heart. She glanced out the window to the moon. Only a sliver was absent. Then it would be full—the day of reckoning.

CHAPTER TWENTY

Nick's paws sank into the damp earth. For one last time he was free to hunt and race and revel in the Beast. His heavy wolf's body quivered with anticipation. Raising his head, he howled at the moon, hanging high and full in the night sky. The golden orb, his jailer and addiction, seduced him with the promise of the freedom he'd denied himself all these centuries.

With a glance back at the house he'd never see again, he raced toward the woods. Antica's sons were on their way to the Balkans, safe now. Somewhere in the darkness Montague waited. Nick would find the demon and rip the flesh from his body and tear out his black heart while it still beat.

Regret and despair triggered the strands of humanity still residing in him.

Kyla.

Lost to him forever. He ran faster, but he couldn't outrun the terrible sadness and injustice that were his eternal companions.

* * * * *

Kyla checked her gun one last time. The chambers were filled with silver bullets, ready for whatever waited for her in the darkness. She slipped the gun into her shoulder holster and shrugged on her leather jacket. No need to stain her face with black tonight. She would face her prey and she would win, or die fighting.

She took inventory of the small house. Her bags were packed, the only evidence she and Todd had been there. Her letter to Todd rested on the largest of the bags where he could find it if she didn't survive the night.

With a silent prayer for Todd, Kyla strode from the house, slamming the door behind her. The time for regrets and recriminations was over. Fight or die.

She jumped into her SUV and drove as fast as the winding road would allow until she came to the trail leading to the deepest part of the forest. She turned off the engine and leaned against the steering wheel, fighting the nausea that plagued her before every hunt.

After consulting with Black Fox, she'd searched her soul and the answer had come to her. She knew what she had to do. As she left the car and headed for the woods, the cross hanging from her neck brushed her, giving her courage. Rubbing the gold and diamonds, she sent up a silent prayer that God would listen to her this time.

The dark night cloaked her with its mystery as she tramped to the wolf circle. The slap of branches hitting her and the swish of leaves underfoot echoed in the quiet forest. Nick had asked her to stay away, but she could no more stay away than stop breathing.

Using skills sharpened through the years, she cautiously surveyed her surroundings. No glowing eyes watched yet, but there was an unsettled rustle all around her as if Nature itself waited for the terror. In what form would the demon Montague appear? She had no demon-killing powers, but she was armed with her gun, her knife and a bloodlust that demanded vengeance. With a grim smile, she patted the knife strapped above her ankle, hidden by her jeans. Comforted by the heavy steel and leather pressed against her flesh, she quickened her pace. The wolf circle lay ahead.

A figure stepped out of the woods to block her path. She stifled her shock and touched her gun, ready to pull it from its holster.

"Strange meeting you here." Sheriff Sanders, her hands on her hips and her feet clad in thick black boots planted firmly on the soft ground, stood before her. The sheriff's mouth slanted in a sneer and her eyes were flat and black, with hardly any white showing.

Kyla tamped down the small kernel of fear that settled in her stomach. "What are you doing here, Max?" She fought to keep her voice even and calm.

"I'm looking for the same thing you are." Max stepped closer and gripped Kyla's arm. When she tried to draw away, the sheriff's fingers dug deeper into her flesh.

"Let me go," Kyla said. Laughing, Max released her. Kyla stumbled back and hit a man's chest. She spun around to face Dan Taylor.

"What are both of you doing here?" She glanced between the two, gauging her odds of fighting them off.

Dan laughed. "You can't protect him, Kyla."

"You've said too much, you fucking idiot." Venom dripped from Max's voice and her eyes flashed anger at Dan. "I wanted to play with her. It's too late now." The sheriff jerked her head at something behind Kyla. "Take her!"

Bright flashes of green sparked around Kyla, burning her eyes and obscuring her vision. When the air cleared, she found herself surrounded by the strange vampire-like creatures that had been in the woods with John Vickers the night her car was almost run off the road.

With strong hands, they grabbed her and held her in viselike grips. Kyla glared at the sheriff. "What the hell are you doing? Make them release me."

"And have you run to Radford?" Madness tainted Max's voice. "We had hoped you might join us willingly, but you've chosen Radford. Again."

Kyla swallowed her fear and confusion. Chosen Nick again? She'd thought Max incompetent. But crazy?

The sheriff moved closer and stroked a cold, bony finger down Kyla's cheek. "You could have spared yourself an eternity of torment had you chosen wisely."

"What the fuck are you talking about?" Kyla turned and yanked her arm, trying to free herself. The creatures holding her gripped her tighter.

Max laughed, an oddly familiar sound that stirred memories in Kyla—harsh memories of horror and loathing and death.

Vicious pain shot through her head. Max and Dan and the vampire-like creatures blurred and wavered.

A young man with hawk-like features appeared out of the mist. His long brown hair, greasy and unkempt, hung to his shoulders. A velvet cloak covered his slim body, and his pale eyes stared with malice at the red-haired woman who held a squalling infant. The woman trembled. At her feet, unmoving, lay the small servant boy. The man snatched the baby from the woman's arms and hurled it to the rocky ground. The woman screamed and lunged for the baby, but the man's bony hands gripped her, pulling her back. "If I can't have you, no one will," he bellowed. "Die, bitch." The man's hands closed around her neck.

Kyla choked as panic rose in her. She felt those same hands around her neck. The vision dissolved. Max and Dan stared intently at her.

"The huntress is prone to visions," Max said in a silky voice devoid of warmth. "Do the visions predict your own torture? When we're finished with you, you'll be too weak to remember your name."

Kyla spat at Max.

"That wasn't very smart of you," Dan said before he slapped Kyla across the face.

She reeled back, but lifted a defiant chin.

Dan grabbed her face between his hands, pressing until blades of pain sliced her. She refused to cry out. The vampire-like creatures laughed and wrapped their hands tighter around her arms.

"I like my women with fight in them." Dan reached inside her jacket and took her gun. His hand brushed suggestively over her breast and he pinched her nipple. She raised her knee and kicked him in the groin.

Rage distorted his features into a cruel caricature of himself. He pulled back, ready to strike her again.

Max grabbed Dan's arm and stopped him. "You'll have your chance with her. We need to go." She turned to the creatures holding Kyla. "Take her to the lodge."

They dragged Kyla along the rutted trail, Max and Dan following. The knife strapped to her leg gave Kyla hope. She tried to memorize the trail and prayed they wouldn't discover the knife. She would fight for her freedom to her last breath.

What would happen to Nick if she died? Could he destroy Montague without her help? Which of the monsters surrounding her was the demon shapeshifter?

An uneasy feeling swept over her as a shadow darkened the woods to black. Kyla looked up and gasped. An enormous stone hunting lodge loomed through the trees before her.

They'd searched this area looking for Todd, but found no house. If Montague had the ability to cloak an entire building, his powers were stronger than any she'd seen. Fear burned through her, shooting pain in her stomach. She fought for calm. She would need all her resources to fight the demon.

They pulled her through the front door of the lodge and up a long flight of stairs. She had a fleeting glimpse of young women bound with chains while men performed various sex acts on them. The young women missing from the nearby towns? Once she and Nick destroyed the demon, she would rescue these women from their living hell.

When they reached the landing, her captors took her to the end of the hallway and threw her into a small empty room, then left, slamming the door shut. She heard the sound of a heavy bolt dropped into place, a death knell. Goosebumps raised on her arms. She fell onto the stone floor and quickly pulled herself up. Stone floor and walls. Dampness. Was this where Todd had been held captive?

Seconds passed. She surveyed the room. A high window let in a slice of moonlight. Too high for her to reach. She checked for her knife. It was still there. When the time came, she would be ready.

She whirled around at the sound of the bolt sliding. The door opened and Dan Taylor slipped in. Grinning, he held her gun up as if inspecting it. "Nice piece. Been in your family long?"

Kyla shot him a glare from narrowed eyes.

"We know who you are, beautiful." His lust-filled gaze roamed her body.

She swallowed her disgust at his leering smirk.

"We've watched your family for centuries," he said. "Your mother was a beauty like you, but she didn't have the stamina for my Lord Montague's lovemaking."

His words set off a raging storm of fury that engulfed Kyla. She trembled and her heart pounded wildly. With an effort, she beat back her anger. They would not defeat her with words.

"You know who I am," she said, folding her arms across her chest and feigning indifference. "Who are you?"

He saluted. "Dan Taylor, NYPD."

"Yeah, right."

He chuckled, a bitter, malicious sound. "You think you're so clever. You want the real me? You'll have him."

His image wavered and his pupils dilated. Beneath his boyish looks, she glimpsed the vile being that inhabited his body.

She pressed against the wall. "How? Why?"

The creature disappeared and Dan stood before her again. Laughing, he strode to her. His breath, hot and smelling of blood, brushed her cheeks. "We could have had fun together. I know things in bed that would have made you sell your soul for more." He pressed against her, pinning her to the wall with his body. "But you preferred Radford."

Kyla pushed him away. "Who are you?"

He bowed. "An angel, created in the beginning of time, until my fall from grace. I now serve my Lord Montague."

"Montague," she whispered. "Who is Montague?"

"You'll find out soon enough, beautiful."

"Where's the real Dan Taylor?" she asked, sliding away from him and playing for time.

"At the bottom of the Hudson." His voice, brutal and hate-filled, pierced the air. "He was almost too easy to lure to his death. So ready to believe I knew who killed his wife."

She studied the monster that was Dan, assessing her

chances of overpowering him. He was a demon shapeshifter, like Montague, with the ability to shift into the bodies of those they killed. He had her gun, but her silver bullets were useless against him. If only her superiors had sent demon hunters, but she was on her own here. She needed to buy herself time to grab her knife. If she disabled him long enough to allow her escape, she could go to the wolf circle and Nick.

The door opened again and Sheriff Sanders entered the room, followed by John Vickers.

"Get me the hell out of here," Kyla said.

"Can't do that," Max said with a cruel grin.

Totally mad, Kyla thought. "Who the hell are you?"

Still grinning, Max bowed low before her. "I'm at your service, milady."

Milady? The word provoked a trace of remembrance in Kyla. She struggled to hold onto the fragment of memory just beyond her reach. "You're not Max."

"You're very astute." The sheriff nodded, as if giving a signal. A sudden, icy draft filled the room. Mist, bright green with swirls of black and gray, rose from the floor, obscuring Max. The vapor funneled, creating a whirlwind that plastered Kyla against the wall. She covered her ears against the mocking laughter that vibrated all around them, bouncing off the walls.

Finally, the laughter stopped and the mist dissolved. Max was gone. In her place, dressed in medieval garb and swathed in a long black cloak, stood the pale-eyed man of Kyla's vision, the fiend who killed the red-haired woman and baby. Fear and disbelief squeezed the air from Kyla's lungs.

"Earl Montague," she whispered. Blood rushed through

her head and blackness overtook her.

* * * * *

Kyla woke to a wicked headache and nausea. Opening her eyes slowly, she scanned her surroundings. Stone walls, cold and damp, met her gaze. It hadn't been only a nightmare after all. Holding her aching head, she struggled to sit up. The room spun and she slid back against the wall, closing her eyes.

Memories flooded her. God help her, she had gone stark raving mad. Her visions hadn't been warnings or disjointed fragments, but a glimpse into a past life, her past life.

It couldn't be. The loud thumping of her heart was the only sound in the room. Sweat broke out on her forehead. She swallowed past the dryness in her throat and opened her eyes again. Instead of seeing the small damp room of her jail, visions of another time and place rolled through her head.

Nicholas, mounted on his black gelding and clothed in black, riding through the dense woods that separated his estates from his friend Cardinal Wolsey's. She'd appeared to him with a warning, an apparition from beyond the grave. But Montague was there. She'd failed to warn Nicholas and his life of hell on Earth had begun.

She saw them all now—Antica, the witch who lived at the edge of their property; Montague, the demon one; and Nicholas, beloved husband. All of them players in a nightmare that had begun five centuries ago. She understood none of it, yet she knew she saw the truth.

The small room came into focus again. Vickers and the demon who was Dan leaned against the far wall and leered at her. Next to them, Earl Montague stood, his pale eyes wide, and a malicious smile on his thin lips.

She had to end this horror, this horror five hundred years

in the making. She was a fighter, a good one, the best. But in all her years of were-hunting she'd never felt the force of evil that touched her now. Defeat was not an option. She tensed and steeled herself for battle.

Her shoulders stiff, she pulled herself up to stand against the rough stone wall. Her knife still clung to her ankle. Too arrogant with their own powers, they hadn't thought to search her for another weapon.

"You," she said, pointing a finger at Vickers. "You betrayed my Nicholas. You told Montague that Nicholas would venture into the woods that night. I tried to warn him, but it was too late." She listened to her words as if hearing someone else speak them.

She looked at Montague. Centuries of hate and rage pulsed through her veins, demanding vengeance. She would have it. "I remember it all. You murdered me and my baby, Jonathan, and my servant Aiden. You condemned my Nicholas. You will pay."

"You can't hurt me." He flung out the words and strode swiftly to her. Gripping her arms, his bony fingers bit into her flesh. He studied her, as if searching for something. "Catherine? You're really my Catherine, come back to me?" Through the madness in his pale eyes, she saw a glimmer of love and longing.

"I'm not your anything, you vile beast."

His eyes hardened and he threw back his head and laughed, revealing an ugly red scar that ran from his jaw line to collar bone.

"The scar," she said, struggling to free herself. "My Nicholas did that. Now I know why Max always wore turtleneck shirts."

"Think I would reveal myself to Radford before I was

ready? I could have gotten rid of this scar long ago, but I use it to remind me of my quest. The quest to forever destroy Radford." His laugh fueled her hatred. He tightened his grip on her. "My master in Hell has seen fit to reward me handsomely for my service." His raspy voice dripped with cruelty. "You died too quickly the last time. I have waited long to punish you as you deserve."

She saw everything in his eyes—his lust and obsession for power. And her own murder all those centuries ago. Her throat closed as if his hands were still around her neck. Coughing, she twisted her body, trying to escape.

He shook her, forcing her to meet his gaze. "I loved you like no other. My desire to possess you drove me to the devil. If only you had become my wife, I would have given you anything you desired."

Memories flashed before Kyla. Defiance stiffened her spine and she thrust out her chin. "You whoremonger and defiler of young women," she spat out. "I remember what you did to those girls from the village. You were in league with the devil long before I rejected you. You think I would choose you over Nicholas?"

He slapped her hard across the face and she would have fallen if he hadn't held onto her. Blood trickled from a cut on her lip. "You will not escape me this time, bitch." She remembered her knife. She couldn't kill the demon he'd become, but she would die before she let him have her.

Red sparked in the depths of his eyes for the space of a heartbeat. "Radford can't save you now. I'll find the boy again too. He can't escape me. You love the boy. He'll suffer."

The boy. The face of the frightened Aiden of her visions pressed into her mind, to be replaced by Todd's features.

Todd and the servant boy, one and the same. As Aiden, he'd tried to save her from Montague. As Todd, he'd been her salvation in this life.

Montague grinned, showing shark-like yellow teeth. "I kidnapped your friend to make you doubt Radford. I thought you'd run to my demon Taylor's arms, but you chose Radford again. I've waited centuries to destroy him and I wasn't going to let a mere hunter bitch have him. Little did I know you're much more than a mere hunter."

His pale, mad eyes gave her a glimpse of the devil that owned his soul. "If only I had known you were my Catherine. You refused to believe ill of Radford. Twice you've chosen him. You'll suffer greatly for that mistake."

His eyes changed to vivid red, then back to pale blue.

She gasped and tried to kick him, but he held her at arm's length. "Red eyes. You're the demon wolf."

He bowed slightly. "At your service. Your bullets can't harm me. You have no power against me."

She stared into his eyes and saw only demonic possession. Any shred of humanity had left him centuries ago. "You murdered my parents. But you won't take me and you won't destroy Nick. His powers are stronger. He has the force of good." And in her heart she knew Nick had fought the darkness of his Beast and won. That was why she loved him now, why she loved him still after all these centuries.

Montague pulled her close. "You haven't lost your love for a fight, Catherine. I like that. I'll give you whatever you need." He bent and pressed cold, thin lips to hers in a violent kiss that forced her lips apart. When he thrust his tongue into her mouth, she clamped down her teeth and bit him.

With a howl, he flung her away. She hit the wall. Glaring at him, she wiped her mouth of the remnants of his kiss.

He gave her a cunning smile. "You'll learn to like my lovemaking, Kyla. Or should I call you Catherine? We've got eternity to know each other. But first, I will destroy your husband. He hasn't the power to fight me and my demon forces."

He stalked to her and squeezed her face until tears of pain filled her eyes. "When Radford's too weak to fight any longer, my demons will drag you to him. Then I'll rape you until you find you like it. He'll die with the image of you begging me to fuck you."

She wrenched free. "I'll never beg for anything from you."

Montague grabbed her arm and pulled it behind her back. "I will enjoy breaking you." He released her, shoving her toward the wall, and turned to Dan. "Guard her. I'll send for her when I'm ready." A swirl of green formed a mist around him. When the mist cleared, Sheriff Sanders stood in his place.

"Where's the real Max Sanders?" Kyla asked.

"Dead, of course. Her soul is rotting in Hell for all I care." Red glimmered in his eyes before he disappeared in another swirl of green.

Vickers, bowing and scraping, approached Kyla. "Milady, I didn't realize you were Lady Catherine come back. My apologies. I will leave you to your memories now. We have eternity to renew our acquaintance." Still bowing, he backed out, closing the door behind him.

She looked around, weighing her chance of escape. She was alone with Dan Taylor, demon. She had to get the hell out of there. Nick needed her.

"Don't even think it," Dan said, swaggering toward her. Her gun dangled from his fingers. "I know your hunting skills and I'm prepared. Radford is ours tonight." His lips tilted in a grotesque grin. "And tomorrow the world belongs to us."

Keep him talking. Hugging herself, she circled the room, forming her plans. She stopped and faced him. "The world?"

"You don't know?"

She shook her head.

He chuckled, the sound more like a cackle. "My lord Montague serves our master in Hell. Montague is our master's instrument in the corruption of the world. Only Radford stands in the way of my lord's total domination."

"Why Nick?"

Dan frowned and she thought he wouldn't answer. Finally with a shrug, he said, "The hag Antica saved Radford, allowing his powers to grow as my lord's have grown. Your demon hunters can't destroy Montague. Radford is the only one with power enough to defeat my lord." He sneered. "But even Radford can't win against the combined strength of Lord Montague and his army of demons. Radford is doomed. Then nothing will stand in our way."

She'd faced evil countless times, but nothing as purely depraved as this. She prayed for strength. "So the upheaval in the demon world is Montague's doing? What do you want?"

"Total control of the world and its souls. The wars, famine, cruelty, and genocide you see around you are the work of my Lord Montague and his army. Soon the world will be flung into total chaos, its governments powerless. Then we will rule. No one will escape us. We will bring billions of souls to our master in Hell."

Kyla's stomach lurched and she took a step back, fighting queasiness. "What happens if Nick defeats Montague?"

Dan shivered and raw terror flashed across his face.

"That can't happen. Our master in Hell has a ferocious anger. He has given Lord Montague one last chance to vanquish Radford. If my lord is unsuccessful, torment in the deepest bowels of Hell awaits us."

He quivered, as if shaking off a picture too horrible to imagine. With visible effort, he relaxed. He moved closer and reached out to touch strands of her hair. She jerked away.

"You're all alone here, huntress." A malicious light shone from his eyes. "You know you can't kill us." He pulled her roughly to him, cupping her bottom and pressing her against him until she felt his hard cock. "My lord will have you later, but I'll have a little fun now." He bent and kissed her.

Kyla tamped down her disgust. Her plan had to work. Melting against him, she returned his kiss. When his body softened, she pulled away and smiled in frank invitation. "I've always been attracted to Dan Taylor. I've wondered what that body looks like naked."

A low growl escaped him. He licked his lips. "You first. Get undressed."

Her gaze on him, she ran her tongue over her lips and bent down as if to slip off her shoes. She quickly raised her pant leg and pulled her knife from its sheath. Knife in hand, she reached up and thrust it to the hilt into his stomach, then pulled it out again.

Shrieking, he clutched his middle as blood spurted from his wound. Her gun flew out of his hand and across the room. "Bitch!" He grabbed for her.

Kyla feinted left and landed a swift kick to his groin, then a hard left to his chin. She couldn't kill the demon, but she could knock him out long enough to allow her escape to the wolf circle and Nick.

The demon's body shook. The figure of Dan Taylor

disappeared and the hideous lump that was his true form stood before her. With a shriek, he lunged at her.

Kyla sidestepped and plunged her knife into his throat. His body folded onto the stone floor. His demon powers would allow him to heal quickly. She had to hurry.

She yanked the knife from his body and grabbed her gun off the floor, then ran to the door and pressed her ear against it. Screams of terror and torture greeted her. Holstering her gun and sheathing her knife, she glanced at the window. Too high and narrow. She had to use the door. Opening the door slowly, she slipped out to the long hallway and glanced left and right. The hall dead ended to her right. Only one set of stairs led out. She raced down the hall and took the stairs at a run.

When she reached the bottom, she hesitated, taking note of her surroundings. The door to the outside and freedom beckoned. She dashed for it, praying no one would notice her. Someone grabbed her arm, pulling her back. She stifled a cry. An elderly man, naked, his skin in folds over his scrawny body, stared at her. "Where are you going, beautiful? The party's just getting started."

Desperate, she glanced around. She couldn't draw attention. She patted his hand and gently extricated herself. "I'll be right back. Why don't you get comfortable and wait for me?"

"Stay." He grabbed her arm again.

It was now or never. She broke free and rushed for the door. Locked. A few of the other men stopped their torture of the women and looked toward her. Damn it! Curtains fluttered at an open window to her left. Several men were now pointing at her. She ran for the window and dove through, landing in dirt. She got to her feet and sprinted away as shouts sounded behind her. She had to find Nick.

CHAPTER TWENTY-ONE

Nick paced the wolf circle. His fur stood on end, a warning that Montague's demons were close. He was ready. His canine hearing picked up the rumble of low growls. He whirled around.

The first wolf, gray fur matted and dirty, leapt into the circle in front of him. Snarling, eyes glowing, the creature pawed the ground, preparing to attack.

Nick crouched low, tensing his body. Clearly, Montague thought to send his werewolves and demons to weaken Nick before the final battle, but his old enemy's band of monsters was no match for Nick's powers.

Montague's werewolf lunged.

Nick sprang at the same time. They collided in mid-air. Nick locked his jaw onto the other's neck and forced him to the ground. Digging his fangs into the creature's flesh, he tore the monster's throat open. Thrashing and flailing in his death throes, the werewolf tried to fight. Finally he lay still.

Panting heavily, Nick watched as the werewolf slowly changed into the youthful mechanic who'd serviced his car. Had the young man willingly sold his soul for a taste of immortality or was he another of Montague's victims? Human sadness fought with Nick's bloodlust.

He had no more time to think as one after another of Montague's demons assaulted him. Some were wolves, mouths opened wide, sharp teeth ready. Others were flying devils, their demonic faces distorted with hate. He battled with his mouth and claws, ripping and biting, but still they came, relentless and evil, ramming into him, tearing his flesh. Blood spurted from his wounds, weakening him, but he would not allow defeat.

Centuries of denying his bloodlust had built up in Nick. Now it broke loose and he fought with strength he'd not known he possessed. Crazed with the scent of blood, he attacked mercilessly. All he knew was to kill and kill again.

At last, he lay shivering under the full moon. All around him sprawled the pathetic brutalized bodies of the demons he'd vanquished. Flames shot to the trees as their bodies incinerated. Screams filled the night air as their souls descended into Hell.

"You can't win, Radford." A familiar, mocking voice jarred Nick and he lifted his head.

A sneering Dan Taylor, with a half-healed gash on his neck, looked down at him. Blood stained the front of his shirt. Grinning, John Vickers peeked from behind the detective's muscular body.

"Your woman escaped us," Taylor said. "She's on her way here, but our magic allowed us to get here before her, and we'll be ready. My Lord Montague will be done with you and take her as his mate. For eternity."

Nick jumped up and growled, prepared for another fight.

Taylor laughed, the sound high-pitched and ringed with malice. His form wavered. Blue lights swirled around him. When the lights cleared, the placid-faced detective had morphed into a hulking demon with a deformed body covered with open sores and peeling flesh.

Nick vaulted toward him. Taylor parried, but Nick was

246

too quick. Energy pumped through him and he easily clamped his jaws on the demon's head and squeezed, crushing his skull with a loud crack. Taylor's body twitched, then he lay still. Fire engulfed his form until nothing existed but a pile of ashes. Terrified, disembodied screams filled the small clearing as he rushed to Hell.

Nick turned to the frightened Vickers. The former squire tried to run, but caught his foot in heavy roots. Nick jumped on him and rendered a killing bite to his neck. Eyes locked in their final horror, Vickers too went up in flames, his soul snatched to Hell with terrified screams.

"I underestimated your powers, Radford." The voice of Charles Ashbrook, Earl of Montague, cut like a dagger through the deadly night.

Nick lifted his head to find his old enemy standing before him. Montague's lank hair hung to his shoulders and his pale eyes shone with evil madness, much as they had on that terror-filled night almost five hundred years before. His hawk-like features were lined and gaunt with the marks of his depravities. He was dressed in black and a heavy velvet cape covered his frame. His thick black buckled boots dug into the muddy earth.

A rushing noise filled Nick's head. Montague and the Maine woods disappeared as Nick was thrust back to that night when his mortal life had ended.

A mist rose to cover him as he rode his gelding through the thick forest toward his estates. A flickering yellow light beckoned through the swirling fog. Then he heard his name whispered in the trees and hurried toward the light. His beloved Catherine, glorious red hair curling in disarray, appeared on the path before him. But she'd been dead for a year. Her mouth formed silent words, and her eyes pleaded.

His horse reared up, almost unseating him. He quickly dismounted and reached for her. He touched air. She was gone.

Out of the mist, his enemy Montague emerged. "Catherine belonged to me," Montague growled. "Now you betray our king by spying for Pope Clement. I will take my revenge and put myself in Henry's favor by killing you this night."

"Catherine was never yours. And I'll not die by your hand." Nicholas drew his short sword from its scabbard. "Come, then, Montague. I'll send you to Hell where you belong."

Lifting his head, Montague howled. The hideous sound scattered leaves and reverberated through the trees. A voice whispered to Nicholas to run, to escape the horror he was about to face. But he wouldn't show cowardice to his enemy. Sword ready, he faced Montague.

Montague's eyes blazed red, and before Nicholas's incredulous gaze, the pale face of the earl shifted and stretched into the canine snout of a demonic creature. Back hunched, Montague went down on all fours. Thick black fur sprouted from his body and the sound of bones splintering and bending echoed into the harsh night. With muscle and sinew stretching, Montague transformed into a powerful wolf, poised to attack.

Frozen in shock, Nicholas mouthed a silent scream and tightened his grip on the sword. Montague pounced, releasing Nicholas from his terror-filled paralysis. The overwhelming stench of animal and decay made him gag. He stabbed the sword toward the monster's throat, but Montague jerked his head, deflecting the fatal blow. Blood dripped from a gash in the demon's neck.

With a roar, the creature knocked Nicholas to the ground

and sent his sword flying. Nicholas threw an arm up to protect his face. He bellowed as the monster slashed his neck with his powerful claws and lowered his snout, prepared to rip the flesh from Nicholas' throat.

"Who goes there?" Antica's son Luka shouted close by.

Montague quickly changed to human form and looked down at Nicholas with eyes that burned hatred. "I have not killed you this night, Radford, but I curse you to walk Earth for eternity, forever a slave to the full moon."

In a whirl of black cape, Montague disappeared. Hands reached for Nicholas as his world turned dark...

Montague's maniacal laugh brought Nick back to the present with a crash.

The demon's features contorted in bemusement as if he read Nick's mind. "The old witch can't help you now. You die tonight, Radford. And Catherine is finally mine. Death won't free her this time." He threw back his head and laughed.

Catherine. Her name filled Nick with hopelessness. She was in Heaven, of that he had no doubt. Montague couldn't taunt him with lies.

"Stupid Radford," Montague said. "You haven't guessed. The huntress is Catherine, come back to life. The body may be different, but the soul belongs to Catherine. This time she'll be my mate. For eternity. Too bad I had to kill her and your brat the last time. I'd only meant to teach her a lesson." He shrugged. "But I couldn't control my rage. I've learned in the years since. No matter now. I'll win this game and Kyla will be mine."

Nick's vision blurred. Kyla was Catherine? No, that couldn't be. His enemy must be trying to confuse him. He'd failed Catherine, but he wouldn't fail Kyla.

He lifted his head and howled at the moon, the hated moon, the source of his power and of his agony. He poured out his fury, his grief and his desperation. Finally, emptied of all feeling but icy hate and an implacable thirst for vengeance, he turned to Montague.

The demon's mocking laugh rang out, spreading his malice over the forest. Pinpricks of red glowed from his eyes. Green, gray and black mist rose from the ground, engulfing him. Demonic shrieks came from within the malignant fog. The mist lifted and the huge black wolf of Nick's nightmares stood before him, muzzle distorted and fangs dripping saliva.

Centuries of bloodlust and hate filled the air. Unnatural silence surrounded them. Nick shifted on his haunches, positioning his body for the last battle, a battle he had to win.

The fur on Nick's back bristled. He and Montague crouched dangerously close. Montague's fur on end, his fangs exposed, he snarled and charged.

Nick jumped first.

The black wolf leaped into the air, straight at Nick's throat. Their powerful bodies slammed into each other and they fell to the ground together. Nick locked onto Montague's ruff and pulled, drawing blood. With a wild yelp, Montague clamped down on one of Nick's ears and bit away a piece of the flesh.

They rolled on the dirt, crushing leaves and branches. Growling and snapping, they clung to each other in a fierce death grip. Montague nipped at Nick's throat and opened his mouth, ready to deliver a fatal bite. But Nick's strength surged and he rolled away, escaping Montague's bloody fangs.

Panting, Nick pawed the ground. A sliver of his human self remained through the haze of hate and revenge coiling through him. He would have his vengeance, for Catherine, for their son, for all they'd lost. Kill or be killed. Teeth bared, he crouched low and sprang.

The black wolf was ready though, and sidestepped. Nick snapped his jaws and caught the monster's right rear haunch. Montague howled.

Nick jumped on the demon's back and clamped his jaws on the back of his neck. With horrific howls that shook the tree branches, Montague spun around, trying to dislodge Nick.

Caught off-guard by Montague's contortions, and weakened by his battles with the other demons, Nick lost his grip and tumbled across the ground. With a hellish roar, Montague jumped onto Nick and pinned him. Eyes flaring with malice and triumph, Montague aimed his mouth at Nick's exposed neck.

Energy spiked through Nick, borne of years of pain and betrayal. With a last surge of strength, he used his powerful back legs to stab Montague in the stomach, sending the demon flying off him.

On all fours again, Montague growled, pawing the ground, his red eyes boring into Nick. Montague sprang. Nick feinted, avoiding the snapping teeth. Montague turned and lunged again. Nick charged.

Shots rang out. The black wolf slid to a halt and turned at the sound. Kyla stood behind them, gun aimed toward them.

With a screeching wail, Montague charged Kyla, hitting her with his powerful body and knocking her to the ground. Her gun flew out of her hand as she fell. Then, she moaned and went still.

Nick's soul splintered. Catherine. Kyla. One and the same. Taken from him by Montague. Rage exploded through him, overwhelming his humanity until he became one with the Beast. He let out a mighty roar and attacked Montague. Death would come for both of them this night.

The demon shapeshifter met Nick's attack head-on. The two wolves locked into a deadly dance. Nick bit down on Montague's jaw. The demon's bones crushed under Nick's powerful teeth.

Snarling, Montague jerked free and smashed Nick to the ground, then leapt on him, holding him down with his body. The breath knocked out of him, Nick felt his strength drain. Montague's army had done his work after all.

The red fire of the demon's eyes seared Nick through the haze of his pain and despair. Growling, Montague lowered his head to render a killing bite.

It was over. Montague would win. Nick had wanted his own death, and now the time had come to find rest, but he couldn't give up on life, not yet.

It would mean the world would be lost. Kyla was already gone from him.

No! Not Kyla. He could not, would not accept that. She was still alive. Nick could feel her robust life force. He let loose a mournful howl and fought to free himself. For her.

* * * * *

Kyla forced her eyes open. Nick needed her. Adrenaline pumped through her veins, obliterating her pain. She struggled to sit. The powerful black and white wolves were locked in a macabre embrace. The white wolf fought valiantly, but he was losing.

She sprang to her feet. Looking quickly around, she found a large rock. She grabbed the rock and heaved it at Montague. It hit him square on the back of the head.

With a shriek, he jumped off Nick and headed for Kyla.

Crouching, she slid her knife from its sheath. Montague pounced. She plunged the knife into his underbelly. Blood gushed from his wound and he fell on her. They rolled together. She scrambled to her feet and yanked her knife free.

Nick vaulted onto Montague's back. The wolves wrestled each other to the ground. With acrobatic gyrations, Montague gained the advantage.

"*Together you can defeat the devil.*" Antica's voice vibrated through Kyla's head.

"*He needs you, little sister. The power of two will prevail.*" Black Fox's voice.

A mist formed, coalescing into dim shapes. Antica and Black Fox stood before her. Their eyes shone with an ethereal light and they chanted, a musical sound that reached out to her and covered her with spiritual armor.

Strength flowed through Kyla, a palpable force she felt in every part of her body. "Yes," she whispered.

Knife held high, Kyla yelled the ancient death cry of the hunters and ran toward the battling wolves.

She rammed her weapon between Montague's shoulder blades. She lurched back when he staggered, allowing Nick to slide free.

Pawing the ground, fangs bared and ready, Nick crouched. He turned his yellow eyes on Kyla. She nodded. Nick attacked the weakened black wolf. He closed his teeth over the demon's throat, ripping into flesh. Montague fought, but Nick clung to him. Finally, with a tortured yelp, Montague's body shuddered and twitched, then lay still.

It was over.

The white wolf stood quivering and stared at the monster sprawled before him. The form of the large black wolf slowly morphed into the cruel features of the human Charles

Ashbrook, the Earl of Montague.

A terrible shrieking rent the air. Demon spirits appeared on all sides of Montague. Kyla watched, horrified, as devils tore at his soul and pulled it away. Montague's spirit fought the monsters, but his powers were gone. With a high-pitched keening, his soul vanished along with the demons. His damaged body exploded in flames, then it too disappeared. The earth beneath them trembled. Montague was where he belonged—in Hell.

Kyla turned to Nick. Blood caked his white fur and patches of skin showed where Montague had yanked the fur from his body. He limped, favoring his right foreleg.

"He's gone." Kyla moved toward him, but he backed away. His yellow wolf eyes impaled hers. She knew what he wanted, but she'd made her decision hours ago. Her superiors at Hunter-Wolf had her resignation.

"No." She shook her head. "It's over, all of it." She swept a hand toward the charred ashes of the demons littering the ground.

His eyes blazed and he snarled at her. Blood dripped from his fangs.

His energy surrounded her, seductive and horrific. Trembling, she stood her ground. Beneath the terrifying Beast who faced her lived Nick, the man she loved.

"You can't scare me." She reached out and touched his fur. His muscled wolf body shuddered.

"I love you," she continued. "I don't care about the curse. I've resigned from Hunter-Wolf. I'll spend my life helping you through every full moon. I won't kill you and I won't leave you. Not ever. We belong with each other. Look at what we did together. We destroyed Montague. We're two halves of a whole."

Ears plastered to his head, Nick growled again and backed away. His gaze begged her, but she wouldn't relent.

She had to make him understand. "Listen to me. My hunting days are over. I'll love you as the Beast, as I love Nick, the man. I've loved you for centuries."

He tilted his head, as if trying to understand. His yellow eyes darkened, the color changing to topaz. Nick's eyes.

Hope blossomed in her heart. "I'm Catherine. Reborn as Kyla. I don't understand it, but I'm here. Little Aiden is here too. He's Todd. This was all meant to happen. We'll be together as long as I live. I'll take care of you."

Tremors rippled through his body. With a yelp of pain, he fell to the ground.

"You're wounded, Nick," she cried out, reaching for him.

Writhing, muscles undulating, he struggled to stand on shaky legs. With a last look at her, he loped away, limping.

He was transforming back while the moon was still full. That meant he was dying. No, she refused to accept that. "Nick, stop, you can't go on."

He ran faster. Heart heavy, she sprinted after him.

He was dying.

She couldn't let him die alone.

CHAPTER TWENTY-TWO

They plowed through the thick woods, Nick limping ahead of Kyla. Branches scratched her face, and, panting, she tripped on the heavy underbrush, but she didn't slow down.

Nick's breath rasped from his exertions and left a trail of mist spiraling into the crisp air. The muscles under his fur rippled and she could hear the sounds of his bones splintering. Skin showed through where his fur had begun to thin. His body stretched, giving a shadowy glimpse of his human form.

Dread coursed through her, forming a knot in her chest. Only dying werewolves transformed back to human form when the moon was still full. Had she found him only to lose him again?

No! Her cry exploded inside her, echoing the emptiness in her heart. She saw his legs give way and she ran faster to catch him as he stumbled.

With a cry, she put out a hand to touch him. He growled and moved out of her reach. "Please. Try to stop it, Nick. Don't let it happen. Don't transform. Please, darling, let me help you." Help how? Only he could stop his transformation. Despair and hopelessness sent pain shooting through her.

He sped away. She raced after him. He was running home to die. "Nick, I love you," she shouted. "Stop the transformation now. Please, Nick." Lungs straining, she pushed herself to run faster.

His breathing grew more labored the longer they ran. His body quivered and he howled. Canine legs began to shape into human limbs and his fur grew thinner as his body elongated. It was all happening too fast.

Fear churned her stomach and tears choked her. Her foot caught in vines and she fell, sobbing, to the ground. She fought to free herself. Nick had disappeared. Heedless of the tears that blurred her vision and the vicious pain in her temple, she stood and ran, violently pushing foliage out of her way.

The full moon cut a path for her. A gentle breeze, carrying the scent of the Southwest desert, brushed against her neck. Black Fox was near. The aroma of ancient sandalwood mingled with the desert scent and she knew Antica hovered close too. Energy pumped through her and hope opened in her heart. She came to a familiar clearing. In front of her loomed the spires of Nick's mansion. Lights were on in all the windows, calling them home.

Nick, half-human now, climbed the stairs, his steps faltering.

"Nick!" she screamed.

He gave her a backward glance. The front door swung open and he fell into the house. She took the steps two at a time and followed him. The door shut behind them with a loud click.

Nick limped into the living room and collapsed onto the floor, writhing in pain. His face, distorted into odd angles, was shadowed with his human image.

"Please, love, you can stop the transformation. I'll be here with you." Desperate to ease his suffering and reassure him, she touched his shoulder. The heat from his body seared her fingers. He shrieked in pain and shifted away from her.

"Nick, fight it." Despair and anguish filled his eyes when he looked at her. He trembled.

She couldn't help him, couldn't even touch him. Tears slid down her face and panic clogged her lungs. She'd never felt so helpless in her life. She wanted to do something, anything.

The scents of the Southwest desert and sandalwood drifted over her then, calming her. Nick must have smelled it too. He stilled and looked at her. Love shone from his eyes. Nick's eyes. There was no trace of the wolf.

His body jerked and a tormented cry escaped him. She put a hand over her mouth to stop her cries from mingling with his.

The sounds of his muscles stretching and his bones cracking tore at her heart and she squeezed her eyes shut. His screams reverberated through the room.

Then all went quiet. Kyla looked down to see Nick, her Nick, bruised and bloody, but human again.

"Kyla," he rasped. His eyes rolled back in his head and his breathing slowed.

"No!" The scream wrenched from her.

* * * * *

The fire in the hearth was long dead and the morning light thrust through the curtains, but Kyla sat as she had for hours, on the floor with Nick's body draped across her lap. She'd tended to his wounds and wrapped a blanket securely around him. She didn't understand it, but somehow he'd lived through a transformation in the midst of a full moon. He'd not awakened since that awful moment when she thought he'd died. But he was alive, his chest rising and falling with his even breathing. She sent a silent prayer of thanks to the God she now knew had never really abandoned her.

While Nick slept, she'd called the state police about the young women in the lodge. The police had found the lodge, abandoned except for the tortured, half-dead women. The demons who'd ravaged the women were gone. To Hell, she hoped.

Nick stirred and moaned softly. His eyelids fluttered open. Joy and apprehension tumbled through her.

"Kyla?" The word came out on a raspy breath. "It wasn't a dream." He struggled to sit up.

Fighting tears, she pressed her hand to his chest. "Don't, Nick, you're hurt. I did the best I could to patch you up, but you need a doctor."

"No doctor. I'll be all right."

She shivered at what she saw in his eyes—disbelief, hope, and above all, love. She brushed a lock of hair off his forehead with a shaky hand. White threaded through the blackness, and bruises and cuts marred his beautiful human face.

"Antica knew," he said.

"It doesn't matter anymore, Nick. Nothing matters but that you're alive." A sob escaped her.

He reached up and touched her face with gentle fingers, skimming over the cut on her lip. "You're hurt."

"I'm fine." She grabbed his hand and kissed his palm, inhaling the familiar scent of him, spice and outdoors. Hope cut through the apprehension that constricted her chest.

He tried to sit up, wincing in pain. "Must tell you." He pushed the words out slowly. "Antica never stopped believing, but I did."

Tears streamed down Kyla's face and dripped onto the

blanket. "You're weak. Rest. We'll talk later."

She gathered him into her arms. His powerful body was hot, so hot it burned through the blanket. "You can't die. I found you again. I won't lose you." She pressed her lips together to stop their trembling.

"Tell you," he said in a weak voice.

Sobbing, she kissed his lips, tasting the sweat that had broken out on his face.

"Don't you dare die on me, Nick Radford," she choked out.

* * * * *

Kyla sat stiffly on the red sofa and cradled her cold mug of coffee between her hands. Despite the curtain of flames in the huge fireplace and the bright late afternoon sunlight streaming through the windows, she shivered. A new day. But was it to be one of deliverance and redemption, or unparalleled sorrow?

She'd helped Nick to his room hours ago. He'd kept mumbling about a prophecy and Antica, but she'd finally gotten him settled into bed. She'd bathed his face in cool water and sat with him until his fever broke and he slept soundly.

Unable to eat, she'd sat on the sofa and drank coffee until she lost count of the number of cups she'd had.

Footsteps sounded behind her. She jumped up and swiveled around. Nick, a tender smile on his face, stood there, dressed in jeans and long sleeved shirt. The coffee mug slipped out of her hands and landed on the rug with a loud thump.

Her heart beat a rapid staccato and she rushed to him. She grabbed his arms, reassuring herself he was real and not a fantasy she'd conjured up. "Nick, you shouldn't be out of bed. You need to rest."

"I've had enough rest," he said, shaking his head. "I feel better than I have in five hundred years. And you did it."

"What did I do?"

His smile tugged at her heart. He pulled her into his arms and kissed her with a hunger that matched the longing deep inside her, a longing that had stayed alive through the centuries. She gripped his shoulders and returned his kiss, giving him the undying love that had waited for him, and only him.

When he finally released her, she looked into his eyes and saw the same wonderment she knew was in hers.

"You transformed back to human form when the moon was full. And you didn't die. How, Nick?"

"Antica's prophecy. I'd stopped believing in it."

"In what? I don't understand. You're not making any sense. None of this is." She touched his lips.

"It's time we talked." He took her hand, and, limping, led her to the sofa. Sitting down, he pulled her with him. Sweat beaded on his forehead and she feared he was ill and in pain.

"You shouldn't be up. You've had an ordeal. Whatever you need to say can wait, love."

He shook his head. "It can't wait. Everything's changed. Montague's gone. He can't ever hurt us again. Whatever evil spell he put on this place will dissipate. The villagers will go back to their routine lives, never knowing the fiend in their midst."

"And I'll protect you," she said, touching his hand. "We can leave here if you want. Start all over. I won't ever desert you. You never have to fear the full moon again."

"My beautiful Kyla. You don't understand."

In his bright smile she saw the young Nicholas she'd

fallen in love with centuries before.

"What don't I understand?" she asked.

He looked away from her, his eyes hooded. She was at a loss as to what to say.

Her whole life had been a series of surreal events, but nothing had really prepared her for this. They'd been torn from each other five hundred years ago. She could wait a little longer while he gathered his thoughts, but the wait was agonizing.

Her visions had told her. But what did that mean to the here and now? Did he still want her?

He turned to her and took her hand, rubbing his thumb over her palm, sending delicious shivers through her.

"I'm sorry I worried you last night," he said. "I felt myself begin to transform. I didn't know what to expect if Antica's prophecy came true. I didn't know if the curse would lift or if I would die."

She blinked back tears. "I thought you were dying."

"I thought I was, too," he said. "That's why I kept trying to get home. I didn't want to die out in the woods."

"Oh, Nick." She kissed him gently, but he took the kiss past simply one of comfort, running his tongue over her lips, building a wild hunger in her before he broke the electrifying contact.

He laughed. "I think you're going to have me around for a while, thanks to Antica."

Kyla drew a deep breath, trying to settle her insides, still trembling from the force of his kiss. "Tell me about Antica's prophecy."

He settled into the sofa and put his arm along the back. She slid closer and he brushed his fingers on the nape of her neck. His touch shot heat along her nerve endings.

He let out a deep sigh. "When Montague cursed me as a werewolf, Antica tried to counter it with a spell, but she didn't have the power. She called on the woodland spirits for help and they sent her a prophecy—I would be saved by a woman who would love me despite my affliction."

He raised his gaze to hers. The pain in his topaz eyes made her gasp and she touched his face, skimming her fingers over the cuts and bruises.

"I thought I'd found that woman once before," he said. "But I was wrong. I'd given up ever finding her, but Antica never stopped believing. I was prepared to die. The Beast inside me was getting stronger and I was afraid I couldn't control it."

He cupped her chin with his hand and looked deeply into her eyes. "Then you came along. Back at the wolf circle, knowing what I was, you said you loved me anyway."

Kyla skimmed a gentle finger across his cheek. "I do love you, and I will forever. I'll take care of you." She tried to smile but her lips trembled. "I know a little something about werewolves. I'll keep you safe."

He studied her and smiled. "You don't need to worry about that anymore."

She furrowed her brow. "What?"

"You gave up your heritage for me." She nodded.

"Why?"

She held his gaze. "You're worth any sacrifice, Nick. I couldn't envision my life without you. Giving up my legacy was nothing compared to losing you."

He closed his eyes and drew deep breaths. When he opened his eyes, tears glistened at the corners. "Your love saved me. There is no more curse. You're the one Antica prophesied."

Kyla licked dry lips. "No curse? What does that mean?"

"I won't ever be the Beast again."

"Never?" She swallowed. Hard.

He looked away from her. "It feels strange. The world looks different when you know you'll leave it someday, much sooner than you'd come to expect, even though I thought I was prepared to die at your hands."

Afraid to believe, her breathing shallow, she said, "You're mortal?"

He turned and gathered her into his arms. She gripped his shirt between her fingers and clung to him. His heart beat sure and steady against her hands.

"Yes, my darling, I'm mortal now."

Blinking back tears, she pulled away.

He took her face between his hands. "We'll grow old together."

Joy surged through her and she laughed. "Old never sounded so good."

His laugh joined hers until the ancient house seemed to vibrate with happiness.

"I love you, Kyla." He stroked her hair.

"I love you, Nick."

They clung to each other. The only sounds were the crackling of the fire in the hearth and the creaks of the house settling around them. The house. The home she'd once loved so much. Theirs again.

Drawing away, she gave him a tremulous smile. "This was meant to happen. All of it. I know that now. I'm Catherine. Reborn. That's why I've had the visions. I don't understand any of it, but I know it's true."

She laughed softly. "What irony. Reborn as a were-hunter. Fate's little laugh at our expense."

He rubbed a finger along her lips. "My Kyla. My love. I can't explain it either, but we've been given our future back and nothing else matters."

His eyes mesmerized her, drawing her into a far-off time and place. Her heart hammered and her head pounded. Visions flew at her, fast and intense. She saw her past life with Nick and their baby, Jonathan, felt the happiness and the sorrow. Felt the cold grave. She began to shake.

"Kyla, love. What's wrong?" He held her close.

Her throat thickened. "I've seen everything, as if it just happened. And I remember it all. I remember when Montague killed me and Jonathan." Swiping tears, she looked up at him. "And little Aiden—Todd now. He tried to save me. I saw my grave too, and you standing over it." She bit down on her lip. "The remembering hurts."

He touched his finger to her lips. "Shush. The past is gone. I love you, Kyla Yaeger, now, in this time. I'll love you until my dying day."

She kissed him, darting her tongue over the fullness of his lips, tasting his strength and his love. Then she rested her head on his broad chest. "I haven't believed in love and goodness for a very long time." Her voice was muffled. "I wonder if Jonathan will come back to us."

Nick rubbed his hand down her back. "We have only good times ahead of us. I promise. And if we believe, our Jonathan will come to us."

She pulled away and stared into his eyes. The love shining in their depths confirmed the truth of his words. Time seemed to stop, hung between their distant past and an uncertain future.

"We loved each other as Nicholas and Catherine," he

said in a soft voice that caressed her. "We'll love each other more as Nick and Kyla."

"Nick and Kyla." The words rolled off her tongue, a promise of new love and new life. She rained tender kisses on his face. "I will never stop loving you."

"Marry me again," he whispered.

Ecstasy pulsed through her veins and settled in her heart. "Yes. Yes." She wrapped her arms around his neck. "I want a simple wedding. Just you and me and the priest. And one guest—Todd."

"Three guests," he said. "Luka and Lycan too. Antica's sons. They've been with me through the centuries."

"Whatever you wish, my lord."

With a husky laugh, he took her lips in a kiss that sealed his vow of long passionate nights and an eternity of love and happiness.

When they finally pulled apart, he stood and held out his hand to her. She placed her hand in his. Together, they walked through the living room and up the stairs. When they reached the top of the stairs, he swung her into his arms and carried her to his room.

"Cursed mates no more," he whispered.

EPILOGUE

Manhattan, one year later

"He's beautiful. Just like his father." Kyla hugged her hours-old son to her chest and smiled up at Nick sitting in a chair pulled up close to her hospital bed.

Nick rubbed their infant's head, then kissed Kyla softly on the lips. "He's beautiful like his mother."

After they married, they'd bought an apartment in Manhattan because Kyla missed the city. They divided their time between their home in Maine, where Todd was a frequent visitor, and their Manhattan apartment. Kyla had wanted their child born in one of New York's best hospital. Thanks to Nick's money, she had a large, beautifully furnished suite and a private nursing staff.

Smiling, her gaze wandered over the room. Balloons and flowers, sent by Nick and her friends at Hunter-Wolf, took up every available space.

A knock at the door drew their attention. Todd poked his head in. "Is it too early to visit?"

Kyla laughed. "His godfather can visit any time."

Todd approached the bed cautiously. He peered down at the sleeping baby in Kyla's arms. "He's perfect."

"He is, isn't he?" Kyla said with a laugh.

The baby opened blue eyes and stared at her. A shiver ran through her at the intelligence and recognition shining from his infant eyes. "Jonathan," she whispered.

"What?" Nick leaned closer. The baby turned to him. "Jonathan." Awe tinged Nick's voice. "He's come back to us."

"Jonathan?" Todd frowned, then his eyes widened. "Your baby." They'd told Todd about their past lives, but he had no memory of himself as Aiden.

Kyla looked at her men, Todd, Jonathan, and Nick. Happiness wound through her. "We're all together again."

Nick took her hand and squeezed. Tears glistened in his eyes. "A family again."

"Forever," she whispered.

****

*I hope you enjoyed *Cursed Mates*. Please turn the page for an excerpt of the romantic thriller, *Murder, Mi Amore* by Cara Marsi.*

MURDER, MI AMORE

CHAPTER ONE

A prickly sensation, like someone breathing on the back of her neck, sent chills slithering down Lexie Cortese's spine. She glanced around the small, exclusive leather goods shop on one of Rome's busiest streets. A well-dressed older woman perused a richly sequined evening bag while a smiling saleswoman looked on. A middle-aged man, dressed in a beautifully tailored gray suit, studied a display case of couture handbags. Nothing sinister. Yet the feeling of being followed had started before she'd entered the shop and had grown stronger in the forty-five minutes she'd been there.

"*Signorina? Carta di credito?*"

Lexie started at the saleswoman's words and turned back to her with an apologetic smile. Although she couldn't speak Italian, Lexie had done enough shopping to know the saleswoman wanted her credit card. She dug into her plain black shoulder bag, pushing aside the bright scarf she'd tied on the handle to liven it up a bit, pulled out her card and handed it to the woman. As she waited for the clerk to ring up the sale, someone jostled her.

"*Scusi, per favore.*" The middle-aged man in the gray suit had bumped her. His flat black eyes bore into hers, as if sending her a message. She backed away.

"No *problema*," she said, hoping she had the Italian right. With a cold smile, he moved on, heading to the door.

Clutching her shopping bag with one hand and holding her shoulder bag tightly against her, she left the shop and joined the throngs of pedestrians on the Via Corsi. Despite the festive atmosphere from shoppers and tourists enjoying an unseasonably warm April day, Lexie couldn't shake the feeling that someone followed her.

Was it the man who'd bumped into her, the one with the dead eyes? She shouldered her way along the crowded street and looked behind her. He wasn't there. God, she was becoming paranoid, letting her imagination run amok. Nevertheless, she tightened her grip on the shopping bag that contained the way-too-expensive pale green designer handbag she'd just purchased. Rome was as well-known for its pickpockets and muggers as for its art and history.

Why would anyone follow her, an ordinary tourist? Then again, she wasn't ordinary any more. Not since she'd come to Rome. And now she had a new handbag to go with her new attitude. In the past two weeks, the cautious and always-do-what's-right-eager-to-please-everyone Lexie Cortese had become a confident, take-charge woman. For all of her twenty-eight years she'd done what others wanted—her parents, her teachers, that louse Jerry. But no more.

Smiling at a vendor selling flowers, she inhaled the heady perfume of early spring blooms and put a little bounce in her step. A good-looking twenty-something man nodded to her as he passed. Lots of handsome Italian men had flirted with her in the two weeks she'd been here. Sure helped make up for what that scum of an ex-fiancé had done.

From now on she'd do whatever she damn well pleased. Spend a month in Rome? Check. Buy a designer bag that cost more than a month's pay? Done. Have a fling with a sexy Italian, then walk away, in control, her heart untouched? Not so sure about that one, but she could hope.

To celebrate the new Lexie, she'd have a glass of wine. Maybe even two glasses. The Trevi Fountain was close. She'd enjoy her drink in the popular piazza admiring old Neptune and his trident. The prickly feeling swept over her again, raising goose bumps on her arms. She stopped and scanned the street. Nothing. Damn it!

Her imagination was in overdrive. It had to be. Thirsty for some calming wine, she hurried toward the piazza.

She found a seat at one of the outdoor tables directly across from old Neptune and ordered a glass of Pinot Noir. The piazza buzzed with tourists snapping pictures and throwing their three coins in the famous fountain. She'd made her three wishes the day she'd arrived. Wish one—that she'd find success in her new job and in grad school; wish two—that she'd come back to Rome, maybe even study here; and three—that someday she'd find real love and happiness. Whatever real happiness was.

When her wine arrived, she held the glass up in salute to Neptune. *Okay, water boy, do your stuff. Grant my wishes and toss a little excitement my way.* With a smile, she took a sip. The rich liquid flowed down her throat, soothing her jumbled nerves. How foolish she'd been to feel so unsettled earlier. Maybe traces of the old, skittish Lexie lingered.

A movement from a side street near the fountain snagged her attention. A man wearing jeans and a hoodie shot from the street, running directly toward…

Her?

Lexie gasped and grabbed her purse from the tabletop as the man raced past and snatched her shopping bag from the ground next to her.

"Hey!" Lexie jumped to her feet. "That's mine!"

The man ignored her, clutching the bag with her new, expensive purse against his chest like a football as he sprinted down a small alleyway.

"Somebody stop him!" she shouted, knocking over the table. The wine goblet shattered onto the cobblestones, splattering red wine all over her black sandals.

The piazza erupted in cries and frantic calls for the police. Onlookers, yelling in several languages, pointed toward the narrow street where the thief had disappeared. Several men ran after him. Lexie started to follow them.

"Stay, *signorina*," her waiter implored, grabbing her arm and holding her back. His eyes, wide and stricken, darted from her to the piazza. "See. The police. They are coming." He pointed out two policemen racing toward the alleyway. "Please, *signorina,* sit, have some wine. No charge." He pulled out a chair at a freshly made up table. Another waiter stood close, holding a full glass of wine out to Lexie.

Reluctantly, she turned away from the chase. "Thank you." She sank into the chair and took the proffered wine, grasping the glass tightly to control her sudden trembling as she noticed people staring. Damn it all to hell! That purse was supposed to symbolize her new attitude. And now some scumbag had stolen it not ten minutes after she walked out of the store with it. What did that say about her chances for a new start?

She looked up to see strangers hovering, offering help in a scattering of languages. She tried to respond, to reassure them she was all right. Her bout of self-pity dissolved with the strangers' kindness. She could handle this.

Fifteen long minutes later, her wine untouched, Lexie stared dismally across the piazza in the direction the thief and his pursuers had taken. Her waiters stood nearby, their faces tense.

"The police will find him, *signorina*. They must."

Then, like ancient Roman warriors returning from battle, the two policemen, followed by a large group of raucous men and boys, materialized from the alleyway. A tall man wearing a suit and holding her shopping bag walked between the policemen. Who was he? Not the thief.

She stood as they approached, wishing she knew enough Italian to ask. His well-cut, dark blue business suit emphasized his broad shoulders and muscular frame as he strode across the piazza toward her. His short dark hair framed a face boasting razor sharp cheekbones and a strong jaw. He might as well have jumped from the pages of a men's fashion magazine into her Roman holiday.

"*Signorina*," Mr. GQ Cover Model said, smiling and holding her bag out to her. He said something totally incomprehensible in Italian, and when she simply stared, he arched one dark eyebrow and tried again. "I believe this is yours?"

His English, spoken with a lilting Italian accent, sent unexpected spasms of pleasure over her. Unwilling to tear her gaze away from that oh-so-charming smile, Lexie stalled. She'd never seen a man so ruggedly beautiful.

She'd been without sex for too long. That was the only explanation.

"*Grazie*," she finally said, taking the bag from him. She opened the bag to make sure her purse was indeed inside, then smiled up at her handsome knight. "Thank you so much. You could have been hurt going after that jerk."

He lifted one elegantly-clad shoulder. "It was nothing. Vermin like that give my city a bad name." He studied her. "You are American." Surprise edged his deep, rich voice.

She nodded, then turned to the policemen, who stood silently by. How odd. "*Grazie* to both of you too."

They touched the brims of their hats at the same time. "We did nothing," the older of the two said. "This gentleman had wrestled your bag from the thief before we got there."

"Where is the thief?" Lexie asked, glancing around.

The policeman shrugged. "He got away, but be assured, we will find him." He smiled and pulled a small notebook from his inside jacket pocket. "Please to give us a little information for our report."

"Of course," she said.

She quickly gave them the information they wanted. "Thank you, *signorina*," the policeman said as he snapped his notebook shut and stuffed it back into his pocket. His partner remained silent and she assumed he didn't speak English. With nods to her, the policemen left.

"Thanks again," Lexie called after them.

She turned to the handsome stranger who'd rescued her bag. "Please, let me buy you a drink as thanks for your help."

"Of course. How can I refuse an invitation from such a beautiful woman?"

Lexie blushed. Italian men sure knew how to make a woman feel sexy. She turned back to her table where her waiter stood. With a smile of gratitude, she slid into the chair he held for her. She put her purse and shopping bag under the table, on the side closest to the wall. Mr. GQ Cover Model sat in the opposite chair and ordered what she assumed was a glass of Pinot Noir in beautiful Italian.

"I'm Lexie Cortese," she said, holding out her hand to shake his.

He took her hand and turned it over, brushing his lips on her wrist. Sparks seemed to fly up her arm and her eyes widened. *This man could charm Neptune's nymphs right out of the fountain.*

Trying her best not to blush again, she smiled and pulled her hand free.

"Domenico Brioni," he said, gifting her with a melt-her-bones smile. Despite his overt sexuality, humor flashed in his eyes, as if he didn't quite take himself seriously. "My American friends call me Dominic."

Oh, yes, she definitely could get used to this. "I hope we can be friends so I shall call you Dominic." The old Lexie would never be so bold with a man she'd just met.

"Of course, we will be friends," he said with another of his smiles. "Cortese. Italian?"

"My great-grandparents came from Abruzzo."

"Abruzzo. That explains your beautiful hazel eyes."

He was a practiced charmer all right. But she liked it.

"Do you speak Italian?" he asked.

"I don't, I'm sorry to say. But you speak beautiful English."

His eyes sparkled with even greater good humor. "Thank you." When the waiter handed him his wine, he held up his glass to her in salute.

Two hours and two glasses of wine later as he walked her back to her hotel—to make sure she arrived safely he'd insisted—she realized she'd done most of the talking. She'd told him about her home in Las Vegas, her new job at the college, her plan to someday earn a doctorate in Ancient Roman studies.

But she didn't tell him about Jerry. She was growing. She was healing.

Her life was far from exciting, yet Dominic continued to listen to her as if she were fascinating. A little niggle of doubt arose as she realized he'd told her very little about himself, only that he was a native Roman who worked in the banking business.

"I would like to see you again, Lexie Cortese," he said when they reached her hotel. His gaze, as warm as the heat of the sun that had made her feel so relaxed and content in the piazza, now sparked another kind of heat in her. When he brushed back a strand of hair from her forehead, jolts of electricity shot to every part of her body. The man had magic in those fingers.

Lexie had always been fond of magic shows.

"I'd love to see you again too," she said, tilting her face up to look at him. He was tall for an Italian, towering over her by about a foot.

He smiled. "It's a date. Dinner tomorrow night?"

"Uh-huh," she said, her mind and her body filled with his smile.

"I will pick you up here at eight," he said.

God, he was gorgeous. Could she put aside a lifetime of caution and take a chance on him? "Eight is good."

He took her hand and kissed her knuckles. "*Buon giorno*, Lexie Cortese. Until tomorrow."

* * * * *

Dominic made sure Lexie entered the hotel, then walked away as casually as possible. He recognized the middle-aged man who lounged against a nearby building, his gray suit blending with the shadows. The same thug had gone into the leather goods shop right behind Lexie. Dominic was sure the guy hadn't noticed him and Ruggiero standing near the shop, nor had the scum suspected one of their female agents was in the store posing as a shopper.

The agent had signaled Dominic when the man slipped

the diamond into Lexie's purse. The hand-off complete, the thug should have disappeared. Yet he'd continued to follow Lexie. Maybe the jewel thieves didn't quite trust her and wanted to be sure she made it to the hotel with the diamond.

Hands in his pockets, Dominic pushed through the pedestrian traffic and crossed the street, deftly avoiding some of Rome's ubiquitous motor scooters, and headed toward Ruggiero, waiting by the bank. They'd been lucky today. The police had almost screwed things up back at the piazza. With his hooded sweatshirt gone, no one would recognize Ruggiero for the street thief who'd grabbed Lexie's bag.

As he headed toward his partner, Dominic's mind replayed the afternoon's events. Lexie Cortese didn't fit the profile of a courier working for international jewel thieves and terrorists. He'd been in the business long enough that nothing shocked him, yet when he'd learned the petite beauty with thick brown hair and big hazel eyes was American, he'd been thrown.

But Dominic knew better. Galina had looked innocent too. Until she'd betrayed them.

Books by Cara Marsi

A Catered Romance
A Cat's Tale & Other Love Stories
(All stories in this anthology are available separately)
A Cinderella Christmas
A Groom for Christmas
Accidental Love
Capri Nights
Cursed Mates
Her Forever Husband
Her Snow White Christmas (Snow Globe Magic Book 1)
Her Frog Prince Holiday (Snow Globe Magic Book 2)
Logan's Redemption (Redemption Book 1)
Franco's Fortune (Redemption Book 2)
Luke's Temptation (Redemption Book 3)
Love Potion
Loving Or Nothing
Murder, Mi Amore
Storm of Desire
Sweet Temptations
Sweet Temptations Boxed Set
The Marriage Coin Boxed Set
The One Who Got Away
The Ring
Wedding Dreams Boxed Set

Coming Early 2016, Her Red Riding Hood Valentine (Snow Globe Magic Book 3)

Read excerpts at www.caramarsi.com
All books available at online booksellers

A Catered Romance, A Groom for Christmas, Cursed Mates, Franco's Fortune, Logan's Redemption, Loving Or Nothing, Luke's Temptation, Murder, Mi Amore, and The Marriage Coin are also available in print

An award-winning and eclectic author, Cara Marsi is published in romantic suspense, paranormal romance, and contemporary romance. She loves a good love story, and believes that everyone deserves a second chance at love. Sexy, sweet, thrilling, or magical, Cara's stories are first and foremost about the love. Treat yourself today, with a taste of romance. When not traveling or dreaming of traveling, Cara and her husband live on the East Coast in a house ruled by a formerly homeless cat who chose them for her family.

Find out more about Cara and her books and sign up for her newsletter at her website at CaraMarsi.com. She's on Twitter, Goodreads, Facebook, and Pinterest and is always interested in meeting new friends.

**